The Thrill of the Stunt

Knowing he had another precious second or two of free action without having to worry about being gunned down, Xander leaped up and ran for the long, curving staircase next to the restaurant. If he could make his way to the bottom of the stairs, he felt certain he could reach the alley and the GTO before Kirill, the sniper, could pick him off.

He ran for the metal handrail in the center of the stairs. Leaping into the air, he slapped the metal serving tray from the restaurant under his feet and landed balanced on the handrail. Thankfully, the serving tray was rigid enough to support his weight, and the rail was slick enough to provide the kind of surface he needed.

The platter ground against the handrail as Xander rode the piece of metal like a skateboard. The screech of tortured metal echoed within the stairway area, and sparks shot out behind him. Bullets broke bricks and tore divots from the mortar, creating a rapid line of destruction that followed him down.

At the bottom of the stairwell, Xander leaped into the air and let go of the serving platter. He dropped to the cobblestones as the platter clattered away.

Kirill watched the stairs where Xander Cage had vanished, but he knew the moment had passed. The rage within him had locked on with talons as unforgiving as a hawk's.

He has escaped.

xXx

**A Novelization by MEL ODOM
Based on the Motion Picture
Written by RICH WILKES**

HarperEntertainment
An Imprint of HarperCollinsPublishers

HARPERENTERTAINMENT
An Imprint of HarperCollins*Publishers*
10 East 53rd Street
New York, New York 10022-5299

ISBN: 0-06-051469-8

HarperCollins®, ■®, and HarperEntertainment™ are trademarks of
HarperCollins Publishers Inc.

First HarperEntertainment paperback printing: July 2002

Printed in the United States of America

Visit HarperEntertainment on the World Wide Web at www.harper-
collins.com

10   9   8   7   6   5   4   3   2   1

This book is dedicated to Vin Diesel,
who rocks the world in action films.
Can't wait to see this one, bro.

And to my kids, who are big fans as well:
Matthew Lane, Matthew Dain,
Montana, Shiloh, and Chandler.

Special Acknowledgment

I want to thank Josh Behar for greenlighting me for this project, April Benavides for keeping it together, and Yulia Borodyanskaya for shepherding us and keeping us on track. And thanks to Revolution Studios for offering up such a crackerjack cinematic feast.

SPY 1.0

I

Prague, Czech Republic

Run!

Standing in the shadows of the alley near the heart of the Old City, Vassily Malenkov pressed back into the stone wall and wished he could turn invisible. Or at least blend into the night with one of the chameleon suits used by his character in his current favorite video game.

Run!

Malenkov's mind screamed at him again, urging him into desperate movement. Fear cascaded inside him, turning his heartbeat into a raging torrent in his ears. His pursuer or pursuers were probably able to track him simply by the sound of his heart beating. Sweat beaded his face and trickled down his body under his loose clothing.

Something scratched along the rooftop above.

For a moment, Malenkov's stomach convulsed and he thought he was going to throw up. He swallowed sour bile. Black spots whirled in his vision and his knees almost gave way under him.

A cat scampered across the rooftop carrying a dead bat in its mouth. The marginal moonlight warred with the light pollution and draped shadows over the building that almost masked the cat.

Predators came out at night in the city. And tonight, Malenkov knew at least one of those predators was after him. Repercussions of the recent political and social upheavals in the surrounding countries continued to roll through the neighborhoods.

Car noises blasted from the street behind Malenkov. He watched the passing traffic suspiciously, expecting a car at any moment to barrel down the narrow alley after him.

And what would he do if one did? The prize he carried had been hard-won, and he'd been paid well for hacking through the Internet to find the information. Upon delivery of the disk he carried, he'd be paid even better. When he'd been hired, he hadn't been told exactly what the information was that he was targeting. The money had enticed him at first, but ultimately the sheer skill level needed to match wits with the complicated security overlays on the military site had drawn him into the game.

Twenty-three years old, skinny as a rail, and possessing no life outside of a CRT monitor, CPU, and keyboard, Malenkov lived for the cat-and-mouse games of computer hacking. He was good at his chosen vocation. That was why people came to him. And he was successful at that vocation. That was why other people—people he'd victimized—came *after* him.

Run!

Struggling, Malenkov ignored the fight-or-flight instinct hardwired into his brain. Running was a primitive reaction to fear and threat, and he knew from experience that running only focused a predator's eye.

He took a final look at the street, and at the Vltava River beyond. Lighted boats and barges moved along the river that threaded through the heart of Prague. Many tourists came to the city these days, and opportunists lined up to take their money. If he hadn't possessed his hacking skills, Malenkov knew he would have been one of those spending their lives toiling for horrible wages. That money was only a pittance against what he made for performing his various contracted hacking jobs.

Those people trafficking in the tourist trade, however, weren't lurking in an alley fearing for their lives, Malenkov reminded himself. The payoff from Yorgi would be enough to keep him safe for a while, though. Once he had Yorgi's money in hand, the young hacker swore he wouldn't take another job for a long time.

Then again, Malenkov thought, smiling a little in spite of the fear that rattled around inside him like tin cans in a windstorm, with the money Yorgi was paying there wouldn't have to be another job for a long time. Malenkov only had his own personal hacking demon to deny.

Bracing himself, Malenkov shoved off from the wall into a stumble that took him farther down the alley. The street noises and the sound of boats farther away lay behind him, but raucous music came from one of the buildings ahead. Yorgi's club was in full swing, and that was where they'd agreed to make the swap.

Malenkov still didn't know why Yorgi didn't have

Viktor or Kolya pick the disk up. That course of action would have been safe and simpler. The young hacker maintained secure living quarters in one of the condemned buildings awaiting renovation that would never come during his lifetime. He rarely left that environment, and wouldn't have deserted his home tonight if the money hadn't been so good.

Of course, there was also the matter of Yorgi's request. Someone who wanted to keep on breathing didn't turn down a request from Yorgi.

Shoving his fists into his coat, Malenkov leaned into the walk. He counted steps out of habit because the habit somehow made the distance seem shorter and the time pass faster. The cadence of the numbers blossomed in his head, keeping some of the fear at bay.

Ahead, he spotted the old cathedral that was his destination. He'd walked by the place before, but never at night. Stone gargoyles clung to the parapets and the rooftop. All of the creatures looked hideous and grotesque. Batwings folded across their backs and leering countenances gave the stone figures a sinister appearance. Looking up at them, he could almost believe the gargoyles might fall from their perches at any moment and swoop down on him.

Something *clacked* behind Malenkov.

Whirling, the young hacker stared behind him. The sound had been sharper than shoe leather scuffing against one of the cobblestones. For an instant he thought that a vehicle had steered from the street and come into the alley. Then he realized that the vehicle's lights would have alerted him first.

He stood frozen, fearing that his heart had stopped forever. Then the next heartbeat thundered through him, urging him into motion. Turning, he quickened his pace and hurried toward the cathedral.

Movement darted in front of Malenkov, a tiny blip of motion that hardly stood out against the dark shadows that filled the alley. But there was no mistaking the sharp *thunk!* that followed. A metallic hum shifted octaves like a guitar string, tightening from a loose basso buzz to a strident pinging that rose above the level of human hearing.

In disbelief, the young hacker gazed at the steel crossbow bolt jutting out from the wall ahead of him. Another foot closer, he realized, and the thing might have pierced his skull. Then he noticed the thin cable attached to the bolt's end.

The cable ran back toward the other side of the alley at a rather steep angle.

Almost hypnotized by the turn of events, Malenkov turned toward the other side of the alley. Somewhere in the back of his mind, his survival instinct was screaming at him to run, but he couldn't because the problem-solving sections of his mind were already at work on the mystery presented before him.

Facing the other end of the cable, Malenkov looked up. Unbelievably, an indistinguishable form seemed to take flight from the opposite building. The black-clad figure swung along the metal cable with a sibilant hiss that grew louder.

Malenkov heard a metallic rasp and the cable hum. The figure swooping down on him shifted. Before the young hacker could move, feet smashed into his face and knocked him backward. He knew he was falling, but he never felt himself hit the ground.

2

Special Agent Jim McGrath of the United States Central Intelligence Agency pushed himself up from the cobblestone-covered alley. Despite the specially cushioned soles of his shoes—never intended for the use he'd just shown them—numbness spread up his feet and lower legs from the impact against Vassily Malenkov. Standing on the building rooftop for nearly fifteen minutes waiting for the young hacker so he could swing down the zip-line and intercept his target had worn McGrath down further. But that was the only intercept point he'd been able to engineer along the way.

Hurriedly, breath rasping in his throat, McGrath crossed the alley to Malenkov. He laid his fingers against the young hacker's throat, checking for a pulse and finding one.

The CIA agent felt slightly relieved that Malenkov wasn't dead. McGrath knew he'd felt bone break from the impact, and he'd hoped that

Malenkov's neck hadn't snapped. During his sixteen years with the Agency, McGrath had killed a number of times. But all those deaths were sanctioned assassinations, or casualties accepted during the course of a mission.

Donnan, the CIA handler overseeing the mission, would have put down Vassily Malenkov as an acceptable casualty but the young hacker wasn't as much of a threat as the men McGrath had been assigned to spy on. The young man hadn't had to die, and McGrath was glad Malenkov lived.

Kneeling, McGrath rummaged through the unconscious man's coat with the practiced ease of a trained thief. The agent found a hard black case tucked into an inside coat pocket. Sitting on his heels, still feeling some of the same old excitement that had drawn him to the Agency while he'd been attending an Ivy League college, McGrath felt for the case's release.

Let it be, he thought.

The case sprang open at his touch.

The data chip inside the protective case lay in a foam rubber cutout.

McGrath didn't know for certain what was on the data chip. Everyone functioned on a need-to-know basis. That was standard operating procedure on all Agency business. For this recovery mission, McGrath's handler hadn't deemed such knowledge necessary.

The CIA agent closed the case. He pulled the ski mask from his head, feeling the cool night brush up against his face. Standing over Malenkov, McGrath stripped out of the one-piece black jumpsuit and dropped the clothing over the unconscious man.

Under the jumpsuit, the agent wore a dark Italian suit. He rubbed the toes of his shoes against the backs of his pants legs, putting a shine back on the Corinthian leather.

Noise from an approaching car engine rumbled into the alley.

Senses alert, McGrath stepped back from Malenkov and flattened in the safety of the shadows clinging to the wall. Looking down at the unconscious hacker, McGrath realized that Malenkov had believed himself safe there as well.

Safety, McGrath remembered from his Agency training days, was an illusion. Self-preservation was the key. He turned and trotted down the alley, staying just ahead of the vehicle's lights burning through the shadows.

Two vehicles, McGrath corrected himself.

A sedan with blacked-out windows drove slowly into the alley. A fully dressed racing motorcycle flanked the sedan. McGrath recognized both vehicles.

The headlights touched Malenkov's unconscious body. Car and motorcycle stopped.

Hurling himself forward, McGrath gained the fleeting safety of the nearest building just before the sedan switched to high beams. The swath of halogen light ripped away the shadows in the alley, leaving a veritable no-man's-land laid bare between the buildings.

Shiny black leather covered the motorcycle rider. He levered his kickstand into place, then switched off his machine. Throwing his leg over the motorcycle, he stood and surveyed the alley with a gunslinger's cold stare. Unconsciously, he pulled his leather gloves tighter.

The sedan's driver got out as well. Although the motorcycle rider was a big, rough-hewn man, the sedan driver dwarfed his companion. His name, McGrath knew from the Intel file he'd been given, was Viktor. The smaller man was Kolya, Yorgi's brother.

All of them, the files in McGrath's handler's briefing had been quick and adamant to point out, were killers.

Viktor walked closer to the unconscious hacker lying in the middle of the alley. The big man carefully stayed out of the light and his comrade's field of fire.

"Is it Malenkov?" Kolya asked in Russian.

"Yes," Viktor confirmed.

Kolya reached inside his motorcycle jacket and took out a semi-automatic pistol. He turned slightly, presenting his profile to the alley like a gunfighter ready to do battle. "Does he have the disk?"

Viktor knelt, taking out a pistol as well. He searched through Malenkov's clothing with his free hand. Due to the light glaring from the vehicle behind him, McGrath couldn't see Viktor's face, but the disgust was apparent in the big man's voice.

"No. Malenkov doesn't have the disk."

"Then someone else does," Kolya declared. "And whoever that person is hasn't been gone long."

Quietly, slowly, McGrath crept back down the building, putting more distance between himself and Yorgi's people. Behind him, the CIA agent heard the sedan door slam shut and the motorcycle's powerful engine blare to life again. He glanced over his shoulder and saw that both vehicles were slowly rolling down the alley.

Glancing forward, McGrath knew that the other end of the alley was too far away. He'd never make the distance—even at an all-out run—before the lights from the vehicle would overtake him and light him up as a target.

Desperately, McGrath looked at the church doors only a few feet away. Having no choice, the CIA agent raced up the steps, aware of the screaming din of the industrial-metal mix growing louder as he neared the doors. Thankfully, no one worked security at the door.

In the next minute, McGrath pushed through the heavy ornate door and strode into hell one step ahead of the hounds that pursued him.

3

Heart hammering, Jim McGrath walked into the club. The industrial-metal band at the center of the performance area rocked the house with deafening intensity. With the cavernous space provided in the church, the building seemed to gather and amplify the noise, becoming a living thing. The amplified music found every nook and cranny, rolling over the church's interior in thunderous waves.

McGrath ran his hands through his hair and tried to smooth everything back into place. The gesture was automatic, a byproduct of Ivy League schools and good hygiene. Unfortunately, both of those criteria separated him from the latex-clad menagerie that danced and maybe fought in the center floor. At least, the CIA agent didn't think all the gyrations out on the floor were dance moves.

The church-cum-concert hall was crowded, and McGrath determined to make that work for him. All he needed was enough time to put some distance between himself and his pursuers. He scanned the walls over the heads of the partygoers for another door out of the huge chamber.

The band, covered in ragged denim, tattoos, and studded leather, slammed through the number they played on a large stage to McGrath's left. Go-go dancers performed bump-and-grind routines in large gilded birdcages. All of the girls were nearly naked hardbodies. Their attire didn't leave much to the imagination, but gazing at the concert attendees, McGrath felt certain that the audience didn't possess much in the way of imagination. The lead singer had been singing the same line over and over since the agent had entered the building.

A mosh pit gathered in the center of the dance floor. Dancers with bondage leather and chains, glittering piercings, and spiked hairdos slammed against one another. Their mouths were open, probably yelling and screaming, but McGrath couldn't hear the noise over the din of the music. The guitar player exploded into a solo that screeched so loudly McGrath expected the stained glass that still occupied the church's windows to shatter at any second.

To the right of the stage, McGrath spotted an arched entryway leading to a shadowed hallway. He scanned the upper balconies around the great chamber, seeing other doors there. The church was honeycombed with doorways, but he knew from past experience that not all of them led outside. Churches like the one he was currently in had been constructed as fortresses, able to provide sanctuary for the priest's flock in times of war and invasion by hostile forces.

Now, McGrath realized, the church was being used to protect the wolves that feasted on the sheep.

Steeling himself, acutely aware of the slight weight of the data chip in his pocket, McGrath stepped into the maze of whirling bodies. Most of the dancers stepped back from him, as if the Italian suit he wore carried some kind of offensive aura. Other dancers glared at him in open rebellion, and McGrath wondered if one of them was going to throw a punch at him. Curses trailed in his wake but the agent ignored them, concentrating on his planned evacuation route.

McGrath glanced behind him as he neared the center of the floor. A forest of waving arms prevented him from seeing the entranceway clearly, but he didn't think the door had opened to admit anyone else. He kept going, picking the path of least resistance, and bumping male and female dancers aside only when he needed to.

"Malenkov is late."

Drawn from his thoughts, Yorgi looked at his companions. The three of them shared a table in one of the balconies overlooking the desanctified church's dance floor. Bodyguards flanked the area and protected his privacy, keeping away the people new to the club who didn't know he was the owner.

Yelena stirred her drink with a finger, gazing at him in open speculation. Beautiful and intelligent, dressed in clothing that showed off her body, she drew the eyes of every male in the club as she passed by. In fact, Yorgi knew from observation, Yelena also drew the eyes of many women in the club.

Seated opposite Yorgi, Kirill leaned back in his chair without a care in the world. Where Yelena was intense and seductive, Kirill was aloof and unrepentant. Most would have pegged him as a poet or a philosopher because of the distance Kirill always seemed to maintain from the rest of the world. But Kirill didn't watch the world from an artist's perception, placing himself outside the mainstream in order to better describe the people and their circumstances. Instead, Kirill viewed the world through a sniper's cold and calculating perspective. Most of the people Kirill had executed had never seen him or even known that death was coming for them.

Yorgi glanced at Yelena to make his reply. "I'm well aware that Malenkov is late."

"You shouldn't have made him come here," Yelena said.

"I have a purpose for doing the things I do."

"Your purpose was to get the data chip."

"I will."

Yelena drew her finger from her drink and placed the digit in her mouth. Her cheeks hollowed as she sucked the liquor from her finger. Her dark eyes flashed.

Yorgi watched her with admiration. She was one of the most volatile women he'd ever met. That fact both excited and angered him.

"Malenkov will be here," Yorgi said.

Yelena raised a speculative eyebrow, but wisely refrained from saying anything.

If Kirill listened to the conversation at all, he gave no sign. He remained slumped in his chair and took another hit off his cigarette. A pile of butts stood in formation in the heavy brass ashtray in front of him.

"Kolya and Viktor are watching Malenkov," Yorgi said. Irritation grated inside him when he realized that he'd voiced that statement more for his own reassurance than for hers.

"Of course," Yelena said.

Yorgi gazed out over the crowd. The concert was in full swing and the attendees were having a good time. That lightened his mood somewhat. All of them had come very far from the war-torn streets and battles fought for governments and ideals that weren't their own.

Having Malenkov deliver the data chip had been a calculated risk on Yorgi's part. Only hours ago, Viktor's sources had confirmed that a team of American agents was looking for the people who had stolen the information Malenkov had taken from supposedly secure military sites. They'd been too late to prevent the loss of the information, but Malenkov had experienced a problem of his own.

In ferreting the information away, the hacker had been forced to break the files into packets and disburse them throughout drops he used in high-user sites, finally bringing all the encrypted coding together again on his own machine and completing the decryption less than an hour ago.

The American agents in Prague wanted the person or persons behind Malenkov, and their commanders had also taken a calculated risk by letting Malenkov keep the information. Such was their conceit that they believed they could retrieve the information safely before the knowledge could be used against them.

Being caught in possession of such documentation would have left Yorgi more vulnerable to a degree, and might have exposed his various operations. The club at the converted church was a front, and everyone knew that. Yorgi had learned to keep his greatest secrets in the greatest hiding places.

Now, with Malenkov in motion, Kolya and Viktor hunted the hunters.

The cell phone in Yorgi's jacket pocket trilled for attention. He lifted the earbud from his jacket and slipped the device into place. Then he tapped the Send button.

"Yes," he said, knowing he didn't need to introduce himself to anyone who called that number.

"Malenkov was intercepted," Kolya announced.

A cold chill spun through Yorgi. "Where?"

"In the alley outside the club."

"What about Malenkov?"

"He's unconscious."

Filled with nervous energy, Yorgi stood and walked to the balcony railing. He looked down at the dancers as the baby spotlights rushed over the gyrating bodies below.

"Kill Malenkov," Yorgi said. From the corner of his eye, he saw Yelena coming up behind him. "Later, burn his hiding place. I'm sure he left nothing behind of the information he retrieved for us, but I want to be certain."

"We will," Kolya replied.

"Who took the chip?" Yorgi asked.

"I don't know, but there is a toy in the alley. A crossbow bolt attached to a cable." Kolya's voice held a smile. "I think Malenkov's attacker slid along the cable and surprised him."

"You think it was the Americans?"

"They love their toys as much as the British," Kolya said. "I also think that the American didn't have a chance to escape. I think he or she fled into the club."

Intrigued by his brother's statement, Yorgi glanced down at the dancers. This time he spotted the man in the Italian suit aggressively making his way through the crowded floor.

Alerted by some primitive instinct that guided hunters and warriors, the CIA agent glanced up, scanning the balconies and finally coming to rest on Yorgi. A faint smile of recognition pulled at the American's lips, then he nodded. Almost casually, he took a protective case from his jacket. He opened the case and took out the chip, then slipped the unit into a small electronic device that Yorgi recognized instantly.

"That's a Tech Deck," Yelena said over the roar of the crowd.

"I know," Yorgi said. With the Tech Deck, the agent could download the information from the data chip, then compress, encrypt, and transmit the files to his handler over the wireless satellite link.

The agent put the data chip away, the contents already scanned into the Tech Deck. He punched a dial-up number.

"Get in here," Yorgi spat into the cell phone. "The agent is here." He folded the phone closed and glanced over his shoulder at Kirill. "I need you."

Without hurry, Kirill uncoiled and took a final drag before crushing the cigarette out in the ashtray. He reached under his coat and dragged out a target pistol.

Yorgi kept his eyes on the American agent struggling to get through the crowd. He pointed at the man as Kirill took his place at the railing.

4

McGrath knew he wasn't going to get out of his present situation alive. When he'd entered the Agency, he'd been told that a day like today might come. At twenty-three, he hadn't believed such a thing could happen. At twenty-three, he'd felt invulnerable, like nothing could ever truly stop him or slow him.

That had been sixteen years ago. At thirty-nine, he'd been shot and stabbed in more than a dozen different countries, with repeats of violence in several of those. All of those wounds and near-deaths had been during service to his country, to a way of life he believed in. He never thought he'd have regrets if the time came when he had to pay the piper.

He didn't have any regrets now, but he knew he had to stay moving long enough for the Tech Deck to complete the telecommunication upload. Once his handler got whatever information Malenkov had been carrying, other agents would visit Yorgi and Anarchy 99, and they'd take their world apart. That wasn't vengeance for the death McGrath knew he was going to have to suffer, but it was close enough.

He stayed low in the crowd, no longer just bumping through the dancers now. He shoved and pushed, used his elbows and his knees to blast through the thronging mass. Feeling the fear thrum through him, trying not to feel ashamed of the emotion, he battled his way toward the stage. If he could gain the stage, he could save some time by racing across the raised platform to the doorway.

Hoarse shouts rang out behind McGrath. Before he could stop himself, the agent glanced back, breaking one of a runner's cardinal rules of never looking over his shoulder.

Viktor and Kolya nearly took the doors off as they charged into the church. Neither of them carried weapons openly, but McGrath doubted the presence of pistols or a rocket launcher would have broken the crowd's mood. The two men lurched into pursuit of him at once, but the crowd hampered their forward progress.

McGrath opened his pocket for a quick look at the Tech Deck. DATA UPLOADING . . . 7%. Steeling his resolve, gasping from the sheer effort required to keep moving through the crowd, the agent fought his way to the stage. He lashed out with an elbow, dropping a young guy like a pole-axed steer. Then the agent grabbed a young woman in front of him and used her as a blocker, ramming her into another group of dancers and sending them all crashing down.

McGrath had little sympathy in his heart. He'd

been told that whatever was on the data chip could threaten the free world, including the United States. And the clubgoers didn't seem like the type to be concerned with the interest of the rest of civilization.

Stepping onto the backs of the half-dozen men and women he'd knocked down, McGrath marched upward, gaining another ten feet toward the stage. The band was wrapped up in their own world and music, oblivious to the fight for survival carried out at their feet.

McGrath's struggle hadn't gone completely unnoticed, though. He found he suddenly had a few fans among the dancers, men and women who cheered him on as he fought his way through the crowd. The agent snap-kicked another man in the groin, doubling the guy over and vaulting to his back. Standing on the injured man's back, swaying with the movement as the man started to collapse, McGrath spotted another guy standing with his hands held in a stirrup fashion at the base of the stage.

The guy's face was covered in piercings and a huge smile that revealed missing teeth. He spoke but McGrath couldn't hear him over the music. His meaning, however, was clear.

McGrath stepped into the man's hands just as the man he was standing on collapsed to the floor. The man holding McGrath's foot levered the agent up, driving him toward the stage in a couple of stumbling steps, aiding what he undoubtedly thought was a crazed fan's effort to reach the stage. Incredibly, the CIA agent caught the raised platform's edge with both hands and started to pull himself up.

Hope surged within McGrath. Maybe he'd been

premature in his assessment of the situation. Maybe he was going to escape.

Yorgi stood silently and watched as Kolya and Viktor rolled over anyone who got in their way. Even as fiercely as his brother and the big man battled, though, Yorgi knew they were doomed to failure. The club was too packed, too filled with people who welcomed violence as a release.

Several of the men and women among the dancers turned to Kolya and Viktor, aiming fists and feet at them, even trying to bite. Kolya and Viktor didn't hesitate and offered no quarter to anyone unlucky enough to be unaware of their approach or those foolish enough to attempt standing against them.

Watching, feeling anxiety pinwheel inside him, Yorgi glanced at Yelena. The woman stood at the railing as well, her face devoid of emotion but her dark eyes ever watchful. She was, Yorgi knew, always watching.

Everything rested with Kirill now.

With a smooth economy of motion, Kirill reached inside his jacket and drew out a silencer and a specially made pistol scope. Looking as though he didn't have a care in the world, Kirill spun the silencer into the threaded grooves a precise two and one-quarter turns, then clipped the scope into place atop the pistol.

Restraining the urge to hurry Kirill, knowing from long practice that such an effort was only a waste of breath because Kirill ignored such things, Yorgi watched as the American agent scrambled to the top of the stage. Several stage divers threw themselves into the crowd, getting carried back on the hands of the audience before the raised platform.

Kirill locked in behind the silenced pistol, arms extended in a relaxed fashion as he sighted through the scope with both eyes open. Then he squeezed the trigger.

The slide popped back only long enough to kick out a single smoking casing. The tumbling brass caught the light for an instant, then disappeared. Without another thought, Kirill lowered and began dismantling his weapon. He glanced at Yelena as if seeking some kind of acknowledgment for his skill, but she—as always—ignored him.

Attention focused on stage, Yorgi thought at first that Kirill had missed. Then he saw that the American agent no longer had control over his body. The man stood stiffly, then toppled backward into the crowd.

Never knowing the man was dead, obviously thinking he was a stage diver, the crowd heaved the corpse backward. The dead man gathered speed as the crowd responded to the challenge of moving him. Other stage divers joined the surfing as the band continued to play.

Yorgi opened his cell phone and punched Kolya's speed-dial number.

"Yes," Kolya responded. On the crowded dance floor, Kolya corrected his course, moving to intercept the dead agent's body.

"He has a Tech Deck in his pocket," Yorgi said. "He was using the device to transmit the files on the data chip."

"Understood."

Yorgi closed his phone and watched as Kolya and

Viktor caught up with the dead American's body. Their hands darted into the corpse's clothing, taking out the Tech Deck and the data chip Malenkov had been delivering.

When he had the Tech Deck, Kolya held the device up in triumph. He made a show of pressing the buttons to break the connection.

Gazing at the dead man being passed back along the crowd, Yorgi watched until the gruesome sight disappeared into the flashing lights and smoke. Then he turned and walked back to their table, followed by Yelena.

Kirill had already resumed his seat. He took his lighter from the pack of cigarettes in front of him, shook out a cigarette, and lighted up. As he smoked, he unbuttoned and rolled up his left sleeve. Despite the dimness of the club, dozens of roughly round burn scars stood revealed on his flesh. Coolly, almost dispassionately, Kirill took his cigarette and pressed the glowing orange coal against his arm in an unblemished area.

The man was counting, Yorgi knew. Over the years, he'd seen Kirill mark each kill in the same manner. Tonight, at least, Yorgi couldn't hear the hiss of searing flesh.

Seated between them, Yelena watched the process and shuddered. She looked away quickly.

Turning his attention to his own drink, Yorgi took a spoonful of sugar from the bowl in front of him. Holding the sugar over a candle flame till the white crystals held a blue glow, he placed the spoon into a glass of absinthe, caught the alcohol on fire briefly, then blew out the cobalt flame. He drank the heated alcohol down in a single gulp, feeling the liquid burn through him. The effects of the drug-laced drink hit him almost immediately, crashing through his senses and opening them up in totally new ways to the world around him.

He gazed at Yelena and almost laughed. She tried so very hard not to appear overly interested in what he was doing, in what the data chip Malenkov had carried meant to them. Now, with the death of the American agent tonight, he knew her curiosity would reach fever pitch.

But she wouldn't ask. No, Yelena was much too careful for that.

Yorgi poured himself another drink and took another spoonful of sugar. He held the spoon over the candle as his senses buzzed. And what if he told her that the data chip involved the end of the world, he wondered. Would she be concerned then? Or would she maintain the cold, controlled exterior at which she worked so hard?

The question begged an answer, and Yorgi almost gave in and told her.

Almost, but he didn't. He would tell her minutes, perhaps only hours before the world ended. Not days. He lit his drink, blew the flame out, then swallowed the absinthe, feeling his nervous system crater and rebuild.

UPGRADING SPY

5

Blue Ridge Mountains, Virginia
United States of America

Special Agent Augustus Gibbons of the National Security Agency, one of the most clandestine agencies operated by his government, sat in the helicopter's copilot seat and watched as Washington, D.C., fell away beneath him. He relaxed, knowing he wasn't going to be hounded by phone calls or questions for the moment, but he focused on the coming meeting.

The face-to-face wasn't just a meeting, though. To Gibbons, the sit-down was a mission. And Augustus Gibbons was all about the mission.

The NSA agent felt the pilot's curious stare and knew the man was sizing him up, probably wondering if the scars that littered Gibbons's face, neck, and hands were from screw-ups and missions gone bad, or if he'd just been in the thick of everything.

The truth was, the scars came from both. He'd earned them while being brave and while being foolhardy; from times when he'd been hard-pressed and times when he'd taken the view that an op was a slam-dunk. Gibbons had paid in blood all the way around—his own and that of others who had trusted him or had made the mistake of believing in him when he'd only been there to use them.

He wore a brown suit that looked nondescript, but he still made the suit look good. He was tall and lean, a tailor's dream for a guy who was supposed to be purely executive material. At his age, Gibbons knew most men started to go to pot, to let themselves go. Hell, there were guys letting themselves go before they ever got to his age.

Gibbons kept himself carefully mastered. Death came for any man who started to let his guard down, or who believed he'd learned enough. The world constantly taught survival skills, and Augustus Gibbons, career warrior, was one of the greatest students.

That was why he was attending the meeting today. A new lesson had been taught in Prague only days ago, and it was time someone picked that lesson up and made something of the new reality.

Gibbons relaxed his mind, concentrating on his reflection in the Plexiglas till the world went away. He no longer heard the throbbing beat of the helicopter rotors or the chirp and bleep of the craft's instruments. As always, he knew everyone who would be at the meeting, and he knew what agenda they were operating from. Today, the opposition was going to have a very bad day. Gibbons intended to take no prisoners.

The complex of black buildings in Virginia's Blue Ridge Mountains remained invisible to casual inspection. Even if an aerial observer happened to notice them, TOP SECRET BASE wasn't advertised in banners.

The helicopter pilot dropped altitude and swooped toward the ground, creating a momentary negative gravity effect.

Gibbons figured the pilot was trying to test his passenger's stomach, and maybe get back a little for the noncommunicative jaunt out into the mountains. The NSA agent didn't care, and the rapid descent didn't bother him in the slightest. The landing on the bull's-eye helipad was picture perfect.

Keeping his head low, Gibbons walked under the rotors. The downdraft pulled at his clothing and stirred microscopic grit from the helipad that stung his exposed skin. He ignored the slight pain, palmed his swipe card, and let himself through the guarded entrance down into the main building.

Uniformed guards stationed at bulletproof checkpoints throughout the complex checked Gibbons out as he passed the primary stations. The security included fingerprinting and retinal scans as well as two men who knew him well enough to ask about family.

After that, he was shown to the special elevator that descended to the basement levels under the building. Disaster-proof and bomb-proof, the basement levels contained computer equipment that watched over the world.

Getting down to the lowest level—at least, the lowest level that Gibbons knew about—took the agent's swipe card, two other swipe cards at two different locations throughout the complex, and a video confirmation from the security station located in the level below.

Gibbons entered the elevator alone. Few other people had clearance to the lower levels, and fewer still had access to the level where his meeting was scheduled. The elevator hummed as the doors closed, then he dropped at a high enough rate of speed to remind him of the helicopter descent.

When the elevator doors opened again, Gibbons saw the double doors ahead of him bearing the National Security Agency seal. Silence filled the long hallway. Gibbons heard his shoes echoing as they struck the floor. He knew he was under constant video and audio surveillance from the time he stepped out of the elevator cage.

A heavy metal door, looking like something that would have been better suited as a submarine compartment hatch, filled the other end of the hallway. Before Gibbons reached it, the door slid open and the agent stepped into the cybernetic nerve center of the underground complex.

Although he'd seen the rows of computer hardware and monitors, the huge screens that filled entire walls with pictures of maps and satellite images from around the world, Gibbons still couldn't help but feel in awe of the whole set-up. If the surface world ended in a nuclear bomb attack at that precise instant, somewhere between heartbeats, the room held enough information and power to run whatever was left of the United States of America, including military installations in other countries.

No one paid Gibbons any attention as he strode through the room. The tech teams manning the various workstations weren't supposed to give any undue attention to field personnel. Besides that, Gibbons knew he was of no interest to the people working the computer stations. After all, he was only flesh and blood, not hardware and software.

Sam Tannick, the grizzled NSA chief, held court in one of the small ready rooms off the main nerve center. Age had put gray in his hair and stooped his posture these days, and had taken a step or two off his game, but Tannick still showed the years of experienced fieldwork that had garnered him a top dog position at the NSA.

Tannick's jacket was open, making him look like a guy who was nearing the end of a long, hard day. He leaned over a workstation and stared at the lines of script covering the monitor.

The man talking to Tannick was Roger Donnan, a field agent who had risen far in the Agency through his political connections. He was prim and proper, showing the influence of the Ivy League schools he'd gone to before taking the position within the Agency.

Seated in the ergonomic computer chair at the workstation, Donnan keyed in data, watching the lines scroll across the screen. "And at 00:30 hours," Donnan said, "the mission deviated from the set parameters."

"It wasn't part of the plan for our agent to get shot in the back?" Tannick asked, laying the sarcasm on. "That's reassuring."

Gibbons paused just a moment as a smile pulled at his lips. He steeled himself, knowing that walking into the situation grinning at Donnan's misfortune wasn't going to play well—especially considering what he was going to try to sell them on.

Donnan bristled at the comment, but didn't try to dodge the issue or shift the blame to someone else. Gibbons gave the man style points. In the old days, Donnan would have tried either avenue, and possibly both before allowing himself to get nailed down.

"McGrath was uploading some data to us when he was . . . cut off." Donnan tapped more keys.

Onscreen, a file appeared, then blossomed into a spray of gibberish that flickered and changed, then continued scrolling down the monitor. Gibbons studied the letters and numerals with increasing interest, making out some of the information.

"We're not sure yet exactly what it was," Donnan went on.

"It's part of a chemical formula," Gibbons announced.

Tannick and Donnan turned to face him. Sour displeasure covered Donnan's features, but the NSA chief smiled a welcome and waved Gibbons into the ready room.

6

Augustus Gibbons stepped into the ready room, ignoring Donnan's challenging stare. Instead, Gibbons kept his attention on the computer screen. He nodded at the information contained there. "Possibly a drug or a biological weapon. There's not enough here to tell. Either way, this is shaping up to be a major problem."

"Gibbons," Donnan said, speaking the agent's name as if speaking about something particularly unsavory that he'd stepped in. His head swiveled toward Tannick. "Sir, what is he doing here?"

"I called him in," Tannick answered without hesitation. "We've lost three agents on this so far. I thought you could use the help."

Gibbons stepped forward, moving dangerously close to invading Donnan's personal space. The Ivy Leaguers were always conscious of personal space. Only respect for Tannick held Gibbons in check.

"I managed to fill in a few blanks from my end," Gibbons said. "The group calls itself Anarchy 99. They started as a splinter arm of the Red Mafiya—"

Donnan pushed himself from the ergonomic chair to a standing position. He was still a few inches short of Gibbons. "I have this under control, sir." His voice sounded strained. "I've got another man prepped and ready to go in."

Silently, Gibbons wondered who Donnan's latest sacrificial lamb was. A slight flush of guilt covered the NSA agent. The men who had died had been good men. They'd deserved a whole hell of a lot better than what they'd gotten. Still, he couldn't let Donnan's comment pass without nailing down some of the responsibility.

Gibbons glanced at Donnan. "Einstein said the definition of insanity is trying the same thing over and over and expecting different results."

Eyeing him petulantly, Donnan retorted, "I must have missed his memo."

"I'd say you've been missing a lot," Gibbons said, heating up a little. "The guys you're after are smarter than you're giving them credit for. They're ex-military. They can smell the training on our agents a mile away." He paused, reaching into his pocket. "It's time we tried something new." He brought the CD out of his pocket, turning the case so that light splintered.

After Tannick and Donnan followed him to his office, Gibbons placed the CD into the drive on his computer. The actual files weren't contained on the disk. A heavily encrypted dial-up program was hidden in the other files loaded onto the disk.

When he had the disk booted, he tapped keys to awaken the program and sent the software out spinning through the Internet to gather the sensitive information he'd compiled in the past few weeks regarding his newest project.

Despite Tannick's easy acceptance of Gibbons's offer to show them the project, Donnan had let his doubt be known. There'd been a lot of grumbling as well. A preparatory strike designed to launch a full rebuttal from, Gibbons guessed. Real effort was required on Gibbons's part not to react to the asinine way that the younger agent acted. Of course, the fact that Gibbons was certain there was no way he could lose helped a lot.

Gibbons offered Tannick the room's only other chair, then took the one behind the desk for himself. Donnan was forced to stand or go get his own chair. Getting his own chair would have implied that he was ready to listen to anything Gibbons had to say, and that was too much. The man chose to stand. Gibbons let him.

Tapping the keyboard, Gibbons started the automatic display feature. Picture after picture of different young men flashed on the computer monitor. None of them fit the crisp, corporate type that the government intelligence agencies had been recruiting for years.

Curiosity fueled Donnan, drawing him closer to the screen. "These guys aren't ours. Who are they? CIA?"

"No," Gibbons said casually, enjoying the moment because he knew he was going to blow Donnan away. "They're civilians." He shrugged. "More or less. Convicts, mercs, contract killers. The top layer from the bottom of the barrel. Each talented in his own way."

Disbelief showed on Donnan's face. A brief glance at Tannick told Gibbons that the NSA chief was still listening.

"You want to send those guys on a mission of national security?" Donnan exploded. He glanced at Tannick, seeking support. "They're the scum of the earth!"

Leaning back in his chair, reminding Donnan that he was the only one not seated and not comfy in the office, Gibbons steepled his fingers, resting his elbows on the chair arms. "They're also programmable. And expendable. It works, and sometimes it's your only option."

"So the question is," Tannick interjected, "can a wild dog be turned into a guard dog?"

A warm glow suffused Gibbons. After years of working with Tannick, the NSA agent knew when the older man was interested in a scheme, and this one had definitely caught his eye.

"Sam," Donnan interrupted, "tell me you aren't considering this. Remember what he tried in Rwanda? And look what that got him."

Anger fired in Tannick's eyes but he kept the emotion from the rest of his face. "That's enough."

Gibbons placed his own anger aside, knowing now was not the time for any of that. Rwanda had been a mistake. This was not.

"Sam," Gibbons grated, "this Ivy League hayseed got three agents dead for a thimbleful of information. Now we can march another man into the rat's nest or we can send a rat instead."

Donnan exploded in apoplexy, and the debate was fully engaged.

Long minutes later, feeling better about life in general and wondering if he'd actually tried to bite off more than he could chew, Gibbons followed Tannick down the hallway to the elevator. Donnan marched beside him, still fully invested in the argument that had begun in Gibbons's office and still hadn't ended.

"Sir," Donnan pleaded, turning sideways and moving quickly to match Tannick's strong stride, "don't let this lunatic jeopardize my operation."

"Things happen in the field that they didn't teach you in spy school, Mr. Donnan," Tannick stated without looking at the man.

"It's a new world," Gibbons couldn't resist saying, "a new era. It's clear now more than ever that the old ways don't always work anymore."

Tannick stopped in front of the elevator, slid his swipe card through the reader, then gazed up at the hidden video camera. The elevator doors opened with a distinct *bing!* The NSA chief stepped inside the cage and turned to face the two men.

Gibbons waited, feeling a little more tense than he wanted to. Donnan shot him a jeering look, reveling in his certain victory.

"The ball goes to," Tannick said, "Gibbons." He shifted his attention to his chosen party. "Get these *scum*, Augustus, and bring them in. Test them, train them—find your man."

Barely restraining an exuberant shout, Gibbons nodded and watched the elevator doors close.

Donnan let fly with a stream of rhetoric that he definitely hadn't learned at an Ivy League university.

Gibbons didn't waste time rubbing salt in an open wound, though the temptation was certainly there. Instead, he turned and walked back toward the command center. The die had been cast, and there still remained about a million details to attend to. Some of those details included kidnapping prospective agent recruits.

7

Los Angeles, California

State Senator Dick Hotchkiss gazed down the long line of cars waiting patiently in front of the country club. Red-jacketed valets scrambled in the late morning sun to get to all the vehicles. Everybody seemed to have chosen to show up fashionably late for the gathering.

Irritably, not patient at all with the turn of events, Hotchkiss checked his reflection in the rearview mirror. He was handsome, still a photogenic favorite of the media, and he enjoyed the role. Hours spent with a personal trainer and under an ultraviolet lamp had left him striking-looking, still the kind of guy who turned women's heads wherever he was.

Hotchkiss knew that some women didn't like the fact that a man knew he drew their attention. The senator didn't care and figured to hell with them. Besides, maybe those women didn't like the fact that he knew what he had, but that dislike certainly didn't keep them from trying to get their share of it.

He took another look at the mirror, then ran his hand through his hair and couldn't help smiling. The tousled look was what he was most famous for—the one that made him look like he'd just crawled out of bed. Of course, speculation about whose bed that had been had filled reams of tabloids and many segments of talk TV.

The young woman in the passenger seat was his latest intern. She was blond and beautiful, blessed with a willowy figure and a high, firm rack that was larger than her IQ. The red dress she wore was just a tad bit longer than obscene, and presented maximum cleavage. No one believed that she just took dictation from him.

She looked at him with doe eyes and an uncertain smile. During their involvement he'd taught her never to make inappropriate touches or use of his first name. Even in bed, he required her to call him Senator so she wouldn't get in the habit of addressing him too familiarly.

And out of a perverse need to keep her guessing where those lines were, primarily so he could berate her in private, Hotchkiss reached out to grab her naked thigh. Her flesh felt warm against his. He took pride in ownership. The bright red convertible Corvette he drove, with the personalized tag VOT4DIK, was one of his most prized possessions. Everyone who knew him knew that.

The young woman started to reach for him.

Hotchkiss hastily drew his hand away and warded off her touch. "Not here," he said. "It would be just my luck that a photographer got a shot of you putting your hands on me. That's all I'd need."

"Sorry," she apologized, pouting a little and looking guilty. "It's just kind of hard, you know, keeping my hands to myself when all I want to do is hold you."

"I know," Hotchkiss said, "but you've got to be strong. For both of us."

She smiled and nodded. The uncertain desperation to please him showed in her eyes, further exciting Hotchkiss.

The late morning heat blasted down. With the top off, Hotchkiss had no protection from the sun and the air conditioner couldn't keep up with the demand. He started to swelter in his suit.

Shoving his head up above the windshield, Hotchkiss peered at the valets working the line hurriedly. Impatient, the state senator leaned on the horn, honking loud and long.

"Come on, Pepe!" Hotchkiss snarled. He turned to the girl in the passenger seat. "Unbelievable. How hard is it to park a car?"

The girl pointed past Hotchkiss.

Before the state senator could turn around, his door opened. Hotchkiss stopped himself short of falling out of the car. Angrily, he stared at the big guy in black pants and the red jacket.

"It's about time," Hotchkiss complained as he got out of the Corvette. He tossed the keys to the big man. "Keep it out of the sun. I don't want that paint to fade."

With an easy grace, the valet slid behind the sports car's wheel. He had a trim physique but showed a weightlifter's build. Tattoos adorned his body, including his hands and arms. The most striking one that caught the state senator's eye was the row of Xs tattooed across his neck at the base of his skull. The outside two Xs were red framed in black, and were a lot smaller than the black center X framed in red that flared out beyond either of them. His shaved head showed the tattoo in all its glory.

The girl in the passenger seat remained sitting, and the smile that blossomed there threatened to split her face.

"Hey," she said.

"Hey," the valet said.

Hotchkiss felt unaccustomed jealousy and thought about saying something, then decided not to. The guy was big and dangerous looking, like the country club had scoured the city's jails or prisons for staff.

The valet nodded toward Hotchkiss but he was talking to the young woman. "Maybe I better park the car by myself. You obviously got a thing to do."

"Yeah," the girl said, her eyes never moving from the valet's face. "Yeah, I guess so. Maybe I'll see you again when we pick up the car."

The valet gave her an easy grin. "Don't think so. This is just a temporary gig for me."

"Too bad." She slid out of the seat.

Hotchkiss looked at her meaningfully. "Don't bother the help. They're obviously behind today."

Coolly, the valet turned and looked at him. Then he started the Corvette and dropped his foot on the accelerator. The tires chirped as they burned rubber, and the Corvette leaped from the line of cars like a spurred quarter horse. The SKATEBOARDING IS A CRIME bumper sticker showed out against the rear bumper.

Hotchkiss watched in disbelief as the car rocketed

over a curb. Then the valet cut the wheel sharply and roared through a line of stone pillars set so close together that both of the vehicle's side mirrors exploded in a spray of mirrored chunks and red fiberglass. In the next instant, the Corvette's fat tires chewed through the landscaped lawn, leaving ruts in their wake. The car skidded up onto the road, pushing the envelope of control but managing to hold traction.

Another valet passed in front of Hotchkiss, his attention riveted on the screeching Corvette fishtailing on the road.

Hotchkiss grabbed the young man by his jacket lapels. "Where's he going?" the state senator demanded.

The valet shrugged.

Frustrated and angry, Hotchkiss took out his cell phone and dialed 911. Whoever the thief was, there was going to be a hell of a price to pay when he got caught. When the phone was answered, the senator yelled, "This is Senator Hotchkiss! Someone just stole my car!"

8

Xander Cage lived for adrenaline highs, and he was working on one now. Stealing Senator Hotchkiss's pet Corvette convertible was only the opening salvo, the first jolt on a planned heart-attack find-and-grind.

It was a shame about the Corvette, though. For an overclassed sports car toy, the vehicle handled pretty damn sweet. Not like pure and classic Detroit muscle, of course.

Reaching into his pocket, Xander took out a cell phone/walkie-talkie combo, keyed the pad, and said, "Yo, Pit Boss."

"Hey, X," Rashonn's rich and melodic voice called back over the handset. She sounded as excited about the stunt as he did. "Pickin' up the story about Senator Hotchkiss's pretty red Corvette gettin' boosted from the country club."

"Yeah," Xander said. "It's a real tear-jerker. You got the crew wound tight?"

"We're at the site now, little man. Come get some."

Xander followed the mental map he'd made of the area. He'd set up the boost and designed the stunt they'd play out. All he had to do was hit the numbers. *Oh, yeah—and get out alive. Don't wanna forget that part.*

A few more turns down a few more streets, hearing the occasional police siren now, Xander spotted the white van the team had. They'd parked next to a truck filled with BMX bikes and towing a bright orange trailer containing a jump ramp.

By the time Xander parked alongside the van and got out, the handpicked pit crew exploded from the van and got to work on the Corvette. The guys in the crew could have worked any NASCAR circuit in the country, but today they were leaving the Corvette stock. However, they were bolting a video camera to the floorboard in front of the driver's seat. Battery-powered electric drills whined as metal screws tore through the Corvette's undercarriage.

The protective crash box with the Plexiglas front had a slim-line design that didn't offer much in the way of comfort, but Xander knew he wasn't going to have to put up with the inconvenience for long. Since the Corvette was an automatic, driving didn't require much fancy footwork.

Rashonn stepped from the van with Xander's street clothes in her arms. She was slim and beautiful. "Hey man, we're goin' off the hook today."

Xander made a fist and bumped knuckles with his friend. Rashonn was Xander's partner in the underground Internet video business they'd set up featuring homegrown extreme sports stunts.

Stripping out of the valet garb quickly and without modesty at the side of the street, Xander pulled his street clothes and stunt gear on, finishing up with wraparound shades and a black woolen beanie.

"I saw the guys with the jump ramp," Xander said, watching as the pit crew finished installing the video camera. "They gonna be in place on time?"

"If they aren't," Rashonn said, "we'll just do it right on the next take." Then she broke up laughing, unable to hold herself back anymore.

Xander laughed too. Both of them knew they only had one shot at the stunt—if they even got the chance. The stunt was the wildest and most legally daring thing Xander had ever done. The sirens sounded like they were getting closer now. He figured someone in the neighborhood had identified the sports car and called in.

"Done," one of the pit crew members said. "Video's confirmed. You're live, dude. Five by five."

"See you when I see you," Xander said to Rashonn.

"After," Rashonn said. "Don't go gettin' dead."

Xander smiled. "Probably sell more videos that way." Then he was moving, the adrenaline singing within him, making him feel alive like nothing else in the world ever did.

Sliding behind the wheel, Xander pulled the transmission into gear, then dropped his foot on the accelerator. The Corvette responded at once, burning rubber. The ass-end of the car slid around for a second before the tires gripped the street and hurled the vehicle forward like an arrow shot from a bow.

A glance over Xander's shoulder showed flashing lights in the distance and closing fast. Rashonn stayed put in the white van, letting the LAPD squad car roll by before pulling onto the street and taking up the pursuit as well.

Xander grinned, then took a CD from his pocket and placed the disk into the player. He cranked the system, filling the car and the neighborhood with the hip-hop techno blast.

Okay, bro, he thought, staring into the rearview mirror attached to the windshield and seeing the police car trying to close the distance, *we're off to the races.*

9

Xander drove the stolen Corvette expertly, weaving through traffic just enough to stay ahead of the five police cars that now followed along his backtrail. *Man, there's absolutely nothing like being hunted.* He felt the grin slide across her face.

He tapped the steering wheel in time with the explosive beat coming from the CD, letting himself really groove to the music. With the adrenaline running so high in him, there was no past, no tomorrows, only the crystal-clear presence of *now.* It was a solid gold rush.

That was where Xander Cage most wanted to live. In the now. That was the only place worth getting to stay in.

The trick with handling the cops was to know how to stay out of any grid they might manage to attempt. Xander had plotted the boost with skill and knowledge, had even taken care to time the lights on the intersections he'd be using, and laid in three alternate courses.

God, he lived for the stunt, and he knew his life would become absolute hell if that ever weren't enough.

"Driver of the red Corvette," a police officer's voice blared from the public address speaker mounted in the marked car. "Pull over now!"

"Yeah, yeah, yeah," Xander replied even though he knew the police officers following him couldn't hear. He checked the rearview mirror on the windshield, then took another corner, just beating out the marked unit that tried to shut off the intersection.

He punched the Release button on the CD player, took out his disk, and carefully put the CD back in the protective case. He shoved the case into his pocket.

Reaching down, he switched on the video camera mounted on the floorboard in the crash box. Seeing the camera's recording light come on, he cleared his throat and said, "This car belongs to the honorable Dick Hotchkiss of the California State Senate. You might remember Dick as the legislator who passed bills on such headline-grabbing topics as the dangers of skateboarding, how rap concerts promote violence, and how movies and video games corrupt the morals of our youth. This from a guy who's never even touched a PS2."

At the next intersection, Xander breezed a yellow light that turned red right before he went through. Horns squawked behind him, the sounds turned to shreds by the approach of the screaming sirens.

"Now," Xander said, continuing his address to

the video camera, "he's trying to bring back the draft for every kid who can't go to college. With a schedule like that, it's amazing he still finds time to sleep with his interns."

Entering another intersection, spotting the street sign announcing Forest Hill Bridge, Xander floored the accelerator and cut off a pair of police cars. *All right, they're definitely amping up the gridlock. But that's cool. The more the merrier, and the bigger the stunt.*

Glancing in the rearview mirror again, Xander checked on Rashonn and the white van. They were still hanging in. And Xander had no doubts that Rashonn was continuing to roll video footage and already composing her voice-overs.

Taking the final turns that brought him to the Angeles Forest Highway, Xander put the pedal to the metal and roared through a half-baked attempt at a blockade. A red-and-white striped sawhorse went flying, ripping a gouge in the Corvette's paint. But the vehicle remained intact.

Okay, baby, Xander thought, *ain't nothing but you and me and the road. And the stunt waiting at the other end.* The wind whipped by him, broken by the windshield. The slipstream howled overhead.

Following the Angeles Forest Highway north out of Los Angeles, Xander kept the Corvette ahead of the pursuing police cars screaming after him. The highway ran through the San Gabriel Mountains and eventually led to Antelope Valley. He wasn't going that far today, and the Corvette would never make that distance.

The Forest Hill Bridge spanned a deep ravine less than two miles ahead. Catching occasional glimpses of the distinctive arched bridge over the valley floor, Xander felt his heart speed up again. *Almost show-time.*

Big-cone spruce and canyon oak trees littered the north slopes of the mountains, visible in Xander's rearview mirror. White rocks gleamed from within the dark emerald chaparral, contrasting sharply with the wide, open blue sky.

The truck hauling BMX bikes and the orange trailer stopped in the middle of the bridge. Men rushed from the cab and off-loaded a jump ramp, shoving the construction onto the bridge in pre-designated spots marked with spray paint. A few inches either way wouldn't make a difference on the jump ramp, but the set-up had to be close.

Xander's stomach tightened as he watched the men shoving the jump ramp back and forth. The distance separating him from the bridge evaporated like night frost under a harsh morning sun. He didn't ease off the accelerator, though. He couldn't. Speed had to be maintained and couldn't be made up, and if he slacked off, one of the police officers behind him might decide to drive up alongside him and try to blast his tires.

Having one or more tires shot out meant the jump ramp—and the stunt—would no longer be doable.

Xander pulled out his cell phone/walkie-talkie and keyed the device up. "I'm coming in hot with a side of bacon. Everybody get ready." He switched the unit off without waiting for a reply, then shoved it deeply into his pocket.

The set-up team abandoned the jump ramp and raced for the waiting truck.

Concentrating and letting go at the same time,

Xander pushed all of the air out of him, clearing his mind and letting his focus become crystal. Part of his attention tracked the arrival of two police cars skidding to halts that blocked the bridge after the truck made a rapid exit past them. But Xander Cage was all about the coming stunt.

Keeping the accelerator pinned, Xander sped from the highway to the bridge, feeling the Corvette's rack-and-pinion steering and low-slung suspension struggle with the harsh change for an instant. *C'mon, baby. Hold together for me for just another couple of seconds.* He kept both hands on the wheel, knowing the shrilling tires were barely maintaining traction with the pavement.

At the other end of the bridge, uniformed police officers abandoned their vehicles and took cover behind the bridge supports on the other side of the ravine. Even if he tried to stop now, Xander knew the effort would have been an exercise in futility. The police officers knew that too. The Corvette's fiberglass body wouldn't have survived the impact, and he'd have been shredded right along with the car.

Xander pulled hard on the steering wheel, hanging onto a thin layer of traction as rubber shrieked in protest. Grudgingly, the Corvette fell into line, hurtling full bore for the jump ramp aimed over the bridge's side. When the sports car muscled up the jump ramp, gravity sucked Xander deeper into the seat. Then he was airborne, hurtling into the blue sky.

That sensation lasted only a couple of thudding beats though, because gravity won and the car fell, floating high and wide, perfectly positioned for all the cameras Rashonn had set up in the area to shoot the jump. And Xander Cage fell with the vehicle.

10

It's not the fall that kills you, Xander reminded himself. *It's that sudden stop at the end.* He couldn't help grinning at his own joke as he unbuckled the seat belt and stood. He glanced around, trapped in the sensory overload of a true adrenaline high—the place where everything seemed to take place in slow motion.

The bridge seemed to fall *up* into the sky, rushing toward the few puffy white clouds hanging in a sea of blue. The shoulders of the valley followed next, surging up like a newly born volcanic island.

Xander pushed himself to the top of the seats and to the Corvette's rear deck, feeling light as a feather. He knew not much effort was needed to kick free of the vehicle. The slipstream pulled at his clothing and tugged at him. He bent and grinned at the video camera, waggling his fingers. "Bye bye!"

Pushing off with a foot, Xander kicked free of the falling Corvette. Amazingly, the car remained upright, like it was going to land catlike on all four tires at the bottom of the ravine.

Xander swooped with the wind, splaying out in a perfect starfish position. If he'd jumped from several thousand feet up instead of just a few hundred, he could have flown for long minutes and enjoyed the exhilaration that filled him even longer. Skydiving was a blast, but he wasn't there to skydive.

He reached up to his chest and pulled the backpack parachute's D-ring. The nylon unfurled overhead, blossoming out into a rectangular sport parachute. He caught the steering lines and toggles, and took control of his descent.

The Corvette slammed against the ground, shattering like a child's toy, scattering in bright pieces against the broken ground. The child's toy analogy, Xander had to admit, was pretty much dead-on. Senator Hotchkiss had prided himself on owning the Corvette.

A classic muscle car convertible sped along the narrow farm-to-market road near the bottom of the ravine. The vehicle fishtailed briefly as the driver pulled off-road, tearing through the green grass and dodging chaparral. Roshonn's white van halted at the shoulder of the road.

Xander pulled on the steering lines and glided toward the white van. A three-man team rushed from the muscle car and started working on the crash cage surrounding the video camera.

Glancing back up at the bridge, growing more and more distant, Xander saw the police officers gathered at the railing. By the time they found the streets leading back to the farm-to-market roads

Rashonn and the others used, Xander knew they'd be long gone.

He angled the parachute's descent again, aiming himself at Rashonn, who stood at the side of the road with a shoulder-mounted video camera. Xander raised his voice, speaking toward the camera. "Here's the moral to the story." He touched down easily, taking a couple running steps to remain upright and to keep the chute cords from getting tangled around him. He thrust his face into the camera lens. "Don't be a dick, Dick."

Rashonn burst out laughing. "Way to fire, little man. You're doing all the good." Turning, she swept the faraway figures standing at the bridge railing.

Xander's nervous system started crashing. Once the adrenaline was past, he came down hard. He was at his absolute best when the chips were down and the odds were against him. Safety and security were alien concepts.

The guys yanking the video camera from the Corvette came away with their prize. They heaved the camera into the rear seat of the convertible and left the passenger seat open to Xander.

Xander stood for just a moment and stared at the wreckage of the Corvette strewn across the uneven terrain of the ravine. Hotchkiss would probably be upset for a few days about the loss of the car, but Xander doubted the senator would show any change of heart. Nope, the reason for stealing the car and driving over the side of the bridge was purely for the rush. And that rush was fast becoming only a memory.

Living in the adrenaline-driven moment was costly, Xander knew. That way of life left an incredible number of other minutes in a day to be filled. Already feeling flattened, he turned from the wreckage, walked to the convertible, and dropped into the passenger's seat. Laying his head back on the seat, he closed his eyes and totally relaxed while the driver sped toward the farm-to-market road.

Hours later, after the sun had fallen and night draped L.A., Xander cruised the streets on his motorcycle. He'd gone looking for action, some kind of event that was going on in an after-hours kind of place, but nothing had caught his fancy.

He was restless and edgy, wanting another adrenaline fix. That was one of the biggest pitfalls in his life: that constant hunger to find the next big and dangerous thing to do.

Whipping through the streets, he watched the city's nightlife lit up in neon around him. The movers and the shakers were out tonight, buying and selling one another and themselves, walking a thin line between life and death. That way of life had called out to him when he was younger, but he hadn't been able to live like that.

Or maybe he just hadn't been able to imagine dying like that. Man, living and dying while fighting over nickel and dime bags would have been a waste.

Maybe stealing Senator Hotchkiss's car was a crime and he'd get busted for the theft if the 5-0 caught up with him, but the crime hadn't hurt anyone. He'd never acted with malice in his heart, and the only people he'd ever harmed had been those trying to bust him or one of his friends up first.

He lived in a dog-eat-dog world. Growing up hard the way he had, doing without a lot because his family barely got by, had taught him that. Extreme sports had saved him from that kind of life. He'd first learned how to skateboard on the streets, then in empty swimming pools and a half-pipe. Then he'd gotten a BMX bike and jumped into other sports. And while he'd learned about the sports, he'd also learned about the equipment. That knowledge led to side jobs repairing and building equipment that kept him financially solvent even as an adult, working for the sports crowd.

A few years ago, Xander had hooked up with Rashonn, and together they'd made history. Rashonn had the underground Internet video biz in place, and she'd made Xander Cage, extreme sports daredevil, one of her hottest stars.

The money hadn't meant anything to Xander, but cold hard cash allowed him to meet life more or less on his own terms. The risks he took, though generally something most people would never do, were his by choice. And God help him if those adrenaline highs from the stunts ever stopped coming because he was afraid there would never be anything else that made him feel so alive.

Eventually, Xander wound up in his neighborhood. He wasn't exactly happy to be there, but he had to be someplace. After the stunt with Hotchkiss's car, he'd blown off steam in some of his favorite arcade areas, playing some of his favorite games and checking out the new ones. Rashonn and her video crew had gone off to work their particular magic on the cameras. Checking out the arcade had been part of the cover they had in place to prevent the prosecution from having an airtight case against him.

Rashonn had come up with the cover. Even though they were planning on releasing the video of the Hotchkiss stunt over the Internet, selling the downloads, Rashonn was going to claim that she'd intercut the video with footage of Xander—as if he'd truly done the stunt. She would claim that the videotape had been delivered to her by an anonymous person, to do whatever she wanted with it. At best, even with the Internet download in hand, the district attorney's office would have only circumstantial evidence. They had plenty of "witnesses" who would say Xander was elsewhere when the car theft occurred.

Xander glanced around at the familiar buildings in the downtown area where he lived. There weren't many streetlights in this part of L.A., and tourists didn't frequent the area after dark. These were mean streets, and the people who walked them during the night were mean folks.

But the rent was right, and he had a whole loft to himself where he could store all his gear and personal effects.

Leaving his motorcycle parked outside, Xander approached the apartment. His gaze swept the number of cars parked in the alleys and on the street. They were street rods, vehicles running NOX systems, painted with computer-tech art, mostly custom jobs with beaters thrown into the mix.

Not exactly coming home to an empty house, Xander thought. He opened the door and went through.

The loft was dark. Only a rectangle of pale moonlight followed Xander inside. He stood still for a moment, letting his senses adjust. For a split second, his nervous system prepared to light the adrenaline fuse that vibrated inside him. His body stayed ready to plunge into overdrive and push circumstances and himself to the limit.

Perfume and body odor hit him, standing out against the usual oil and graphite smells in the apartment. He wasn't alone in the loft, but he wasn't in danger either.

"I hate you guys," Xander said, reaching for the light switch.

" "

Rows of lights cascaded across the loft's ceiling between the skylights. Thunderous hollow explosions of electrical current surged through the transformers. The harsh illumination revealed motorcycle parts and weight-lifting equipment scattered throughout the living area, barely leaving room for the bed and the mismatched couches and chairs.

Posters of extreme sports heroes like Dave Mirra, Tony Hawk, Biker Sherlock, Danny Way, Andy Hetzel, Lairde Hamilton, Debbie Evans, Jamie Burge, and Eva Sandelgard, all featured in their respective sports, covered the walls. A half-pipe vertical ramp occupied one wall, competing for space with a homegrown sound system wired into speakers throughout the loft.

A crowd of people erupted from hiding as the darkness was stripped away, transforming the loft into ground zero for party central. Black and white,

Asian and Hispanic, domestic and foreign, the crowd was a melting pot, all of them bound by their love of extreme sports.

"Surprise!" they yelled, led by Rashonn, who was decked out in party gear.

"Big surprise," Xander said. "There's so many thrasher cars parked outside it looks like a demolition derby."

Full-bore party mode took over. Someone lit up the sound system and speed-driven metal crashed through the loft. If a sonic boom could have leveled the loft, Xander knew the place would have been gone in an instant. Instead, he let himself go. If he couldn't get a buzz from an adrenaline high, a party was the next best thing.

Rashonn stepped forward and took Xander by the arm, tugging him into movement.

"You know," Xander said, "I don't even know a lot of these people you got here." He accepted a drink from a pretty brunette and reluctantly remained in step with Rashonn.

"So get to know them," Rashonn said. "Later. Right now, we gotta talk." She leaned in close and whispered. "We're gonna make bank on this video, little man."

Xander waved the comment away. "Let's not talk business, Rashonn. You're wreckin' my party."

"Over here. I got something to show you." Rashonn kept Xander moving, though, leading him through the thronging crowd back toward the big-screen TV at the far end of the loft.

Gazing at the screen, Xander realized that the video of the stunt with Hotchkiss's Corvette was playing. He watched the video, noticing that Rashonn had pieced the film together in triple play and multi-angle, showing slow-motion cuts of all the action.

A crowd of partyers stood rapt in front of the screen. When the Corvette smashed against the ground, a cheer went up that was heard over the throbbing techno beat.

"Look at that," Rashonn said, her dark eyes flashing. "These people are crazy for your shit. This new video is gonna move *beaucoup* units. Once it does, then I can pay you."

A stunt mixed with a little payback from the extreme sports people, Xander thought. He'd planned on doing the stunt; Rashonn had been the one who insisted on taping it. But watching the stunt again, he felt dulled and leaden inside. There was no residual excitement for him. The only glow he ever got was during the stunt itself. He sipped his drink.

The widescreen showed a close-up of his face. "Don't be a dick, Dick."

When the video ended, starting immediately again, a guy in grunge clothing and a skater haircut looked at Xander. "That was off the hook! You're psycho, bro."

"Hey," another guy said, "when do we get to see that new freestyle move you been talkin' about?"

"The corkscrew Superman seat grab?" Xander asked, nodding. "I'm still working on it."

A third guy shook his head, pushing long hair out of his face. "Forget it, dude. Some things can't be done on a motorcycle. It's impossible."

Xander grinned, feeling himself rise to the challenge. That was where the adrenaline began, always stirring and bubbling beneath the surface, waiting for the chance to push the envelope, to lay it all on the line again.

A young woman with piercings and tattoos turned to face Xander. She grinned broadly, eyes aflame with excitement. "You know, an athlete like you really should have his own video game. I could hook you up. If you're nice to me."

Laughing, Xander leaned in and kissed the young woman on the mouth, cutting off whatever else she had in store as a sales pitch. The video game producers had chased him for a while. They were aware of the fan base he pulled in as a result of the Internet videos he and Rashonn had made, and from the competitions he'd been involved in. He left the young woman standing there and moved on through the partygoers.

"He ain't never gonna sell out, girl," Rashonn said behind him. "That's why he's him. He's the last of the old-school holdouts."

Xander snagged another drink and kept walking. His mind had already turned to working out the corkscrew Superman seat grab. When he had a full burn going on how to get his body to stunt, he could stay lost in the images, playing them over and over again in his mind until his body reacted like he'd been doing the stunt for years. He was almost there with the corkscrew Superman seat grab.

Rashonn came up from behind Xander and took his arm. "X," Rashonn said, "listen to me. This is for real. I'm cutting you an advance on Internet presales." She pointed at a poster on the nearby wall. "I want you to go down to Pago Pago for a while. Relax, meet a girl, get busy. Have a vacation."

Xander couldn't believe his friend's suggestion.

"That's Bora Bora. And since when did you get so generous?"

A worried look filled Rashonn's face. "You need to clear town until the heat's off."

Xander shook his head. "No way."

"Man, you wrecked a senator's car, X."

"So Hotchkiss gets upset and the insurance companies take a bath. Hotchkiss deserves it, and the insurance companies can afford the loss. That's what they're in the business of doing: affording losses. And they still make the big bucks. Besides, we have our alibi in place, right?"

"I got an underground website to run," Rashonn said. "We got more tapes to make, and it's gonna be a lot easier to do if you ain't in jail. I'm serious." She glanced up at the widescreen television as the senator's Corvette plunged over the side of the bridge again. On-screen, Xander kicked free of the sports car and the rectangular parafoil blossomed overhead. "Heads are gonna get busted over this one."

"You worry too much, Rashonn," Xander chided.

A tall guy Xander recognized from the BMX trails joined them. He was covered with tattoos, and scars marred some of them. "Yeah. Don't worry about it, X. They'll never catch you."

Xander started to toast the guy and rag on Rashonn for being such a nellie, but an explosion blew the loft's front door off the hinges.

12

Although prepared to risk their lives at whatever extreme sport suited their particular jones, the crowd gathered in Xander Cage's loft carried a healthy paranoia with them.

Xander knew that because he carried the same paranoia. As extreme sports fans, they lived life on the edge, on the fringes of polite society. Their tattoos and piercings and language marked them as different from the normal populace. Those things also marked them as targets for authority figures.

The invading force that followed the splintered door into the loft represented the epitome of that paranoia. Clad in black body armor, faceless behind the dark shields of their helmets, the invading riot squad filled the living quarters. They carried assault rifles and pistols with black matte finishes, but they lashed out with heavy flashlights, martial arts batons, and jackboots.

Though hardened by the serious physical side of

the sports they enjoyed, the partygoers went down before the invading force. Xander didn't blame them even though he couldn't agree with the philosophy. A sports freak could fight the mountain, could fight the water, and could defy gravity, but there was no fighting city hall.

More black-clad stormtroopers crashed through the skylights and dropped to the loft floor from ropes. Complete destruction followed in the wake of the armored men as they fought their way toward Xander. They crossed the intervening distance with predatory swiftness.

"Uh . . ." the guy who'd been talking to Xander said, glancing at the new arrivals. "Never mind." He hurried away, trying to stay clear of the field of fire.

From the way the men approached him, Xander knew they were after him. He had no clue why. Even nicking Hotchkiss's toy sports car shouldn't have netted this kind of attention or retaliation. No, this was definitely something else.

Rashonn started to step in front of Xander, definitely in conflict with her better judgment. Xander caught her, laying one gentle hand against her hip, and kept her clear as a pair of WWF-sized guys in black armor rushed him.

Xander let them come. No matter what kind of shitstorm had just flooded his loft, Rashonn knew lawyers. Keeping her out of general lockup was important.

The two men grabbed Xander's wrists and hustled him back against the nearest wall. Xander rolled his shoulders and tilted his head forward, keeping the back of his skull from smashing against the wall when they threw him there. The two men held him, leaning their body weight against him.

"Let me guess," Xander said laconically. "This ain't about the stereo."

Neither of the men holding him replied.

"Get these people out of here!" one of the black-suited figures ordered, indicating everyone else in the room.

The partygoers went more or less willingly. A few of them tried to put up a front and resist being ousted, but the invaders beat them down with rifle butts and batons. People too hurt or too dazed to walk out on their own got dragged out.

One of the men grabbed Rashonn, lifting her from her feet and carrying her away. She mouthed, *I'll get you out of this. Don't worry.*

Xander wasn't worried, though. Not really. With the way he was doing things, the kinds of stunts he'd been pulling, getting taken down by the police could only be expected. He'd been locked up before. Getting locked up was no biggie. Given the things that he'd done, the door would open again. Nobody was looking to put him away permanently.

Only after everyone was cleared from the loft, none of the black-suited figures broke out a badge and started reading anything remotely Miranda-sounding. That was definitely ominous.

Xander smiled, and he knew it was one of those smiles other people told him he had right before he stunted. Rashonn had labeled the expression an FTW—fuck the world—smile, and said there'd been no reason to put overdrive on an adrenaline addict.

"Alone at last," Xander said with grim defiance. "Better break out the nightsticks, boys, cuz I ain't going without a fight." Moving quickly, he stomped his foot against the side of one of the men's knees, feeling cartilage stretch and possibly even snap. The guy tumbled away, and Xander knew the invader wasn't going to be getting up again.

One of the stormtroopers in front of Xander drew an oversized pistol from a holster belted to his thigh.

Struggling against the other man holding him, Xander couldn't believe the guy was actually going to shoot him. It didn't make sense. None of the other guys looked like they were going to stop the guy with the pistol.

The pistol jerked in the guy's gloved hand, but there was no report.

At first, Xander thought the pistol had somehow misfired. Then he felt the sharp, stinging pain in his chest. *Silenced,* he realized, glancing down at his chest to see what damage had been done. He tried to convince himself that he was going to be all right. *People get shot in the chest all the time. If you don't take one through the pump, you can make it. Hell, it happens on TV and the movies all the time.*

Only instead of a bloody bullet hole, Xander saw a chrome dart jutting out of his flesh. *What the hell?* Then a wave of wooziness slammed into his brain, chipping away at the adrenaline firing through his nervous system. The world suddenly started retreating, pulling back into a long tunnel. *They drugged me.* He struggled against the sedatives flowing through his bloodstream, but he knew the fight was a losing battle.

The black-clad man with the big pistol stepped closer.

"You . . . pussies . . ." Xander tried to go after the man, determined to achieve a little get-back of his own before he went down for the count. But he tripped over his next step, falling toward the floor but crashing through oblivion before he hit.

SPY 2.0:
TRAINING MODE

13

A throbbing headache woke Xander. He kept his eyes shut tight, gathering his mind out of the cottony fog at the edges of his returning consciousness. A cool slick surface pressed against his forehead. It took a moment for him to realize he was seated.

If you're sitting down, Xander told himself, *then you didn't wipe out too badly. A guy falling to pieces, the docs don't just prop him up and expect him to tend to himself.*

Over the years, he'd been in a few hospitals after a shredder or two down a street on a motorcycle that came off wrong. Stitches and gauze, having broken bones set and casts, he'd been through them all. Healing time was healing time. If a guy played hard and fast, he had to factor in the healing time.

Slowly, memory of the loft invasion returned to him. He kept still, kept his eyes closed. Not moving when he first woke was a survival skill he'd learned from crashing and shredding. If no one was there to tell him he was okay to stand, he had trained himself to wait until he knew he wasn't going to hurt himself getting up.

Pain was an important thing to notice. Pain indicated broken bones and torn flesh. A wrong move could send a broken rib through a heart or a lung, rendering a serious injury into a fatal one. A wrong move could mean spilling something vital out of a body cavity that might not go back in so easily, like intestines.

Xander didn't smell blood, which was a good thing. He'd learned to recognize the scent while stunting. He'd also learned the stink of burned flesh, his own and that of other guys.

No blood. Pain's just in my head. Hell, we're doing okay so far.

He listened, hearing the gentle buzz of conversations around him. A sizzling sound came from in front of him, mixing with a roll of heat. He smelled frying bacon, hamburger, orange juice, yeast, and fresh-baked bread.

He cracked his eyes open and discovered he was seated at a counter. In front of him, a skinny kid cleaned a flat grill, then poured four pancakes. The kid glanced nervously over his shoulder and nodded.

Craning his head around, Xander took stock of the booths against the front wall on either side of the entrance. PANN'S DINER was written backward on the glass doors. Hard afternoon sunlight glared off the street on the other side of the big plate-glass windows. He narrowed his eyes against the light, feeling the throbbing inside his head increase.

Glancing down at himself, he saw that he was in

the same clothes he'd been in at the loft. "What the hell?"

Hard-soled shoes clicked against the worn black and white squares of linoleum covering the diner's floor. He looked up from the shoes and the legs of the middle-aged woman in the waitress apron and small peaked cap. She looked at him, her face pinched and tired-looking.

"Hey," Xander called out to her. "How did I get here?"

The waitress took a pot of coffee from a warmer on the counter, slipped a few packets of artificial sweetener and sugar into her apron, and turned to Xander. "Two big guys dropped you off ten minutes ago. They told me to look after you. They said to tell you they were sorry, and that you were the wrong guy."

Wrong guy? Xander snorted and shook his head. *No way. Not with the way those guys came on like gangbusters. They knew who they were looking for.* But hell, they hadn't called him by name and things like that had happened before. Police guys, and Xander was certain that's what the men had been, were known to break into the wrong house before.

He gazed out the window again. He didn't recognize the neighborhood, so he had to wonder how far the invaders had gone before dropping off their "mistake."

"Those sons of bitches," Xander muttered. He gazed around the room.

A trucker sat against one wall in a booth by himself. The guy was huge, with long dirty hair and red-rheumy eyes. He wore jeans, a cowboy hat, and a sheepskin vest over a plaid shirt. He chewed with his mouth open and gazed at the waitress's legs with intense interest. Farther back, a guy in a plain black business suit sat holding a *Financial Times*. A dozen other people, men and women and two guys in hip-hop clothing, sat in the booths eating and talking.

"You want a cup of coffee?" the waitress asked. "You look like you could use some."

"Sure," Xander replied.

The waitress turned to get a cup from the stack beside the coffee pots. She filled a cup. She almost dropped the saucer, but managed to recover it and place it under the cup. Hands shaking, she placed a spoon on the saucer as well, took a paper napkin from her apron, and sat the cup in front of Xander.

"You all right?" Xander asked. He'd wanted to ask her if guys were in the habit of dropping unconscious strangers off at the diner, but her apparent nervousness caught his attention instead.

"Fine." The waitress smiled at him, but the effort seemed strained. "Just fine." She pushed the coffee toward him, slopping some of the dark liquid over the rim.

Daylight outside, Xander thought, picking up the cup. *Wonder how long I've been out?* The headache was starting to subside. He figured he'd probably be feeling pretty good about now—if all the other weirdness hadn't been going on around him. He checked the trucker and the guy in the suit again, wondering why he was getting a weird vibe off of those two men. Hell, the whole situation was weird. Including the waitress's—

His thoughts froze as he looked at his paper napkin. There, inscribed in shaky blue ballpoint, were the numbers 911.

14

Adrenaline smashed through Xander's nervous system. The headache disappeared and his breathing leveled out, letting him take oxygen deep inside his lungs, getting pumped up.

He placed the cup back over the message, hiding the numbers from view. Casually, he gazed around the diner again. This time he noticed the bulge under the truck driver's vest. There was probably a list of things that could have made a bulge like that, but one immediately came to Xander's mind.

Continuing to check out the diner, Xander saw the nervous eye-darting on the part of the guy in the business suit. He had the newspaper pulled up to his nose now, peering over. The effort was almost comical.

Xander didn't feel amused, though. *Somebody's playin' you, bro,* he told himself. *The only thing that ain't wrong with this picture is you.* Then he became aware that the trucker was staring at him.

"What?" Xander demanded. On closer thought, he decided maybe he should have just kept his mouth shut and minded his own business. Getting up and getting out of the diner wasn't a bad idea, either. And maybe he would have tried to find out if they would have let him—except he felt like pushing back a little. Hell, truth to tell, maybe he wanted to push back against somebody a lot.

"I said," the trucker snarled, "you got a problem, boy?"

Xander bristled. With the adrenaline flowing this strong, the need to do something was almost explosive. "Problem? No, no problem. You go right ahead."

That caught the trucker by surprise. "With what?"

Xander shrugged.

"I said, go right on ahead with what?" the trucker demanded, swapping looks with the guy in the business suit.

"Whatever, dude," Xander responded. They'd dealt the cards, and he was going to let them play out the hand.

The trucker looked at the guy in the suit again. Without another word, they stood. The businessman dropped his paper and revealed the cut-down .12-gauge pump shotgun. The pistol grip slapped into his palm as he brought the weapon around.

Reaching under his vest, the trucker brought out a Beretta 9mm pistol and spun to face the rest of the diners. "All right, nobody make a move!"

The waitress backed away, cringing in fear.

Glaring at Xander, the trucker said, "Shoulda walked away when you had the chance, dumbass."

"Forget him, Buck," the guy in the business suit said. "Let's just do it."

"Shut up!" the trucker ordered the other man. Then the big guy turned his attention back to Xander. "You keep still or I'm gonna make damn sure you stop breathing today. Got that?"

Xander shrugged. He felt loose and ready, riding the high, waiting for an opening. *It's all about the timing, bro. All about the timing.* "All right, *Buck.* Whatever you say."

The waitress moaned, acting like she was about to drop from a nervous attack.

"Keep your goddamn mouth shut and empty that register!" Buck commanded the waitress. "Couldn't just let him leave, could ya? You know what I'm gonna do to ya for that? Huh? Do ya?"

"You ain't gonna do nothing," Xander told the trucker flatly.

Savagery spread across the trucker's features as he turned to shove the pistol into Xander's face.

Xander uncoiled like a released spring, feeling the adrenaline burning in him now, his muscles surprisingly loose and ready in spite of being drugged. He chopped down on the trucker's wrist with the edge of his hand, popping the Beretta loose, raking his other hand across the man's face and breaking his nose, then sweeping the trucker's legs. Xander thought of going for the pistol, but the guy in the business suit swung around with the shotgun.

Moving with lightning-quick reflexes, Xander crossed the intervening space, then shoved out a hand and caught the shotgun barrel on the fly. He curled his fingers around the gleaming metal and yanked the weapon out of the man's hands. Before the guy could move, Xander reversed the shotgun and racked the slide, then pointed the barrel at the center of the guy's forehead.

Everyone in the diner froze, and Xander knew they were all waiting to see if he was going to pull the trigger. He waited, not knowing what was going to happen, but believing he was ready for anything.

But the applause he received, then the standing ovation from one of the diner's patrons, came from way out of left field.

The scar-faced man slowly approached with an amused smile on his lips. He let his hands hang to his sides.

Xander whirled, pointing the shotgun at the center of the man's chest.

"Very well done, Mr. Cage," the man said.

15

Looking at the scar-faced man standing at the business end of the shotgun, Xander asked, "Who the hell are you?"

"My name is Gibbons," the man answered calmly. He didn't seem afraid of the shotgun pointed at him.

For an instant, Xander wanted to bust up the guy's stone-cold review, wanted to bring a little of the uncertainty and paranoia that was now crowding into his own life to the guy. After a short mental debate, Xander pushed those thoughts out of his head. He kept a firm grip on the shotgun, using the weapon to keep the man at bay. Xander wasn't afraid of the guy, but the man's calm demeanor and honest amusement triggered an innate wariness.

"You seem upset," Gibbons said. "Is there a problem?"

Xander turned the question over in his mind. He couldn't help wondering if the situation he now found himself in had anything to do with Hotchkiss, but he couldn't accept that. The state senator was low in the political food chain. Whoever had put the diner stunt together had spent considerable time and money. And how would anything that happened here hold up in a court of law?

"What is this place?" Xander countered.

Gibbons looked around as if truly noticing the place for the first time. "Looks like a diner."

"Diner, huh?" Xander retorted. "You had me going for a while, I'll give you that. It sure looks real."

Gibbons looked at him with increased interest.

"Then I started noticing things," Xander said. "You got a *stockbroker* over here dressed up and reading the *Financial Times* on a Sunday morning when the markets are closed."

The guy in the business suit regarded Xander blankly.

Xander moved on to the trucker. "Okay, fine. I can go with the paper thing. I can even go with the stick-up man packing a cop-issue Beretta. But you know where you blew it?"

Amusement deepened on Gibbons's face.

"With her." Xander pointed at the waitress.

The woman still pretended to be somewhat cowed by the recent events.

"My aunt was in food service all her life," Xander said. "There's no way in hell a career waitress is coming to work in a hard-soled platform shoe. She'd be beat before the lunch rush. So if she ain't a waitress, then this whole thing ain't what it seems." He jerked a thumb at the trucker. "That's how I knew Bozo wouldn't get a shot off even if I gave him all day." He leveled the shotgun at one of the plate glass windows at the front of the diner. Without hesitation, he pulled the trigger.

The shotgun's blast ripped through the quiet of the diner, but the window remained unmarked.

"Cuz there's nothing but blanks in these guns," Xander said. "And no offense, but their performances were terrible." He tossed the shotgun on the counter. The adrenaline-high still buzzed within him, but he kept the feeling on a short leash. There were still a lot of things he didn't know, including who the scar-faced man really was.

The diner "patrons" looked at Gibbons. The scar-faced man gave an almost imperceptible nod. Immediately, the people around Xander started clearing out of the diner, acting like factory workers whose shift had ended. The waitress leaned back against the counter and smiled a little before pouring herself a cup of coffee.

"Not bad," Gibbons commented. "Not bad at all."

Xander could tell the man really meant the compliment. "Now it's your turn, pretty boy. What the hell is going on?"

"It was a test, Mr. Cage," Gibbons replied. "One that you plowed through like a rhino through wet tissue paper."

Another man in an off-the-rack suit who looked like cop material joined Gibbons. He was twenty years younger, but still had the same cynical, hard-eyed glare of the older man.

"This is Agent Polk," Gibbons said.

"He seems to have a bit of an attitude," the newcomer suggested. "Should we throw him back?"

Xander bristled at the suggestion. There wasn't a

cut he hadn't made. Then he reminded himself that he wanted no part of whatever gig the scar-faced man had going on. He just wanted to get back to what was left of his loft.

"Hell, no," Gibbons said. "I like his attitude. Let's take this one to Phase Two."

"You ain't taking me nowhere," Xander said.

Gibbons turned and walked away.

"Hey," Xander called, starting after the man. "I'm talking to you!"

"Get on the Sat-Com," Gibbons said to the younger man. "I want to rendezvous with the team in two hours."

Xander matched Gibbons's pace as they walked back toward the center of the diner. The guy was becoming a major pain, and Xander was about ready to strike out to alleviate that pain.

"I want this place swept down and everyone out in ten minutes," Gibbons ordered. Then he pointed at the truck driver. "And get a damn towel for Mike. He's bleeding all over the floor."

Xander stepped in front of Gibbons and invaded the man's personal space. "I don't know who you people are," Xander grated, "but I want some answers and I want 'em now."

Gibbons stared back, making no move to answer.

"Don't make me wreck you, Hopalong," Xander threatened.

Turning his attention to the waitress, Gibbons said, "Shut him up."

Xander tried to move, catching sight from the corner of his eye of the big pistol the woman drew. He turned, senses alive and humming, torn between diving for cover and trying to reach her. He did neither because there was simply no time.

The waitress brought the pistol up and fired with the skill and speed of an arcade twitch game master. Fast as she was, she was dead-on target, too.

Xander felt the pain bite into his stomach with vicious rat's teeth. His fingers found the tiny, cylindrical object that had sunk into his flesh. Pulling the object out, he recognized the shiny chrome dart at once. He threw the dart down, already feeling the sedative invade his body and strip him of reasoning and motion.

"Why is it always the assholes who pass the tests?" Gibbons asked, sounding a long way off.

Yeah well, asshole, Xander thought as his senses swirled and faded, *you must have passed some tests yourself to be standing on the other side of whatever the hell this is.*

Then everything went black.

16

Droning jet engines and the familiar shiver of an aircraft woke Xander. He kept his eyes closed for a time, trying to glean more information from his surroundings, then finally gave up. The engines and the quaking of the airplane were everything. He opened his eyes, noticing the dim red glow at once.

Military bird, Xander thought, looking around the huge cargo area available in the airplane. *This has gotta be a C-123 at the least. Man, this bird is ancient.* He was familiar with the airplane's design and history from some of the old paratrooper guys he'd gotten to know while skydiving and skyboarding. The C-123 had come out in the 1950s and almost been discontinued until the Vietnam War started up, requiring cargo ships that had a need for a shorter runway than the C-130 troop transports required. The C-123s had also started getting outfitted with small jet engines instead of propellers to shorten that distance.

After the war, the surviving C-123s had been sold off to private businesses and individuals. The American government had also kept some of the planes around to use in clandestine operations, such as Air America.

Looking at the dark shadows filling the cargo hold, barely held at bay by the dim red light, Xander had the feeling that he wasn't exactly in the hands of the police anymore. There was no way. This was strictly government biz, but he couldn't figure out what they were doing with him. Accepting that Hotchkiss was somehow behind his incarceration in whatever games Gibbons—if that was the scar-faced man's real name—was involved in just didn't scan.

Xander found that he was lying in the middle of the cargo bay. He still wore the same clothes, and they were starting to get rank now. That didn't bother him too much, but not knowing why he was in the air did. The small wounds in his chest and stomach ached and drew his attention to the constriction around his upper body and crotch. He ran his fingers along the harness equipped with a D-ring.

A jump-rig? That didn't make any sense either, but Xander was familiar with the harness.

A man groaned beside Xander. Curious, Xander watched the guy sit up and hold his head.

The guy was Hispanic, short and broad. Gang tattoos marked his arms and face and neck. Like Xander, he was dressed in street clothes and the harness.

Another man, this one white and hard-bodied, a little grizzled and unkempt, sat up at Xander's feet. He cursed for a short time and rubbed the back of his neck.

Xander couldn't help himself. Before he could stop, he was chuckling, finally laughing aloud at the sheer ludicrousness of the situation.

"What's so damn funny?" the Hispanic sneered.

Xander got hold of himself and asked, "Been to any good diners lately?"

The white guy cracked up, whooping and slapping his thigh.

Then Xander felt other people's eyes on him. The narcotic still swimming in his system threw his night vision off. He glanced around, noticing the foldout bench seats ringing the cargo area's walls.

Soldiers wearing camou BDUs sat silent and still on the benches. All of them looked like hard men. They carried their M-16 assault rifles in a relaxed manner, but not one that suggested the weapons would be easily taken from them. Black camou greasepaint shadowed their faces, making death's-heads of their features.

None of the soldiers cracked a smile or looked particularly interested in anything Xander or the other two men did.

"Nobody told me this was a costume party," Xander said. He sat loose and casual, his arms locked around his legs, making no effort to get up. This was someone else's game, maybe Gibbons's, but it for damn sure wasn't his. He was through playing.

"Heads up, man," the Hispanic yelled. He pulled at the harness, trying to unlatch it. "What is this thing?"

The special ops soldiers stood and trained their weapons on the Hispanic. The meaning was clear enough. One of the soldiers stepped forward and clipped a long bungee cord to the D-ring on the man's harness.

"Hey, don't touch me!" the Hispanic yelled, slapping at the man's hands.

The soldier standing in front of the man aimed his weapon at the Hispanic. The ruby-red eye of a laser-sighting device dawned on the man's forehead. All resistance ended immediately.

Abruptly, the red lightbulb over the cargo door located at the rear of the C-123 changed to green. One of the soldiers split off from the group and trotted to the back of the plane. He pressed a button and the rear-mounted cargo ramp yawned open, dropping down from the tail assembly above.

Bright sunlight streamed into the cargo area, glinting off the dark metallic surfaces. The view through the cargo hatch was split between blue sky and emerald jungle. Air swirled into the plane, and the noise of the jets increased to loud thundering.

Judging from the clarity of the leaves and branches he could see on the trees below, Xander figured they weren't flying much above tree-top level. *Where the hell did they find so much jungle vegetation so close to L.A.?* A sinking feeling suddenly materialized in his stomach. There was no problem finding jungles if a guy didn't stay in California, he realized.

A moment later, as the C-123 locked into its final course, a dirt road cleaved the verdant growth of the jungle. The road twisted and turned across mountaintops, scrawling a ragged scar through the vegetation.

The C-123 angled down slightly, losing more altitude.

Xander made himself stay loose. Whatever was going to happen was going to happen damn quick. One of the soldiers clipped a bungee cord to Xander's D-ring while another did the same to the remaining members of their tiny, disenfranchised group.

The cargo plane touched down with a jarring bump, bounced back into the air, and came down again. Dust clouds roiled behind the plane, kicked up by the landing gear, then shoved violently by the jet engines.

One of the men signaled the soldier standing by the cargo door. The soldier reached behind him and pulled a hunk of nylon into his arms. He turned and threw the bulk outside where the wind caught the material and belled the folds out, revealing the parachute shape.

As the parachute caught the wind, coils of bungee cord started paying out. Xander stared at the three piles of cord and three men in the cargo area with cord clamped to their harnesses. The math was easy to do.

The Hispanic put everything together as well, but way too late to do anything to save himself because his cord was linked to the first parachute. The bungee cord grew taut and yanked him from the C-123. Xander heard the man's screams even over the jet engines and the noise of the landing gear skidding over the uneven dirt road.

The other man went next, somewhat more composed but definitely not happy about the situation.

With a lithe move that was only a little slow and awkward because of the drugs still in his system, Xander stood. He faced the black-clad soldiers as they stared at him. He wondered if they thought throwing him from the back of a moving plane was torture or psychological warfare.

The soldier standing by the cargo door threw out the third chute and the bungee cord uncoiled with an electric hiss.

Defiantly, Xander flipped off the black-clad squad and grinned. "I live for this shit," he growled in a loud voice. He timed the disappearance of the cord and jumped up just as the bungee cord attached to the D-ring on his harness grew tight and yanked him out of the transport plane.

17

Although there was some play in the bungee cord, Xander hit the end of that rapidly. He held onto the harness, knowing he was going to hit the ground hard. Keeping his body loose, forcing himself to breathe even through the choking cloud of dust around him, he watched the C-123 keep rolling along the dirt road. The pilot kicked in the jet engines and lifted into the blue sky just as Xander slammed against the ground.

That initial impact only proved to be the first of several. Pain flooded Xander's senses, but the feeling was an old friend and he didn't fight. The adrenaline filling his nervous system covered some of the hurt. In fact, getting thrown out of a plane and dragged by a parachute in God only knew where turned out to be a hell of a charge. He skidded across the ground like a stone skipped across a lake.

Gradually, he and the other two men overtook their parachutes, rolling and sprawling till they ended up tangled in the cords and the nylon. *Man, what a rush*, Xander thought as he recovered and fought his way free of the parachute. He got to his feet and started unbuckling the harness.

"Not bad," Xander commented, looking at the other two men.

The C-123 was a speck flying high under a noonday sun.

Pain stabbed into Xander's eyes and he knew that was from residual effects of the drugs his captors had used on him. He squinted against the harsh sunlight and gazed around at the almost impenetrable jungle on either side of the dirt road.

"This is strictly a military op," the white guy said.

Xander shrugged out of his harness. "You think?"

The guy nodded toward the tangled parachutes and bungee cords. "That was a LAPES."

"Low altitude parachute extraction system," Xander said. "I know."

The white guy looked at him with new respect. "You military?"

Xander grinned and shook his head, regretting the movement instantly as a new wave of pain hit him. "No way, man. Too many rules for me. You were, though, right?"

The man nodded. "Navy."

"You out now? Or are you here to do some kind of observation? See how this works out for us?"

"I'm no volunteer," the man said. "I got into trouble in civilian life, they forced me into the military. I got into trouble in the military, they forced me back out again. Then one day I come home to my girlfriend's apartment and get kidnapped."

"By the black suits," Xander said.

"Yeah."

"They weren't police, were they?"

The man grinned. "Not even close. You meet Gibbons?"

"Yeah."

"The guy's CIA. Or maybe worse."

"Worse?"

Nodding, the man said, "The government's got black ops squads buried deep inside the country and outside. Those guys that took us? I think they're off the books, man. Nobody knows what they do. Nobody wants to know what they do."

Xander considered that. "Then what do they want with us?"

"Don't know, bro, but I can bet it ain't nothing good." The man extended a closed fist. "My name is T.J."

Xander dropped his own closed fist onto the other man's. "Xander."

The Hispanic roared out curses, unable to free himself from the parachute and bungee cords.

"Guess he's new to this," Xander said, grinning.

Xander and T.J. followed the Hispanic, whose name turned out to be Virg, up a small rise beside the dirt road. They'd stayed with the road because even though they could eventually figure out the cardinal compass points from the descending sun, they had no clue where to go.

Virg, although he cursed like a sailor, wasn't ex-military like T.J. He was pure gangbanger, and he wasn't happy with his situation or the company. Xander and T.J. didn't much care.

The sun beat down on Xander, drawing the moisture from his body in rivulets of sweat. He cursed the men who'd dropped them there, thinking that leaving a canteen of water wouldn't have been too much to ask for. His stomach grumbled, too. Without knowing how long he'd been out, he had no way of knowing how much time had passed since he'd last eaten. He didn't think much time had passed, otherwise he'd have been in worse shape. But the shape he was in now was bad enough.

The thought that not much time had passed brought up another cold realization. Whoever was moving him around wasn't wasting time. Evidently, the *tests* were important to somebody. Whoever that somebody was, Xander decided, was going to be sadly disappointed from that moment on. He was done playing games.

At the top of the rise, Xander stared out at the lush field someone had chopped out of the surrounding jungle. Green plants stood in long rows, the broad leaves waving a little in the slight breeze. What looked like migrant workers dressed in thin and ragged cotton garments tended the field with hoes and rakes. Others plucked leaves from the plants and stuffed them in cloth sacks tied to their waists.

Several of the workers stopped hoeing and raking and plucking to stare at Xander and his companions.

Xander looked around, wondering where the guys in the black suits were hiding. If this was all a test, those guys had to be nearby.

Beyond the fields, ramshackle buildings stood under camou netting that blended them into the foliage. Some of the structures were evidently living quarters, but they were worse than anything Xander had ever seen in the projects in which he'd grown up. Other buildings held rusted farm equipment, most of which seemed to be broken down. Big pots hung over open fires. Men and women stirred the contents of the pots with long wooden paddles while workers dumped in more sacks of leaves.

Xander felt like he'd stepped back in time somehow. "Where the hell are we?" he asked.

"Holy shit!" Virg said in an awed voice. "A whole field of Colombian fun flakes!"

Xander and T.J. looked at Virg.

Virg shook his head as if not believing they had no clue what he was talking about. "Cocaine, man!" he said. "These are coke plants!" He ran down the rise to the field. Reaching the plants, he began plucking the leaves off and stuffing them in his pockets.

"Oh," Xander said, "and now we're supposed to believe that we've been dropped off in the middle of some cocaine cartel baron's private reserve. Now I know where our tax money goes. Tests." He looked at T.J., expecting the guy to get the humor in the situation.

T.J. pointed.

Following the line of the ex-Navy guy's arm, Xander spotted dust trails spitting down from the other side of the field. Jeeps, ATVs, a dirt bike, and even a guy riding a horse made the trails.

Okay, Xander admitted, *Scarface went all out on this one. Put in all the bells and whistles. If I didn't know better, I'd think I really was down on the farm with a bunch of Colombian dope traffickers.*

"Test or no test," T.J. commented in a dry voice, "I'm getting the hell out of here."

"Yeah," Xander said sarcastically. "Good idea."

T.J. ran back the way they'd traveled along the road. Virg joined him a heartbeat later. Both of them disappeared over the rise in a flurry of small dust clouds.

Joke's over, Xander thought as he strolled toward the nearest stand of farm machinery. He took a seat on some kind of thresher, kicking his feet up and going into total relaxation mode. Making the cut was one thing, but being tested like some kind of rat in a maze wasn't going to happen. *Let that scar-faced bastard worry about his own ass for a while. Noncompliance is my middle name from here on out.* Defeating the last test hadn't gotten him anything. It was time to find out what losing would net him.

The guy on the horse reached Xander first, but two Jeeps filled with guys toting AK-47 assault rifles quickly flanked the man. At the horseman's nod, the armed men fanned out and surrounded Xander. Two other Jeeps vanished over the top of the rise, evidently pursuing T.J. and Virg.

"You boys are too good for me," Xander said, lacing his fingers and placing his hands behind his head. "Guess I failed this test, huh?" *Okay, Scarface, what're you gonna do about this?*

The man on horseback spoke briefly to the guy on the dirt bike, then pointed at Xander. The dirt bike rider grinned coldly, revealing a full set of gold teeth.

Xander remained relaxed. The test was over. They weren't getting the reaction they wanted. Idly, he wondered how far the guys were going to go to try to get him to react the way they wanted him to.

Without a word, the gold-toothed man rammed the AK-47's butt into Xander's stomach, driving the air from his lungs in an explosive blast. Almost passing out from the pain, Xander fell from the thresher and landed on the ground, slamming his head against the hard-packed earth. Before he could get up, determined to take a pound of flesh of his own, the gold-toothed bastard hit him again, driving the rifle's buttstock into Xander's temple and scattering his senses.

18

Xander fought his way through layers of darkness. *Damn, I'm tired of waking up like this.* Something constricted his wrists, and the air wherever he was held took on a moldy thickness that required a little more effort to breathe. Nothing moved around him.

His hands had grown numb from the constriction, but pain sawed at his wrists and arm sockets. He opened his eyes and gazed around at the interior of a small room. Double doors lay at either end and stalls occupied one side. Fifty-five-gallon metal drums filled a lot of the space.

Okay, I'm in one of the barns, Xander thought. *Guess we're not through testing this little scenario after all.* Chains bound his hands. Looking up through the darkness clinging to the barn's peaked roof, he saw that the chain was hooked over a naked rafter.

He also realized that he'd been out for a while because the darkness gathered inside the barn wasn't from shadows. Night had fallen outside.

He worked his jaw as he stood to relieve the weight on his bound hands. Surprisingly, his jaw wasn't broken, but his head hurt like hell. *If I see that gold-toothed asshole again, I'm gonna do a little testing of my own.*

Gazing around the room, Xander figured the place hadn't been used for animals for a long time. The barn hadn't been cleaned out, either. Dark smears that looked like bloodstains mottled the walls. Some of the stains still looked fresh enough to hold a glimmer of red from the weak kerosene lantern sitting on a small table. The moldy hay scattered across the earthen floor held pools of dark liquid.

The lantern burned steadily, revealing lumpy shapes under a bloodstained beach towel. Behind the table, T.J. and Virg, showing bumps and bruises of their own, lay hog-tied and gagged on the filthy hay.

"Nice to see you again, fellas," Xander said. He nodded toward the bloodstained walls. "They're really going all out on this one, huh?" He curbed the anger inside him, knowing that yelling and demanding to see the scar-faced bastard who was evidently in charge of everything would only satisfy the people he was sure were watching him.

Voices sounded outside, growing louder, then the barn doors opened. A single man entered the room. He wore expensive clothes and an overabundance of gold jewelry. He glared at the three captives with the arrogance of someone used to command.

Xander almost laughed. *Man, this guy is seriously overplaying the role. Shoulda stamped* MYSTERIOUS BADASS *on his forehead.*

Wordlessly, the man walked to the table. He

lifted the lantern long enough to yank away the bloodstained beach towel. Knives, chisels, bolt cutters, a hacksaw, and a blowtorch—all of them blood-encrusted—lay on the table.

Definitely going for the Halloween theatrics here, Xander thought. *Man, who thinks up this stuff?*

The man dropped the towel and placed the lantern back on the table.

"What's on the menu tonight, *jefe*?" Xander taunted, unable to get into the role of the victim. "The old blowtorch-to-the-family-jewels routine, I'll bet. Hey, you want roasted nuts, let's break out the Planters."

Despite the fact that they were gagged, T.J. and Virg cracked up, nearly strangling with the effort.

The well-dressed man shot the two bound men a withering glare. Then he looked back at Xander. "Do you know what we do with people come round here?" His voice was deadly earnest, surprisingly soft. "You know what we do with people come in our business?"

Xander ignored the threat. He concentrated on flexing his hands, working the blood back into them. Pinpricks of pain showered his fingers. The numbness faded, but the pain wasn't a big improvement. Still, he could deal with hurt. He'd been doing that since the day he was born.

The torturer ran his hands over the tools with the love of a craftsman. Xander had seen the same attitude in jocks who loved their hardware.

Finally, the torturer picked up a wide-bladed machete and ran his thumb along the edge. Bright blood welled up from his flesh. He put his thumb in his mouth and sucked the blood away. Letting the blade hang down loosely at his side, he approached Xander.

"We cut the Achilles tendon," the torturer went on. "Your feet flop around like a marionette." He paused, cocking his head. "Or maybe instead you wanna tell me something."

"Okay," Xander said, "I'll tell you something: for a guy who's supposed to be Colombian, your accent sucks. Where'd they find you? Central Casting?"

Virg tried to talk but only unintelligible sounds got past the gag.

Xander nodded toward Virg, playing to the audience now. The experience was nowhere as good as stunting, but at least it was something. And hopefully Scarface would get pissed off. "My buddy agrees. He says you're a fruitcake."

The torturer's eyes flared, and for a minute he was selling the whole role. He kicked Virg. "Shut up!" he ordered. "I said, shut your stinking mouth!"

"A minute ago," Xander said, "you told us to talk. Now it's shut up." He put a weary, bored tone in his voice. "I'm not trying to be a nitpicker, but this is not a very professional torture session."

The man's backhanded slap caught Xander across the face. The impact split his lips and he tasted salty blood.

Anger stirred inside Xander, amping up the adrenaline levels. "Don't push it, chief," he warned. "You slap me again, I'm gonna throw you a beatin'."

The man's hand moved even faster the second time, coming hard enough this time to turn Xander's head.

Chill out, Xander told himself. *Your time will*

come. He shrugged. "I hope you get paid extra for this."

"Now," the torturer said, "you're gonna make me enjoy this, funny guy." He lifted the machete to Xander's face, resting the blade against Xander's upper lip. "I think maybe I'll take your nose first. Whatchu think of that?"

Xander breathed in, keeping control through a supreme act of willpower. The familiar coppery tang flooded his nostrils, making his scalp prickle.

"You know what's funny," Xander said. "That smells like real blood." *Is Scarface the kind of guy who would have gone all-out like this?* Doubt worried at the base of Xander's skull, then scurried right on up into his mind and blossomed like a mushroom.

The torturer stared coldly. "Do you like it? That's the last thing you gonna smell."

The last vestiges of doubt about the reality of the situation vanished from Xander's thoughts. "Awww, shit."

A grin spread across the torturer's face, but the low thumping noise that filled the barn checked him, drawing his attention.

Xander recognized the noise easily. That familiar beating noise could only belong to helicopters. From the sudden increase of thundering echoes, there were a lot of helicopters. In the next instant, gunfire erupted, breaking up the hammering *whop-whop-whop* of the helicopter rotors.

Berserk rage filled the torturer's face. He drew the machete back and swung at Xander's legs.

19

Move! Xander felt the sudden onslaught of adrenaline rip through him. Overcharged, mind redlining, he exploded into motion, throwing himself to one side. The torturer's machete missed him by less than an inch.

Still in motion, Xander ran toward the nearest wall. Thankfully, the chain wrapped across the rafter was loose enough to slide. The links rattled as they skated across the thick timber.

The Colombian pulled the machete from the ground and pursued.

Not breaking stride, Xander ran up the wall, fighting gravity, one of his eternal opponents. His boots thudded into the wall. With his senses in overdrive, he could almost hear the lessening of each impact as his weight against the wall dropped down to near-nothing.

The Colombian almost reached the wall, starting to put on the brakes and draw the machete back for another blow.

Xander kicked against the wall and took up slack in the chain around his wrists, kicking himself over in a back flip. As he twisted, he launched a kick that caught the Colombian in the face. The blow wasn't enough to knock the guy down, but he staggered back a dozen steps.

Off-balance, Xander tried to keep his feet under him but failed. He fell, watching as the Colombian charged again, lifting the machete back over his shoulder for a full-stroke shot.

T.J. rolled and lashed out with his feet, tripping the Colombian. The torturer toppled, skidding across the hay-covered earthen barn floor.

Synapses firing, Xander leaped up, caught the chain as high as he could, then used his hands and his feet to propel himself up to the rafter. Holding onto the loop of chain hanging from the rafter with his feet, he arched up and caught the rough timber in both hands. Releasing his feet, holding his grip with his hands, he flipped himself up and locked his legs around the timber. He hung upside down like a bat, the knot of chain accessible before him. He said silent thanks because the chain was only tied together there, not welded or locked. He saw the Colombian getting to his feet just as the last knot in the chain around his wrists came apart.

The Colombian slipped a pistol from the back of his waistband. He took a two-handed grip on the weapon, aiming up into the barn's rafters.

Xander swung down from the beam before the Colombian could draw a bead on him. Spinning like a gymnast, Xander planted both feet solidly in his opponent's chest as he came down, driving the Colombian to the ground, watching the guy go limp immediately.

Outside, the battle sounds escalated like world war had been declared. Cannon fired, breaking up the harsh crack of selective fire and the steady yammer of machine guns on full-auto.

Xander was still trying to wrap his head around everything that had happened to him. Was he really in Colombia? There was no freaking way. Who was Gibbons? And damn his scar-faced ass.

Grabbing up the abandoned machete, Xander cut T.J. free and helped the ex-Navy guy to his feet. A burst of gunfire tore through the barn wall. Spurred by survival instinct, Xander dove to the ground for cover. He wrapped his hands over his head, watching as T.J. stumbled and dropped to the ground.

Bright blood gushed from the ex-Navy man's side. When he put his hands there, they came away covered in crimson.

"I'm hit!" T.J. yelled incredulously. "I'm hit!"

Xander scrambled over to T.J., tearing the man's shirt away so he could better see. Miraculously, the kerosene lantern still burned on the table with the torture tools. There was enough light to see that T.J. wasn't going to get far without medical attention.

"Jesus Christ, man!" Virg shouted. "It's all for real!"

Xander looked up at the gangbanger in disgust. "No kidding." Although he didn't care for Virg, he crawled over to him and cut his ropes off.

Virg shook off the ropes and pushed himself to his feet.

Crossing back to T.J., Xander hooked one of the man's arms across his shoulders and helped the ex-Navy man stand. "Sorry about this, bro. I know you're all busted up, but we can't stay here."

T.J. nodded weakly.

Virg crept over by the barn door.

Xander looked at the man. "Help me with this guy."

"Hell with that," Virg responded. "It's every man for himself." Turning, he wheeled and dashed through the door.

Angry, Xander shouted, "That only works if you're a man!"

Virg didn't make a reply, and didn't hesitate, vanishing almost instantly into the night outside the barn doors. Red and purple tracer rounds glowed like supersonic fireflies as they hurtled through the air in the view afforded through the opening.

Although every nerve in him was screaming to run and hide, Xander stayed with T.J. The wounded guy struggled to help himself but wasn't too proud to accept help. He leaned heavily on Xander.

Pausing at the door, Xander peered out, not liking their odds at all. Somebody was attacking the Colombian drug farm but Xander had no idea who. Nobody was identified.

An SUV was parked out in the open thirty feet away. The target was tempting, but there was no damn cover and Xander was betting nobody had left the keys inside. He was certain he'd be dead before he was able to hotwire the vehicle.

The drug guys were trying desperately to set up a skirmish line, but none of the troops had enough heart to stick. When one of the men went down, the group of guys nearest him scattered like a covey of quail, sometimes leaving a wounded man behind yelling and screaming for help.

Still, the adrenaline pounded within Xander. This wasn't his turf, but the chances of escape offered the usual odds. He was drawn into the firefight, wondering if he could stretch big enough to cover the play—especially while carrying a wounded man.

Six helicopters suddenly swooped into view. The rotors beat the air, throwing down a rotor wash that flattened plants in the field and knocked over empty fifty-five-gallon drums. Shingles ripped from the buildings, and Xander heard them tearing loose atop the barn as well.

The pilots stayed close to the ground, allowing gunners the freedom to pick targets in the darkness. Night Suns, miniature high-intensity spotter lights, glared from the helicopters, marking targets and tracking the movements of the men they hunted. Tracer rounds slammed into a group of barrels filled with chemicals. Evidently something in the mix was flammable because all of the barrels exploded, throwing fire high into the night sky.

Xander knew they couldn't stay there. The people attacking the drug traffickers might be rivals. If they were, they weren't going to be picky about who they killed. He glanced at T.J. "You up to this?"

"Yeah." The ex-Navy tried to take a step but his knees folded under him.

Another fusillade of bullets slammed into the barn, piercing the ramshackle walls easily. One of the bullets hit the kerosene lamp, shattering the reservoir and spreading a pool across the hay-covered floor. Flames chased the kerosene at once. Only a few feet away, the Colombian who had shown up to torture them stirred and sat up.

"We got to go, bro," Xander said. "Sorry about this." Before T.J. could move or say anything, Xander bent down and picked him up in a fireman's carry.

20

With the wounded man across his shoulders, Xander took a last look at the open space before him. *Damn, that's big.* He pushed his breath out twice, breathed in deeply both times to charge his body with oxygen, then sprinted forward.

A line of machine gun bullets chewed the ground in front of Xander. He stopped, struggling with the extra weight, then changed directions. He ran, putting one foot in front of the other, swaying with T.J.'s added weight.

A series of 20mm Vulcan cannon blasts struck the coca fields. The explosions threw the ragged bodies of traffickers into the air and left gaping craters in the ground. Resistance among the cocaine outlaws was diminishing, and the farm was going to be totaled.

Strained by carrying the burden of T.J. and still suffering the effects of the beatings he'd taken and the drugs he'd been given, Xander couldn't handle the pace anymore. Gasping for breath, on the out-skirts of the farm now, Xander dropped to his knees behind a stack of crates. Gently, he slid T.J. from his shoulders. He checked the man's side and found that the blood of his wound was starting to coagu-late.

Covered with sweat, panting for breath and shak-ing from the exertion, Xander looked at the wounded man. "You'll be all right."

T.J. nodded and firmed his jaw. "It's not the first time I've been shot. Thanks, man."

"No problem," Xander replied. He pushed away the slight guilt he felt. He was done; there was noth-ing more he could do for T.J. *And it's not like I owe the guy any favors. This place is about as safe as it gets around here, and it's for damn sure neither one of us is gonna make it with me trying to pack him outta here on my back.* "This is where we split up, though. Okay? The *soldados* will patch you up when this is all over. Just keep your head down."

T.J. offered his hand.

With only a momentary hesitation, Xander took the man's hand and they shook. Then Xander turned and ran, not looking back over his shoulder because he didn't want to remember leaving the man there like that. *Not my responsibility,* he told himself. *We can't both survive this thing. Gotta look out for my own ass. Just his bad luck, that's all.*

Xander kept running, feeling light on his feet now that he didn't have T.J. draped over his shoulders. That absence of weight was noticeable, though. Xander stayed with the shadows, skirting the build-ings and taking the cover that was presented.

Glancing back, Xander saw the Colombian sprint

from the barn. Flames twisted up through the barn's roof, but that lasted only a moment because a salvo from one of the helicopters' 20mm Vulcan cannon ripped through the building and tore the structure to shreds.

The next salvo of cannon rounds struck the SUV just as the Colombian was scrambling aboard. The vehicle jerked with the impacts, then leaped up as the gas tanks ruptured and blew. The Colombian shoved his hands through the driver's-side window and tried to climb out. Another explosion, this one smaller, shook the SUV. Flames reached out and the Colombian dropped back into them like he was melting wax.

Xander fled, spotting a scattered line of traffickers beating feet through the coca field. *Okay, gotta be a reason for that,* Xander thought. He launched himself in pursuit, trying to stay low. Acrid smoke lacing the air burned his lungs and made his eyes tear.

Less than a hundred yards from the main farm buildings, a camouflage canopy covered a small cluster of structures. More important, the canopy disguised a line of Jeeps, pickups, and trucks.

Motor pool, Xander thought. *The traffickers were bright guys for deciding to keep those away from the rest of the farm.* He kept running, hoping all the movement and the night's darkness would help keep him disguised long enough to get his hands on one of the vehicles.

Covering the ground in long-legged strides, Xander reached the vehicles at the same time as most of the traffickers. Maybe he was going to have to fight for one of the vehicles, but that was—

Helicopter rotors sounded overhead, giving Xan-

der a split-second of warning. He threw himself to
the ground just as the cannon rounds struck. Shield-
ing his head with his hands, he peered up at the
flaming debris that had been the line of vehicles.
The Night Suns played over the destruction, then
the helicopter returned to blast the big pieces of
what had been left over.

A flicker of light on metal in Xander's peripheral
vision caught his attention. He turned, hardly daring to hope, and spotted the gold-toothed bastard's
dirt bike leaning against the side of the nearby
building.

Pushing up, Xander sprinted for the dirt bike.
More cannon rounds hammered the ground behind
him. Dirt and rock peppered his back when he
reached the motorcycle. A quick glance assured him
that the dirt bike didn't have a key ignition.

Xander threw a leg across the motorcycle, then
reached down and flipped out the manual starter.
Pulling in the clutch, he stood up and jammed his
weight on the starter, feeling it slide like a stick
through thick mud. Before he reached the bottom of
the kick stroke, the dirt bike started with a throaty
roar that belched blue-gray smoke.

Yeah, baby, Xander thought enthusiastically.
We're going mobile now. He gunned the engine and
popped the clutch, pulling the dirt bike up in a
wheelie.

A disorganized group of traffickers plunged toward him through the coca field. Only a short distance away, Xander spotted the dirt road that he
had followed to the farm. The traffickers reached
the dirt road and began running.

Xander followed them, cutting across the field till

he reached the dirt road. Pulling onto the road, he glanced over his shoulder to where he'd left T.J. Guilt washed over him like a wave slamming him after a wakeboard wipeout. Before he knew what he was doing, he jammed the brakes and came to a stop, leaning on his left foot to support the bike.

"You had to be a decent guy, didn't you?" Xander asked. Knowing what he was about to do had to be in his Top Ten List of Stupid Things to Do, he wheeled the bike around and sped back toward the farm. Avoiding the dirt road, knowing he'd be an attractive target in plain sight there, he went crosscountry, slamming through the coca plants.

A light flared out of the darkness, streaking across the coca plants ahead of him, then backtracking till the light focused on him. In the next instant, the helicopter descended from the dark heavens. The aircraft jinked around to bring the 20mm cannon to bear.

Xander was grimly aware of his shadow riding behind him. The harsh light made seeing difficult, stripping him of his night vision.

"Shit," he said.

Then the helicopter's 20mm cannon opened up with thunderous booms.

21

Xander twisted the dirt bike's throttle and accelerated. The powerful engine growled and rose to the challenge, muscling forward across the uneven terrain and through the coca plants.

A salvo of 20mm cannon rounds pulverized the area where Xander had been. Rocks pounded his back hard enough to leave bruises. Twisting on the seat, he glanced over his shoulder and saw the helicopter swinging around to come after him.

Despite the need to turn around, the helicopter's speed was greater than the dirt bike's. Xander rode in a half-crouch, keeping his body balanced on the pegs, leaning back and forth as he needed to bring the front wheel up or shove it down. Having to keep looking over his shoulder was doubly risky, but not looking would have been suicidal.

A line of green tracers flamed the air, followed by explosions that pocked the field. The line Xander was leaving through the coca plants looked like a connect-the-dot game with the way the cannon rounds slammed the ground.

When the cannon rounds were less than ten feet behind him and gaining, Xander leaned hard to the right, putting a knee out to drag the bike over in a tight turn. The ground was mushy and loose, giving way too easily under the knobby tires. His knee hit the ground, bouncing across the ripped earth. For a heartbeat, Xander thought he was going to lose the bike, but he accelerated again and opened the turn a little. The tires grabbed hold again, pulling him away as the line of cannon rounds hammered past him.

Okay, dammit, Xander said as he watched the helicopter suddenly juke around to come for him again, *let's see what you got, bro. Maybe you're the hawk and I'm the mouse, but I'm one freakin' tricky mouse.* He was amped now and he knew it. Adrenaline flooded his senses and fear didn't exist anymore. *It's all about the timing, baby. Don't you ever forget that.*

Xander held the motorcycle loose and ready, rocking his body to fit the contours of the land, making the rough terrain work for him. He became an impossible target, juking and weaving, diving and darting.

Without warning, the Night Sun's beam caught the fence in front of Xander. The harsh light revealed the plant-covered barricade that seemed to stretch endlessly in either direction.

Knowing he'd never be able to stop in time, Xander spotted a dirt mound in front of the fence on the left. Evidently the traffickers had cleared the land and pushed the excess back to leave a flatter field to aid in irrigation. Nearly twenty feet separated the dirt mound from the fence. Xander didn't know if the mound was high enough or close enough, but he was all out of options.

He pulled the dirt bike into line with the mound. As he gazed at the shadowed mass, he wondered briefly about cutting back on the acceleration. If the grade was too steep, he was going to drag the bike frame and lose momentum, and if he cut speed, he might not be able to get the distance he needed out of the jump.

More speed, Xander assured himself. *More speed is better*. His senses were singing as he hit the mound. The Night Sun flared an ellipse around him, casting his shadow on the ground just ahead of him and letting him know the helicopter was burning up his back trail. *Second place? I don't think so, bro.* He twisted the throttle.

Cannonfire pounded the base of the mound as Xander leaned into the climb, almost hanging over the handlebars as he kept the dirt bike locked down. The bike rocketed from the top of the mound and the rear wheel screamed as the resistance faded and let the tire spin freely.

In the air, Xander throttled down, then kicked the right foot peg, turning the dirt bike in midair to achieve a tabletop aerial. With the dirt bike twisted horizontal to the ground, he presented a smaller target to the helicopter's cannon and managed to get the height he needed to clear the fence by a handful of inches.

He came down on the other side of the fence, twisting the dirt bike again to land on both tires. Gunning the engine, he grabbed the necessary traction and shot forward just as cannonfire reduced the fence to kindling.

The helicopter roared by again, and for an instant Xander was out of the Night Sun's glow. *One hell of a mouse*, he congratulated himself.

But the helicopter pilot wasn't giving up. The tail rotor spun the aircraft around for another approach. This time the gunner opened up as he streaked toward Xander, trying for an interception kill.

Xander found another dirt mound, this one partially reclaimed by the jungle and showing signs of new growth. He roared up the hill. As he crested the jump, he saw that the helicopter pilot had seen the hill as well and had accounted for it. The Vulcan mini-cannon came around, getting target lock from less than fifty feet out.

Kicking free of the pegs, Xander yanked the handlebars straight up, dropping the dirt bike's ass-end down till the machine stood up vertically in mid-air. He pulled himself over the handlebars, pushing his body straight out behind him. Mike Jones had branded the "Kiss of Death" aerial in the motocross circuit, but Xander's form was perfect.

The 20mm cannon rounds screamed by, passing only inches over Xander's head. He was grinning, feeling the adrenaline burn as he recovered the dirt bike and landed with both wheels down.

A guard tower stood out against the jungle background less than a hundred yards away. Muzzle flashes proved that the traffickers hadn't all gone. Xander changed course, heading for the guard tower and hoping to borrow a little covering fire.

Instead, the trafficker in the guard tower switched

from aiming at the helicopter to firing at the motor-cycle.

Xander didn't waste his breath cursing the guy. Staying alive took all his concentration. One slip and he knew either the trafficker or the helicopter gun crew would have him. He hit another mound, powering up the incline, driving straight for the guard tower.

The trafficker didn't flinch as the motorcycle streaked right at him. He pulled the assault rifle to his shoulder and took aim.

Knowing his life was measured between heart-beats, Xander pushed up and swung forward over the motorcycle's handlebars. The move was called a can-can aerial in BMX circuits, and had a similar move called the candybar aerial in motocross. He drove his feet forward to clear the seat as bullets cut the air where he'd been. Then he swung around and crunched both feet into the trafficker's chest.

When the man opened his mouth to scream as he fell from the guard tower, Xander recognized him as the gold-toothed bastard who had hit him with the rifle stock. *The wheel turns, bro. Payback's a bitch.*

Xander was back astride the motorcycle by the time he hit the ground. The trafficker landed imme-diately after. Pieces of the guard tower rained down over them as 20mm cannon rounds blew the struc-ture to hell.

The Night Sun speared through the solid wall of jungle ahead of Xander. The brief glance proved there was no escape in that direction. And T.J. was back the other way.

Xander dropped a knee and tapped the brakes, bringing the dirt bike around in a tight turn, then began a wide loop that took him back toward the farm. He roared cross-country, pursued again by the helicopter.

Skirting the edge of the jungle canopy, he also managed to stay mostly out of the helicopter pilot's sights. But that just seemed to encourage the pilot to continue the pursuit.

This far into the attack, the drug farm looked like a small corner of hell. Flames danced atop and within most of the buildings. Whoever the attackers were, they didn't intend to leave anything standing.

Knowing time was running out for T.J., Xander steered for the building where he'd left the guy. Taking a brief glance over his shoulder, Xander saw that the helicopter was doggedly staying with him. Looking forward again, he spotted a large drainpipe sticking out of the hill behind the building where he'd been held. The drainpipe was about five feet across and probably used to funnel the boiling water away from the farm after the leaves were thoroughly soaked.

A desperate plan formed in Xander's mind when he spotted the wrecked SUV still sitting in front of the building. He changed directions at the last instant, shedding speed and pulling to the right hard enough to skid for just a moment before he managed to get traction again. He aimed himself at the SUV.

The SUV sat on four blown-out tires. The front end was mashed down, crushed by the concussion of a near miss. The angle looked right, but Xander knew he wouldn't know for sure until he was into the stunt. By then, he wouldn't have any time to stop, and no margin for error.

A line of 20mm cannon rounds devastated the

ground only a few yards away. Dirt showered Xander and left a moldy taste in his mouth. He ignored the distraction and concentrated on the stunt. He twisted the throttle till it wouldn't go any farther, winding the dirt bike's powerful engine out.

All or nothing, bro, Xander told himself. *All or nothing. Timing is everything.* He was conscious of the helicopter again, like he could feel the gunner's sights in the middle of his back. But there was no time now—no time for anything but the stunt.

The adrenaline was slamming through Xander when he hit the crushed front of the SUV, leaned forward as the machine scrambled up the rugged climb, then went airborne, heading for the peaked rooftop of the building behind the vehicle.

22

Xander stood on the motorcycle pegs as he sailed more than fifty feet through the air. He'd built up more speed and caught a better angle than he'd thought. When he started coming down, he discovered that he'd overshot his target, landing on the downslope of the barn's roof instead of the upslope.

Even as he landed, 20mm cannon rounds thumped into the other side of the roof. Machine gun fire, glowing with red tracers, ripped through the wooden shingles around Xander. The bullets hammered the shingles to shreds and started a small avalanche of wood toward the roof's edge.

Xander passed the falling shingles and shot over the barn's edge. Overflow from the pipe he'd spotted on the way in had turned the ground to mud. The bike was going way too fast when he hit the mud. Struggling to control the dirt bike, he ended up stuffing it instead. Laying the dirt bike over, Xander managed to keep a death grip on the handlebars and stay with the machine as he skidded through the mud.

An instant later, the barn exploded. A concussive heat wave slammed into Xander. Evidently the barn had stored more inside than he'd seen. The sky lit up with bright yellows, oranges, and reds as curling flames tongued the sky.

Despite losing the dirt bike, Xander saw that he'd been dead-on course. He and the bike both slid toward the large pipe, shushing through the smelly glop and ending up inside the pipe. He stood and pulled the dirt bike on into the concealment offered by the pipe just as another series of explosions ripped through the barn.

Patient only because he knew he had no choice, Xander squatted on his haunches and stared at the burning building. All the chemical fires and the explosive cannon rounds left a white haze and falling powder hanging in the air.

Xander dealt with the pain that filled him. He breathed regularly and flexed cramped muscles. The bruises and strains would heal. But only if he grabbed T.J. when nobody was looking and they escaped.

The helicopter hovered over the building for a short time while someone flashed the Night Sun over the area. While the aircraft hung there, smoke and chemical haze filtered into the interior. After a short wait, the helicopter drifted away.

Xander gave the situation another minute count, then gathered up the dirt bike and pushed the machine out of the pipe. He kept pushing the bike until he reached the place where he'd left T.J.

The ex-Navy guy remained in a seated posture.

Both of his hands pressed wadded material from his shirt against his wounded side.

"Let's go, man!" Xander said. With the bike, he was certain they could both get away. He liked that a lot better than T.J.'s chances of finding a sympathetic party at the cocaine farm.

T.J. remained seated, but he glanced around pointedly behind Xander.

"What?" Xander demanded. Then he heard a rustle behind him. Spinning quickly, he spotted the black-clad troops that had kicked him off the C-123. He released the dirt bike and tried to set himself up in a defensive posture. But it was too late. He was winded and tired, and the black-uniformed men were too quick and too many. They grabbed hold of him and took him down to the ground.

Xander sat handcuffed to a chair in one of the few remaining buildings on the drug farm. From his position, he was able to see most of the activity outside the window. Dawn had broken less than an hour ago and torn away the shreds of night that had been left after most of the buildings had burned to the ground.

The helicopters belonged to the Colombian military, and they were operating with an American special ops task force. The Colombians hadn't exactly been enthusiastic about taking prisoners. A few of the traffickers had been rounded up and marched under guard onto buses. Any resistance on the part of the traffickers had been an excuse to execute them.

Xander gathered there was no love lost between the Colombian military and the drug traffickers. He

still didn't know what had kept him from getting
locked up with the traffickers, but he had his suspi-
cions. Three of the black-clad American soldiers
guarded him. More of them were stationed outside
the door.

The scar-faced guy, Gibbons, hadn't put in an appearance yet, but Xander knew the man had to be
around.

Smoke from the smoldering heaps of the burned
and gutted buildings left wine-dark smudges against
the rose and lavender-streaked sky above the tree-
tops. Another helicopter took off, rotors growling,
and stirred the smoke. Walkie-talkies bleated and
squelched, and snippets of angry and short conversations echoed over the farm.

Virg stepped out onto the street wearing handcuffs and leg irons. Taking short, hobbling steps, the
gangbanger looked back over his shoulder and spotted Xander. Maybe it was only wishful thinking, but
Xander thought Virg looked a little ashamed.

A moment later, two black-clad special ops guys
carried T.J. by on a gurney. Xander felt a little better
about that. He and the ex-Navy guy had been separated as soon as they'd been taken into custody. He
hadn't known if T.J. had survived his wound.

Weakly, T.J. looked at Xander, then gave him a
thumbs-up. The special ops guys carried the gurney
toward a waiting American helicopter.

As they loaded T.J. onto the aircraft, a figure
strode through the smoke that roiled through the
street. Although the man was dressed in a tropical
suit, Xander recognized Gibbons at once.

Gibbons crossed the road between the burned-out
husks of the buildings, skirting the craters and over-

turned cars and corpses that had been left by the 20mm cannon rounds. Somehow, the guy looked totally at home in all the chaos.

Xander pulled on the handcuffs locking him to the chair, then made himself relax. So far, this was all Scarface's game, but the payback wheel turned in mysterious ways.

Gibbons entered the room and looked at Xander.

Xander returned the man's gaze full measure. "If you have me shot with another one of them darts, I'm gonna bust your ass."

A slight smile flickered briefly at Gibbons's lips. "Easy, X. You just graduated at the head of your class." He nodded at one of the black-clad special ops warriors. "Unlock him."

When the cuff was off his wrist, Xander stood and squared off with Gibbons.

Agent Polk, the younger man who had been at the diner, entered the room and stood at Gibbons's side.

"What the hell are you talking about?" Xander demanded. *Head of the class, my ass.* "You almost got me killed out there. For what?"

Polk shrugged. "We knew the Colombian army was moving in. They thought our idea of three decoys was a good one."

Anger spun through Xander. Control evaporated from him the way snow crust did under a falling body during a snowboard wipeout. Stepping forward, Xander headbutted the younger agent before the guy even knew the attack was coming. The impact caused black spots to whirl in Xander's vision, but the pain was worth the effort.

Polk staggered back, crying out and pressing both hands to his bloody nose.

Xander tried to go after the guy, willing to vent his rage at being set up and used. T.J. had been hurt bad, and for what? As a decoy? Before Xander took a second step, Gibbons slid a foot forward and leg-jammed him, making him trip over his own feet.

Off-balance, Xander crashed to the hardwood floor. Before he could roll to his feet, Gibbons put a foot on his throat, adding just enough weight to let him know how easy crushing his throat would have been.

Gibbons's face was hard and cold.

Xander had no doubt that the man would kill him if he had to. But Gibbons was choosing not to kill him. Xander chuckled. "Not bad for an old man."

Gibbons held his foot in place a little longer, allowing Polk to step farther away. Then Gibbons removed his foot. "Let's take a walk."

Xander rolled to his feet with difficulty. He was beat up and hurting all over, but he damn sure wasn't going to let anybody in that room know. He followed Gibbons, aware that they were getting down to the bottom line now.

23

Xander dusted himself off as he trailed Gibbons out of the building and into the smoke-laden area between the structures. He also made an effort not to let the agent see him limping. Gibbons surveyed the battlefield, but Xander couldn't tell if everything met the guy's expectations or not.

A Jeep carrying Colombian soldiers in battle-dress green camous roared by. Xander had to step out of the way, but they never came close to Gibbons. The agent never once flinched.

Gibbons spoke in a controlled, level voice. "I'm one of those guys that believes that, under the right circumstances, a man can change."

Xander didn't rise to the bait, not truly knowing what the man expected. Scarface was a conundrum.

"Last night," Gibbons said, "you of all people showed leadership, courage, and a willingness to protect a man you hardly knew."

"So give me a medal," Xander said.

"I'd rather give you a job."

Though Xander was hurting and stranded and didn't know how in the hell he was going to get back home, he laughed. He couldn't stop himself even though he knew he might piss Gibbons off.

"Dude," Xander said, "look at me. Do I look like a fan of law enforcement?" He shook his head. "Forget the tests. You shoulda just asked me. I woulda saved you a lot of trouble."

"Oh, I don't know," Gibbons replied, unperturbed. "I think the tests work pretty well. Sometimes they give me answers you wouldn't admit to in a million years."

Irritation filled Xander. "Why don't you cut the crap and get to the sales pitch?"

Gibbons smiled, but the effort was cold enough to frost lava. "It's your lucky day, Xander. This is your chance to pay back our wonderful country for all the freedom you enjoy. The job's not complicated. I just want you to meet some people and find out whatever you can about them."

Vague interest stirred inside Xander, but the emotion was liberally mixed with suspicion and a certain lack of trust. If he'd died during the Colombian test, he was positive Gibbons wouldn't have shed any tears over him.

"What type of people you want me to meet?" Xander asked.

"Dirty, dangerous, tattooed, uncivilized," Gibbons answered. "Your kind of people."

"And you want me to pull a Judas?" Xander shook his head. "That's not my style. So how's about you just kiss my ass, Scarface?"

As if by magic, a pistol appeared in Gibbons's hand.

Xander started to move, but he knew it was already too late. If the man wanted him dead, that was how things were going to be.

"Normally," Gibbons said in a light tone, "I'd just press this up to your head and ask you very nicely to do what I want. But you're not the type that's afraid of death. So that sort of puts us in a quandary."

"I guess we'd better call it a day, then."

"Oh, not just yet." Gibbons paused, keeping the pistol out in the open but not pointing the weapon at Xander. "You ever watch the lions at the zoo?"

Xander didn't reply.

"You can tell which ones were captured in the wild by looking in their eyes. The wild lioness, she remembers the open plain, the thrill of the hunt. She's four hundred pounds of killing fury stuck in a box. After a few years, her eyes start to glaze over and you can just tell her soul has died."

Xander knew that. Seeing the animals in captivity was a primary reason he didn't much care for zoos. Society was like a zoo, and that was one of the reasons he broke the rules.

"Same thing happens to a man," Gibbons went on. "Leavenworth Federal Pen is no joke. They'll take a wildman like you and put him in solitary just for fun. Lockdown twenty-three hours a day for the rest of your natural life."

Despite his effort at control, Xander's stomach churned. Death held no fear for him. But being trapped like that, locked down and kept away from everything he loved, that was worse than anything he'd ever imagined. And he had no doubt that Gibbons could make it happen.

"No more mountains," the scar-faced man said. "No more ocean. Just a six-foot-by-eight-foot concrete cell with no window. Without anything except a bucket to shit in." He paused, letting his words have full impact. "Of course, you can avoid all that by doing me this small favor."

Xander shook his head. "You got nothing on me. You'll be lucky I don't sue your ass."

"Oh, really? I see you got three Xs on the back of your neck. That's appropriate, 'cause you're looking at three strikes." Gibbons counted them out on his fingers. "Grand theft auto. Reckless driving. Avoiding arrest. Your little adventure just made you a three-time loser." He grinned mirthlessly. "You could call yourself *Triple X*."

Cold realization filled Xander. The feeling wasn't fear, only the heavy weight of reality. For a brief moment he felt like he was back in the projects, growing up having nothing, wanting something. But there had been no opportunities in the projects that didn't offer a quick trip to the graveyard.

Guys he'd known who had tried to make something of themselves by getting out usually got busted up by the rest of society and sent home with their tails between their legs. Guys who tried to pull in the benjamins by trafficking in drugs ended up dead, shot by law enforcement personnel or by other traffickers looking to take over more territory.

Extreme sports had provided Xander a vision and an outlet. And he'd made that skill and talent work for him. Partnering up with Rashonn might have led somewhere, might have been his ticket out. The stunt with Hotchkiss's Corvette had been just that: a stunt. And maybe part of it had been about a little payback for Hotchkiss's stance on extreme sports and video games.

Now the stunt was a noose around Xander's neck. Part of him wanted to say screw it and let the chips fall. But he knew without a doubt that Gibbons would follow through on his threat.

Xander gazed at the destroyed drug farm, weighing his options. None of them seemed attractive. Lockdown or being a narc? Either option totally went against everything he lived for. How could he compromise in either direction without losing himself?

"If you find out what I want to know," Gibbons said, "I'll forget about your recent criminal transgressions and let you get on with your pathetic excuse of a life."

"Why would I go back to that when I could be like you?" Xander asked sarcastically. "Get all shot up for the old Stars and Stripes. I bet the flag's a real comfort every time you look in the mirror, Crispy."

Gibbons held his gaze for a moment. "A small price I paid for putting foot to ass for my country. And I'm fully prepared to continue my good work right here if that's what you want."

"Let's say I agree to go. How do I know you'll keep up your end?"

"One thing you will learn about me," Gibbons said in a flat voice, "is that I keep my word." He gestured.

Before Xander could turn around, one of the black-clad special ops warriors stood at his side. The way the guys moved was incredible.

The warrior shook out his hands, letting the handcuffs and chains he carried slide down to their full length with a clanking jangle.

"So tell me, Triple X," Gibbons said. "You wanna get on a plane? Or is 'Kiss my ass, Scarface' your final answer?"

SPY 2.0: THE MISSION

24

Seated in the last row of seats on a jet aimed at Eastern Europe, Xander reached into the backpack Agent Gibbons had given him when he'd flown out. The departure, the soonest Gibbons could arrange, hadn't been a tearful good-bye.

Xander had caught a red-eye flight out that was already packed with weary travelers who had been flying for hours. After take-off, once the flight had leveled out, everyone went to sleep. Even the flight attendants appeared to have settled in for the night. Only blackness and silver-limned clouds showed outside the window.

Despite the fatigue that enveloped him, Xander couldn't sleep. He was too edgy, too conflicted inside in ways he'd never experienced before. None of the bad times he'd had at home when he was growing up had prepared him for what he was about to do. He'd never figured himself for the jet-set crowd, and he'd for damn sure never figured himself for a rat.

Xander took out a small chrome-finished personal DVD player and headphones from the backpack. Gibbons had put all the mission information on a DVD. Xander opened the compact player and keyed up the menu, then punched in his access code. He flipped through the photos and maps, then queued the briefing.

As the briefing began, the bathroom door opened beside Xander. He glanced up and saw a young boy stepping out of the small room.

The kid was ten or eleven, skinny and all eyes. He stared with avid interest at the DVD player Xander held.

"What game is that?" the kid asked.

"Huh?" Xander asked. Then his mind caught up and he realized the kid thought he was using a personal gaming system. Xander didn't want to be rude. Growing up as he had, being around his aunt and the restaurant where she'd worked, he'd always felt kids were special. The only problem was they got their innocence ripped away from them too early. "It's called *Anarchy 99.*" He returned his attention to the player.

The kid stood there and stared at the player screen.

Xander glanced around the passenger cabin, looking for someone who might be missing a kid. Nobody seemed concerned.

"What's wrong?" Xander asked the boy. "Can't sleep?"

The kid frowned. "I'm stuck between my mom and her boyfriend who snores."

"Oh." Xander nodded. He understood all about moms and boyfriends and getting lost in that particular shuffle. His heart went out to the kid. And, truth to tell, maybe he was starting to feel a little lonely and lost on the flight himself. The kid understood and loved games. It was a commonality. "Well, why don't you check it out?"

The boy came closer, eyes focused on the player screen.

Xander turned the player a little more toward the boy. "Sweet graphics, huh?"

Cautiously, the boy sat in the empty seat beside Xander. "Is it a first-person shooter?" the boy asked.

Xander considered his answer, remembering the kind of people he was going to be dealing with. If Anarchy 99 found out about him, there was no doubt what they'd do with him. "Unfortunately, yeah. My guy is an undercover agent who deals in stolen cars."

"Cool." The kid nodded and cracked his knuckles in anticipation. "So the bad guys must be Anarchy 99?"

The debriefing was in full swing, showing pictures of the five primary members of the terrorist group Gibbons had put Xander onto. Most of the footage was shot during the civil wars that had ripped through Prague and the rest of the country. The four men were shown in military uniforms. All four guys looked deadly and intense.

"Ninety-nine," Xander said, "that's how many people they killed taking over their crime syndicate. In one night." Every time he thought about that, the fact seemed more and more unbelievable, something that would come from a video game. "This might be harder than I thought."

The footage kept rolling. More shots of the four men showed them in civilian dress, joined by a beautiful brunette who looked to be two parts sex kitten and one part hardcase.

"Damn," the boy said, then caught himself. "I mean, who's she?"

Xander smiled, knowing the boy was just now getting into the whole awareness of the opposite sex. "You like her, huh? Do you have a girlfriend?"

The boy looked embarrassed. "No."

"Hey," Xander said, trying to make the boy more comfortable, "there's nothing wrong with appreciating beautiful graphics."

The boy nodded. "Any cool weapons?"

Xander stopped the briefing, then clicked on the inventory menu selection. He'd checked out the section before, and as he watched the compilation of weapons and vehicles available to him and that Anarchy 99 was known to use, he was still blown away.

"Just about anything I want, I guess," Xander said.

A grin split the kid's face. "Hardcore."

"It's gonna be tough, though," Xander said. "I've never played before. Plus, I gotta get it right the first time through. No Game Shark, no Prima Strategy Guide, no nothing." He hadn't meant to say that. Those thoughts were his, and thinking like that felt odd. Before every stunt he did, he always felt like he was on top of the world.

This bit, though, just felt bad all the way around.

Xander blinked, realizing that the kid was talking to him.

"That is a tough game," the boy said.

"Serious," Xander agreed. "You'd better get back to your mom. Take it easy."

The kid got up and started walking down the aisle. Then he stopped and turned around. "What does your guy get if he finishes?" the boy asked.

"I dunno," Xander admitted. He hadn't even thought that far.

"I bet by the end he gets something," the boy said.

"Like what?"

The boy shrugged. "He gets to be the hero." He turned and kept going, disappearing into one of the rows.

Hero? For ratting people out? Xander thought about what he'd just told the boy, and about the context in which he'd put Anarchy 99. *Man, it's not that simple. Life ain't about black and white. Not when you start figuring people into the equation.*

But part of him envied the boy. With his view of the world, all good guys and bad guys, the boy would have fit right into Gibbons's little God-Save-America mentality. But somebody liked the boy, someone who was so sure about what he was doing and why, wouldn't stand a chance against Anarchy 99. So Gibbons had blackmailed Xander into the job, and Xander didn't much care about the rest of the world. How fucked up was that? And what did it say about him?

Pushing the thoughts from his mind, Xander turned his attention back to the DVD briefing. Prague was only a few hours away now, and he had to hit the ground running there.

25

"This is some welcome to Prague," Xander said. He gazed out the windows of the beat-up car that had picked him up at the airport only minutes ago. The two men who had met him at the arrival gate after he'd cleared Customs hadn't been overly friendly. In fact, they'd acted like he was a disappointment. But they'd had police I.D. and the names of all the contacts that Gibbons had told Xander to ask about.

The city was a lot different from L.A. Old buildings occupied the downtown area rather than modern buildings and expensive landscaping. Prague didn't just look old; the city *felt* old. The buildings towered in an oppressive manner, seeming to block out the sky because of the narrow and winding cobblestone streets. The car's tires bumped over the uneven surface and through the burial crypt–sized potholes.

With the gargoyles perched on all the buildings and the Gothic architecture, Xander kept thinking that Romania wasn't that far away. His imagination had no trouble imagining the city's alleys filled with vampires and ghouls after the sun went down. *Nightlife around here must be a trip,* he thought.

Scars showed on the buildings and the streets as well, though. In several places, new brickwork and mortar stood out against decades-old walls and buildings. Tanks had rolled through Prague at different times, and the treads had splintered and shattered the cobblestones. That was where some of the potholes had come from, Xander guessed. Other places showed patchwork replacements of differently colored cobblestones.

The long years of war and general unease showed in the faces of the people living in the neighborhoods. Pots of flowers hung from canopies, sat in windows, or were grouped on tiny patios. The effect was an illusion of innocence and relaxation, though, because the windows and doors were filled with watchful and worried eyes.

Maybe this place isn't so different from L.A., Xander told himself. He turned his attention to the two men sitting in the front seats. They'd dumped him in the back seat with his luggage. There was a lot of luggage compared to how he normally traveled. Gibbons had made sure Xander was outfitted before he'd left.

Xander locked eyes with the driver in the rearview mirror. "What's your name, slick?"

"My name is Ivan," the man said. He could have been twins with the man in the passenger seat. Both of them were at least six feet four inches tall and looked like they were made of four-by-four timbers tied together with barbed wire.

Xander shifted his gaze to the man in the passenger seat.

"My name is Ivan," the second man said.

"That's gotta be confusing on Valentine's Day," Xander stated. "So where are we headed?"

Neither man answered.

"Fellas," Xander tried again, in case they hadn't actually heard over the rattle of the car, "I said, where we headed?"

The driver just glanced at him in the rearview mirror but didn't say anything.

"Yeah," Xander said, disgusted. "Whatever." He tried to make himself comfortable amid his luggage. The car was small enough that the two big cops would have probably strained the comfort zone. Xander and his luggage had no chance at all. *Scarface, when we talk again, I'm definitely gonna tell you how much this little assignment blows.*

A few minutes later, Ivan the driver turned off the main streets and wound through what seemed to be a series of alleys. The part of town they ended up in looked like it had caught some kind of fungus disease and should have been amputated years ago.

Trash piles littered the alleys, overflowing onto the sidewalks in front of the crumbling buildings. The surrounding structures all had missing masonry. From the looks of the mortar jobs and mismatched bricks, the residents habitually stole bricks back and forth from each other, mortaring them into different empty places that became occupied.

Ivan the driver pulled the rattletrap car to a halt in front of a particularly malodorous and cancerous-looking building. Ivan riding shotgun got out, opened the back door, then heaved Xander's luggage out onto the garbage-strewn sidewalk.

Xander stepped out into the cold wind without a word. Griping and complaining weren't going to do anything but get someone's head busted. Even if he could take the two Ivans, which he thought he could, he'd end up in a foreign country without resources. At least the Ivans were friends. He glanced at the luggage sitting on the sidewalk. Maybe they weren't good friends.

The Ivans headed for the building.

Taking a look down the street, Xander saw a group of winos warming themselves around a trashcan fire. Above them, a mean-faced old woman scowled at Xander and shook her head in disapproval.

Welcome home, Xander thought wryly. Even Prague had project neighborhoods. He gathered his luggage, taking his time because he saw the Ivans waiting inside the building ahead of him. With some reluctance, he followed them inside, then began the long trek up narrow stairs.

Three stories later, one of the Ivans opened an apartment door.

Xander entered the room and found his temporary living quarters were every bit as bad as he'd thought they would be. Small and cramped, the room held an overstuffed chair and a couch sitting lopsided because the block of wood under one corner hadn't been cut to fit. Roaches crawled through the peeling wallpaper. Years of collected dust coated the cracked windows, which let the wind whistle through. A sagging, iron-framed bed occupied a third of the room near the windows overlooking the street.

Oh, yeah, Gibbons, me and you are gonna have us a heart-to-heart next time I see you. Xander dropped his luggage in the middle of the floor. A layer of dust billowed up from the ragged throw rug.

A trim guy with an intense expression and a suit that would have looked at home in a retro collection specializing in ugly and bizarre sat in the overstuffed chair. He might as well have had COP written all over him. Turgid smoke drifted from a rank-smelling cigar that somehow cut through the stink of the apartment.

"So," Xander said, "do you talk? Or are you all big on the silent tough-guy act like the Ivans?"

26

Detective Milan Sova of the Prague police department stared in near open-mouthed amazement at the American standing before him. Since agreeing through diplomatic channels to yet another Central Intelligence Agency man, he'd expected someone like the others he'd worked with. But this man couldn't have been a trained agent. In a lot of ways, he looked as bad as any member of Anarchy 99.

Steeling himself, maintaining the control that he was known for, Sova shifted his flat gaze to the Ivans. "Idiots!" he snapped in his native tongue. "Where is the American agent?"

"This is him, sir," Ivan said.

Sova glanced back at the American. There was no way that this man was one of the United States' best agents. He looked like a street thug, and had the demeanor to match.

"They must be giving up on this operation," Sova said.

The American glanced around the apartment. His displeasure was evident on his face. Then he shifted his gaze to Sova, pinning him with his eyes. "What's up, guys?"

Sova was even more surprised. The new agent didn't even speak the language. How the hell did the Americans expect the man to survive in the city, much less up against Anarchy 99? Sova took a hit off his cigar, then spoke in English, "Sit down."

The man considered the order for about the space of a heartbeat. "I've been on a plane for twelve hours. I think I'll stand."

Sova made himself ignore the fact that the American had disobeyed an order, not simply passed on a suggestion. "My name is Milan Sova. I am a detective with the Czech secret police."

"Xander Cage," the American said.

Sova chose to ignore the niceties and pleasantries. "When you are here, you are under my jurisdiction. You take my orders. You do what I say. If you become any kind of an inconvenience, I'll shoot you."

A smile crossed the American's face. "Hey, take a number."

Pretending he hadn't heard, Sova continued. "You're here because your government is putting pressure on my government. This is an internal affair. A Czech affair. I will warn you once: Don't shit on my lawn. Get whatever information your government seeks and get out."

"First of all," the American said, "I don't wanna be here any more than you want me here. Two, if you had the authority to shoot me you would've done it by now. Three, the person you oughta shoot is whoever sold you that suit."

Sova stared at the man.

As calmly as if he were in his own home instead of a roach-infested apartment half a world away, the American walked to the bed and laid down. He laced his hands together behind his head and stared up at the ceiling.

Rather than push the issue, Sova got up and walked to the door. He decided not to lose his temper with the American. The man wouldn't last long in Prague anyway. None of the other CIA agents had.

Sova glanced back at the American. "Be ready in three hours," he said. Then he turned to the Ivans and spoke in Czech. "Watch him."

Both men nodded and remained in the room.

Sova took a final look at the American on the bed. The man had his eyes closed. The slow, regular rise and fall of his chest indicated that he was already asleep.

Amazing, Sova thought as he turned and walked out the door. He was convinced the man wouldn't last twenty-four hours.

As weird music flooded the street out in front of the massive building in downtown Prague where Sova had brought him, Xander looked around, feeling the strange rhythm throbbing inside his head. The neighborhood was a million miles from anything he knew, and the music sounded like it came from another planet. He didn't even recognize the instrument.

Night had fallen over Prague a couple hours ago. The shadows around the city had gradually deepened, then given way to occasional street lamps not damaged by war or neglect. Traffic on the street in front of the building was lively. Cars were already parked in the empty lots around the building, and a steady stream of them kept coming.

Xander accompanied Sova. The Czech detective still hadn't broken out with a case of the friendlies, but at least he was informative. Anarchy 99 was supposed to be inside the building.

The Ivans had followed them in the rattletrap car they had, but they'd vanished. Xander was willing to bet the men were still around somewhere, though. They were the kind who could fade into the woodwork and reappear whenever they wanted. Xander figured the Ivans would have felt right at home with Gibbons's black-clad military crew.

Two big men in leather coats worked the entrance to the building where the techno music was coming from. Xander recognized them as bouncers immediately.

Sova nodded to one of the men as he paid the cover charge. The bouncer nodded back surreptitiously.

Inside guy, Xander thought to himself. His estimation of Sova rose. The guy had a few balls in the air. According to the Czech detective, the building was one of the clubs Anarchy 99 owned. Xander couldn't help wondering if the club was the one where the last CIA agent had gotten killed.

"Everybody in here has two things in common," Sova said as he led Xander through an outer room, then down stairs that led to a basement. "They're filthy rich and they're outlaws."

"Good," Xander said. "Half of me will fit in."

The club located in the basement was definitely

upscale. Guys in expensive business suits and Rolexes sat drinking with women way too young and too beautiful for them. *Mistresses,* Xander guessed, *and probably not a wife in the bunch.*

The décor was distinctive, and probably meant something to the people seated at the plush booth, but definitely wasn't the kind of environment Xander was used to. He idly wondered if Gibbons would have felt at home there. But the décor also let Xander know that the CIA agent he'd been told about hadn't died there. That agent had been shot in an industrial metal club.

Xander turned to Sova. "You don't know me."

"I wish I didn't," the Czech detective agreed.

Xander stared at the guy.

Sudden understanding dawned in Sova's eyes, followed by angry glints. He nodded and walked away, but his deliberate eye contact let Xander know he'd be watching.

Splitting off from Sova, who was scenting the air like a hunting hound, Xander walked over to the bar. The bartender was a beautiful woman with incredible cleavage. She flashed Xander a smile, then asked a question in Czech.

Xander shook his head. "American. Sorry, I don't speak the local lingo." He grinned.

"Too bad," the bartender said.

"Yeah," Xander agreed, running his eyes over her body. "Looks like it's a beautiful language."

The bartender smiled and leaned over the bar, exposing more of her ample cleavage. "What do you want to drink?"

"A beer."

Turning, the bartender drew a draft and handed

the glass across the bar, revealing her charms once more.

Xander took the glass and paid for the drink, stuffing a couple of bills into the tip jar. He was working off of Gibbons's fun money; he could afford to be generous. He sipped the beer, taking stock of the bartender again. "Nice hops."

She smiled and moved away, called by another customer.

Standing at the bar and sipping the beer, Xander turned and surveyed the crowd. According to the briefing he'd had, Anarchy 99 owned five clubs, and it made sense that they would keep an eye on the operations. Sweeping the second level of the club visible through the large hole that had been cut through the floor of the ground level above, Xander spotted the group he'd been sent for.

All five of them, the four men and the woman, sat at the edge of the second floor. Bodyguards ringed their table, creating space between the crime members and the club patrons.

Terrific, Xander thought. *I'm gonna have to be carrying some weight if I'm gonna make it past those clowns.* But that was okay with Sova along. He could kill two birds with one stone.

Suspicious and still angry, Sova watched the American agent standing at the bar. The man stared off like he'd been hypnotized or his brain had locked down on him. Of course, assuming his brain had stopped working was being generous—Sova didn't even know if the man had a brain.

Sova had to admit that the idea of the two of them acting like they didn't know each other while in the club was a good one. The way the American agent was working, he was going to be found out at any time. When Yorgi and his comrades discovered whom the American really was, the Czech detective figured the farther he was away from ground zero when the killing occurred the better.

Seeing the American still staring galvanized Sova into motion. The Czech detective made his way to the bar and stood beside the American. He ordered a drink from the bartender, paid for it and added a small tip, and promptly got ignored for his efforts. He kept his back to the American agent, then spoke only loud enough for the agent to hear him.

"That's them," Sova said. "Anarchy 99. In the middle, Yorgi, he's the leader. He owns this club and five others like it. How do you say, all 'cash cows'? In American terminology."

When there was no answer, Sova turned to glance at the American agent only to find that the man had eluded him and was already walking up the stairs leading to the second floor and Anarchy 99.

"Oh, no," Sova gasped in disbelief. The fool wasn't going to rest until he got them both killed.

27

As Xander neared the table where the members of Anarchy 99 sat in the club, two blocky bodyguards turned and moved on an interception path. Both of the guys reached under their jackets.

Xander raised his hands slowly, showing that they were empty. He felt the adrenaline flooding his nervous system, amping him up. He was surprised that he was starting to feel like he was about to launch an unplanned stunt, something that sometimes happened when he was poppin' air and pushing himself to the max in a half-pipe. Although totally unexpected, the feeling was welcome. He leaned into it, deciding to go big. *Gonna break it or get busted up,* he thought. With an event like this, there was nothing in between.

"Hey, Yorgi!" Xander yelled loud enough to be heard across the floor.

The Anarchy 99 leader looked up.

The bodyguards kept coming, closing the distance quickly now.

"You're the man I'm looking for," Xander yelled. "I heard you're the G around here. I need cars. Expensive ones. A lot of them."

Yorgi spoke in Russian. Although he couldn't understand Yorgi's words, Xander couldn't mistake the dismissive gesture the man made. Everyone else at the table watched Xander with only passing interest.

Xander recognized all the players from the mission briefing he'd watched several times on the DVD player on the plane. Yelena sat near Yorgi with Kirill nearby. Kolya and Viktor sat across the table.

"This is hilarious," Xander exploded. "You got a cop hanging at the bar and *I'm* not welcome?" He paused and looked at Yorgi. "You understand *cop*?"

Yorgi held up a hand. The bodyguards froze like well-trained Dobermans. At the table, Viktor stood. *Bro,* Xander thought, looking at the big man, *this guy seriously did* not *look that big on the DVD.*

"What cop?" Viktor asked in English.

Xander pointed back at Milan Sova standing at the bar. The Czech detective was watching the action happening up on the second floor of the club. Sova tried very hard not to appear interested. Of course, that only made him appear even more interested.

"See that stooge wearing the suit made outta motel drapes?" Xander asked.

Milan Sova saw the American agent pointing him out to the Anarchy 99 members. He couldn't believe it. Was the man insane? Then the Czech detective's survival instinct kicked in and he looked away, turning his attention back to the female bartender flirting with the customers.

Sova swallowed his drink and watched in growing trepidation as four of the bodyguards came down the stairs and toward the bar. The four men didn't hesitate, moving like heat-seeking missiles for their target.

The weight of the pistol snugged in shoulder leather under his arm lacked the degree of comfort that Sova generally expected. With the four men bearing down on him, the detective felt like the weapon was a handicap. If they found the weapon on him, they'd be less likely to believe his story or be merciful. Even with the Ivans outside, he didn't like his chances.

Hands trembling slightly, Sova finished his drink and sat the empty tumbler back on the bar. He considered all the years he'd served the Czech police department, all the risks he'd taken against criminals who consistently lived better than he did. Suddenly, that time seemed like such a waste. What had he gotten for his time and troubles and pain? *Nothing*.

He glanced at the bar mirror, watching as the men came for him. He'd been betrayed by his department, understaffed by his superiors, and now set up by the Americans. His life, as the Americans would say, totally sucked.

"Sir," one of the bodyguards said politely.

Cautiously, expecting to be gunned down at any moment, taking little solace in the fact that Yorgi had never ordered anyone killed in this particular

club, Sova turned. "Me?" he asked, and his voice
was so dry and tight that the word cracked.

"Yes. You will come with us."

"Is there a problem?" Sova asked, trying his best
to look like a total innocent. "I paid for my drink. I
was about to leave a tip." Before he could say another word, one of the men grabbed him by the upper arm in a grip that felt like a vise. The detective
thought about the pistol under his arm, but he
knew that going for the weapon would be the absolute worst thing he could do under the circumstances. Maybe Yorgi had never ordered anyone
killed in this club yet, but all the other clubs had a
death count. Two of them even proudly posted the
numbers.

Reluctantly, his feet feeling like lead weights,
Sova crossed the club floor with the four men. He
knew the group drew the attention of several of the
patrons, and he was surprised at the embarrassment
that filled him. All of the men in the room flirted
with the criminal community in the city, broke laws
with impunity. Yet here he was worrying about how
he looked to them in the suit over which the American had insulted him. The situation was ludicrous.

The bodyguards herded him up the stairs and
stopped him in front of Yorgi's table. The four men
glared at him with hot suspicion.

Beads of sweat rolled under Sova's clothing. What
the hell had the American agent told them? Didn't
he understand that every one of those men was a
cold-blooded killer? Sova tried to smile, but the effort was weak and awkward.

"What is this all about?" Sova asked politely. He

didn't have to fake the nervousness in his voice. "I've done nothing."

The American agent leaned into him. No emotion showed on the American's face. "Who you working for?" the American demanded.

Astonished, Sova stared at him. The man was using him to effect a better cover with the Anarchy 99. That made sense on the surface, but the Czech detective couldn't help thinking he was being sold out once again. The American was plainly a thug, not far removed from the life of a street criminal himself. Was the American exposing him to Yorgi and the others to help his cover, or was he actually offering information in exchange for favors?

"What do you do for a living, dickhead?" the American agent demanded.

For a moment, only a brief moment, Sova considered blowing the American agent's cover as well. Then he realized trying to do something like that might only succeed in getting them both killed.

"Me?" Sova asked. "I work in a bank." He tried to put on a bit of an edge. "So what?"

"Bank my ass," the American agent said sarcastically.

Without warning, the American grabbed Sova roughly by the lapels of his jacket and shoved him backward, driving him in quick steps across the floor. Before Sova knew it, the railing was against the backs of his legs and he was hanging out over the first floor while the American's free hand searched through his clothing. The American left the pistol where it was, but he took the detective's badge case.

"Look what we have here," the American agent announced, releasing Sova and stepping back. He held the badge case up in triumph, flipping the cheap leather holder open to reveal the badge within.

Shame burned Sova's face. All the years of dedication he'd spent, all the risk he'd taken, were represented in that badge. Suddenly, the badge seemed like such a cheap trophy for such a prolonged battle.

"Czech Five-O on the mack," the American agent said.

As the light struck the badge in the American's hand, Sova knew beyond a doubt that he was a dead man. The American agent might as well have shoved a gun to his head and pulled the trigger.

28

Xander watched as Viktor started forward. A killing rage burned in the big man's eyes. Doubt filled Xander and he wondered if burning the Czech detective had been the right thing to do.

He hadn't wanted Sova hanging all over him, and he knew the man wouldn't have been able to step back. Sova was hooked on the job and was all about trying to pull the rug from under Yorgi and the rest of Anarchy 99. If Xander was going to do the infiltration job Gibbons had sent him on, he couldn't have Sova hanging onto his shirttail. Maybe this was somebody else's game, but Xander decided he wasn't going to play by somebody else's rules. If he was going to stunt, he was going to stunt his way.

Still, getting the guy killed wasn't in the plans either. Xander knew if the play came down to that he was going to have to do something.

Yorgi lifted a hand and shut Viktor down. Grumbling and cursing, the big man took his seat again.

Yorgi stood and crossed to Xander, studying him with renewed interest. The Anarchy 99 leader held his hand out for the badge.

Xander handed the badge over.

Briefly, Yorgi studied the badge, then cut his eyes to Sova. "I would like you to leave my club. Right now."

Sova started to protest, then closed his mouth.

Yorgi handed the badge case to one of the bodyguards, who gave it back to Sova. When Yorgi nodded, the four bodyguards herded the Czech detective back down the stairs and out the door.

Looking at Xander, Yorgi said, "Cops. Like a plague. No matter how many you pay, there's always another with his hand out."

Xander nodded, and said, "I know all about cops. I'm from L.A." He knew there was no chance in hell of him passing himself off as a local. If he was going to stand out, he was going to stand out his way and be true to himself.

"I appreciate you bringing this to my attention," Yorgi said, looking directly into Xander's eyes. "My only question is why?"

Xander shrugged. Nobody did anything for free in the world. He understood that, and he knew Yorgi shared the view. If he didn't have an ulterior motive that Yorgi understood, the man would wonder.

"Now that I done you a solid," Xander said, "maybe we can do some business." He left the fact that Yorgi owed him something hanging in the air.

Kolya spoke up from the table, then stood and came around to join Yorgi.

Xander remembered from the briefing that the two men were brothers. He stood still as Kolya walked around behind him. Kolya pulled down his coat collar so he could see the three Xs tattooed across the base of Xander's skull.

"What's he gonna do?" Xander asked. "Hump my leg?"

Kolya stepped back to Yorgi and an argument ensued.

Xander tried to stay relaxed, but he was grimly aware that the club bodyguards ringed him. If everything went to hell, he knew he wasn't getting out of the club without a fight. And even if he fought, there were no guarantees.

Kolya pointed at Xander and kept arguing.

Yorgi finally roared a single word. The argument ended. Kolya didn't look happy about the situation.

Turning to Xander again, Yorgi asked, "What's your name?"

"Cage," Xander answered. "Xander Cage. Friends call me X."

"I knew it!" Kolya exploded excitedly. He was grinning like a madman. "You sick crazy on a snowboard, on a motor bike! Everything!"

Bro, Xander thought to himself in disbelief, *are we talking about a fan here?*

Kolya's announcement drew interest and speculation from the group. Viktor grinned expansively and nodded. The woman, Yelena, looked at Xander with renewed interest. Kirill's expression didn't change at all.

"My brother here is a great admirer," Yorgi said. "He has seen your videos many times, X. Now, what was it that you were looking for?"

Xander shrugged, enjoying the unexpected glow of the change in atmosphere. Still, the adrenaline pumped through him, reminding him that he was popping air over a yawning chasm. One slip could totally shred him.

"Ferraris," Xander said. "Lamborghinis. High-end pasta rockets for the most part. Ten to start." He pulled a list from his pocket. He'd written the list on stationery he'd cribbed from the airport. Gibbons had provided a list, but that list had been totally bogus.

Yorgi took the list and read quickly. "This one," he said, tapping the paper. "Number ten will be very difficult to find in Europe."

"Yeah," Xander agreed. "That one's for me. I like Detroit steel."

Nodding appreciatively, Yorgi commented, "You certainly know your cars."

"Cars, boats, planes," Xander replied. "I like anything fast I can do something stupid in."

Yorgi waved to the table. "Please. Join us."

Kolya and Viktor scooted around, making room at the table.

Xander looked at the table, locking eyes momentarily with Yelena. The woman looked even better in person. He smiled at her, then noticed the slight tilting of Kirill's head as the man turned his gunsight eyes toward Xander. Kirill lit a fresh cigarette from the butt of his old one.

Oh, Xander thought, reading the proprietary interest the man had in the woman. *So that's how it is. Unrequited love with the boss's main squeeze. That, bro, is a seriously dangerous cocktail.*

And even as he realized that, Xander realized more deeply how dangerous his own situation was. For a second, he thought Yorgi might not have bought into the cover at all, even though Kolya had vouched for him. Yorgi could seat him at the table, then have Kirill shoot him. Or maybe Yorgi would slit Xander's throat with a dinner knife.

The rules were out the window on the mission and Xander knew it. He kept remembering that the last agent to get close to the Anarchy 99 crowd had ended up shot dead and his body dragged out into the street like rejected carrion. But that uncertainty, that specter of death that hung over the group there at the table, made Xander as much interested as wary.

And in the end, the amount of risk drew Xander on the same way a killer mountain or a motocross trail he'd never ridden drew him on. The desire to see what happened next, and whether he could beat it, rose to a fierce heat. He took a seat at the table next to Kolya, sandwiched with Viktor on the other side.

Time to play, Xander thought. *And I got game, bro.*

29

The beautiful brunette, Yelena, took the list from Yorgi and started reading. "Ten cars is hardly worth the effort," she said disparagingly. "We're talking a lousy million-five U.S."

Xander accepted the bottle of dark German beer Kolya handed him and nodded thanks. "I have American buyers who are looking to move a fleet," Xander said to the woman. "If you have the quality of merchandise they're after. And it's a mill, max."

Yelena looked over the top of the list. Her dark eyes narrowed. "Make it a million four."

Xander grinned, enjoying the byplay. *Man, she's easy on the eyes*. "A million two," he agreed magnanimously, "and you're ripping me off."

Yelena glanced at Yorgi, who nodded. She transferred her attention back to Xander. "Do you know what a wire transfer is?"

Xander looked at Yorgi as if he couldn't believe

what he'd just heard. He jerked a thumb at Yelena. "Is she for real?"

Yorgi only smiled, but Xander noticed that Kirill frowned slightly.

"Honey," Xander said, looking back at Yelena, "maybe you should quiet down and let the grown-ups have a conversation." The tension of the moment, the adrenaline high lying almost within reach, kept him wired. The woman seemed to be the key to getting inside. Kolya was already showing enthusiasm.

Yelena's arched eyebrows rose in feigned surprise. "My goodness. *Conversation?* A word with four syllables. Perhaps you'd like some ice to cool off your overheated brain."

"Sure. Just chisel some off your heart. If you can find it."

Shaking her head sympathetically, Yelena smiled. "Poor man. For your sake I hope the rest of you is not as limp as your wit."

From the corner of his eye, Xander saw Kolya start to react, looking like he was about to enter the argument. A quick hand signal from Yorgi cut him off. Xander turned to Yorgi.

Unexpectedly, Yorgi burst out laughing. "Don't look at me, X. Yelena handles all the financial details."

Xander shrugged and leaned back in his chair. He folded his arms over his chest, knowing she would read the challenge and defiance in his posture. "Tell you what, princess. This might work faster with an account number."

Scarcely missing a beat, Yelena reached for a cocktail napkin. She took a pen from her purse and quickly scrawled a series of numbers. "You have forty-eight hours to complete the transfer." Pushing the cocktail napkin across the table, she locked eyes with him. "Don't waste my time."

Xander took the napkin. "Wouldn't dream of it. I'm even gonna throw in a few extra bucks to send you to charm school."

Kolya burst out laughing, spitting his drink out, then mopping his face and chin with his sleeve. Yelena glared at Xander.

Xander grinned back at the woman, enjoying the moment. His pulse was elevated a little and he knew it. Maybe working the undercover ploy Gibbons had forced him into wasn't quite the same as a stunt, but the act of sitting down at a table surrounded by mass murderers was something of a rush.

Kirill stared at Xander over the burning coal of his cigarette. Smoke wreathed the man's head and he never blinked. His gaze was as steady as a sniper scope.

Xander returned the stare for a moment, then passed on. Maybe Kirill would think he was backing away from the pressure, but Xander knew the time wasn't ripe to pony up to the unstated challenge. Yorgi had snakes in his house and didn't even know it. And for his business there, Xander decided he really didn't need to be stirring up the snakes.

"All right," Yorgi bellowed. "Now that business is finished, we party!" He clapped his hands. "Bitches, come!"

A dozen women dressed in sexy evening gowns approached the table and draped themselves over all the men except Kirill. Yelena leaned back from the table, folding her arms across her breasts and closing herself off.

Xander's arms suddenly filled with warm, feminine curves as a beautiful and willing woman leaned into him. She grabbed his face and kissed him deep and long. Her breath tasted sweetly alcoholic, and he felt his adrenaline level bumping up another notch.

Servers brought platters of food and drink, covering the table with a feast like Xander had never seen before. Yorgi ignited his drink, blew out the flame, then raised it in a toast.

Xander reached for one of the glasses on the table. He hoisted his drink, joining Yorgi. "I believe I can hang with you fellas for a while." If he was going to die tonight, at least he was going to die on a full stomach and in total party mode.

30

Augustus Gibbons stood his ground in the command center outside his office. His eyes flicked across the screens that were the spying eyes and ears on the world.

Other NSA handlers watched screens, too. Over the years, Gibbons had learned most of their names, but never what they worked on unless he got invited in or until what he was working on spilled over onto their territories. Never once had he picked over the broken bones of a busted operation that wasn't in his purview.

During his years at his present position, he'd earned enemies. Any guy who carried weight in the agency earned enemies. Some of them were based on politics, but a number of them were personal.

That was how things were between Gibbons and Roger Donnan. They'd never mixed; oil and water. Donnan had been in charge of the effort to bring down Anarchy 99 until the hacker had ripped through firewalls and Internet countermeasures at sites Gibbons had under observation. That act, and that trail, had led Gibbons to Anarchy 99.

Donnan wasn't able to get around the fact that Gibbons hadn't simply muscled into the op because he'd succeeded in getting three CIA agents killed. Maybe the friction hadn't started out as personal, but Donnan was definitely pushing the confrontation in that direction.

Gibbons had spent the last eighteen hours in his office, catching a few hours of sleep. He knew that Xander Cage was on the ground somewhere in Prague, and hopefully getting close to making contact with Anarchy 99. The relationship the American agencies had with Detective Milan Sova, the point guy for the Czech police, was an arm's-length one at best.

So far, Gibbons had chosen not to try to contact Xander. The guy was wild and uncivilized, and any reminder that he was currently being held on a short leash was only going to antagonize him.

Agent Polk, his broken nose covered by a bandage and dark bruises under both eyes from the encounter down in Colombia a couple days ago, hurried into the room. He held a paper in one hand. Spotting Gibbons, Polk hurried over, making an effort not to draw the attention of Donnan.

Of course, Donnan noticed at once and started over.

"Problem," Polk said, extending the paper.

Gibbons took the paper and quickly scanned the print. The bank they'd set up to handle the transaction Xander was supposed to coordinate with Anarchy 99 was requesting permission to transfer one million two hundred thousand dollars.

Anger stirred inside Gibbons, but he didn't let the emotion show.

Donnan read the note over Gibbons's shoulder, then whistled. "A million two, huh?" Donnan asked. "I thought you authorized four hundred thousand on this buy."

Gibbons didn't say anything.

"Smooth move," Donnan said. "Your boy's slicker than a crate of K-Y jelly. He's probably figuring that when you come across with the cash, he'll give Anarchy their cut, then pocket the rest for himself. Then he'll vanish and you'll never see him again."

Pocketing the note, Gibbons walked to the nearest communications console and punched in the number for Xander Cage's Tech Deck. Maybe Xander was in Prague, but he wasn't out of Augustus Gibbons's reach. Not yet, anyway. Not without the money.

A shrill ring woke Xander. He lay in a tangle of bedclothes that smelled stale and unwashed and on a bed that swayed so much it felt like sleeping in a half-pipe. He was also freezing his ass off, something that didn't happen in L.A. After all the drinking at the party last night, he had a hangover, too.

Staring at the luggage scattered across the floor, he tracked the irritating ringing noise to a gym bag containing his personal effects. He was pretty certain Sova and the Ivans had gone through his stuff while he was at the club, but that hadn't mattered.

There wasn't anything in any of the bags that would tell the Czech police anything they didn't already know.

He reached into the gym bag and pulled out the oversized cell phone Gibbons had given him and told him not to use. As rich as the American federal government was, Xander couldn't believe that Gibbons hadn't gotten him a slimline cell instead of something that could have doubled as a brick.

He pressed the SATLINK button, which he thought sounded a little ostentatious. Immediately, a small video screen slid out of the device. Once the screen was fully extended, the gray surface juiced, then coalesced into a full-color image of Gibbons.

Seeing the scarred face, Xander drew back from the screen. "Damn! I thought this was just a cell phone." *Okay, like, that face is one of the last freakin' things a guy should have to wake up and see.*

Gibbons wasn't exactly chatty. "Have a nice rest, Triple X?"

The broadcast level was harsh, too loud and grating on the ears. Xander found the volume control and cranked the level down. "Yo, dial it down. I just got to sleep an hour ago."

Yorgi's party had never seemed to end. And when the festivities had finally given way to fatigue, they'd been pulling out survivors. Xander had walked out of the club on his own two feet. One of the Ivans masquerading as a taxi driver had picked him up and taken him back to the apartment.

"You were given a specific list of cars to go after," Gibbons stated. "Who told you to alter that list?"

"The cars on that list sucked," Xander said. "They woulda seen right through it."

"I authorized four hundred thousand dollars."

Xander shrugged. "I authorized a mill-two, and I saved you money over what they wanted." He watched the screen, wondering if this was going to be a deal-breaker between them, and figuring the hell with Gibbons. There was only one way to handle business with the kind of people he was dealing with—on *both* sides of the squeeze he was in. Maybe he'd been blackmailed into this gig, but he didn't have to be stupid about working it. Especially not when being stupid about the situation was also going to get him killed.

Xander watched Gibbons's face, but the agent didn't give anything away. Paranoia settled into Xander as he awaited the man's response, and he almost wanted to look over his shoulder to see if anyone was sneaking up on him with a dart gun.

31

"Real winner you picked here, Gibbons," Donnan taunted. "I guess the ball goes back to . . . *Donnan.*"

Ignoring the other agent, Gibbons stared at the monitor. He tapped the keyboard, accessing the other video cams that had been installed in Xander Cage's room.

The monitor screen split into quadrants, picking up the Tech Deck's transmission as well as the three angles afforded through the video cams planted in the room. On those screens, Xander pushed himself out of bed, pulled his boots on, and slid into a long fur coat.

Gibbons knew the fur coat hadn't been part of the package he'd sent over.

Xander shivered slightly, then crossed the room to the notebook computer sitting on a small nightstand. The computer's modem was hooked into a phone jack that had been worked on by the electronics team Gibbons had on-site in Prague. With surprising speed, Xander tapped the keyboard.

Gibbons heard the modem chirp, then the shifting buzzes of the connection.

"You should think about changing travel agencies," Xander said. "Oh, I got the info you wanted."

Gibbons nodded at Polk, who took a seat at the console. Tapping keys on the board in front of him, Polk opened another screen, this one overlying the video feeds. The new screen showed his mail server.

As Gibbons watched, a piece of mail appeared. Polk dragged the cursor over to the new mail and double-clicked on the icon.

Immediately, the mail opened, spewing out lists that were arranged with neat precision that Gibbons wouldn't have expected from his newest operative. As he read, the NSA handler couldn't help smiling.

"Names, birthdays, ranks in the Red Army, organization, favorite foods," Gibbons said with a trace of pride he knew would chew into Donnan. Those lists were more information than the teams Donnan had been using had gotten in months. Xander Cage had gotten it all in one night. "How the hell did you get all this?"

"Kolya," Xander explained. "Yorgi's younger brother. He's an extreme sports fanatic." He smiled into the Tech Deck viewer. "In fact, he's a fan of yours truly. Pretty cool guy, but when you kill a bottle of vodka in three swigs, you're gonna talk too much."

Gibbons glanced at Donnan, watching the other man draw back.

"Oh, yeah," Xander said. "I got something else."

"What?" Gibbons couldn't even guess what else the young guy might have.

"Their personal bank account number." On the screen from the video cam feeds, Xander checked the pockets of the fur coat. "Got it somewhere." He brought his hand back out with a crumpled napkin. Then he leaned forward and typed the number into an e-mail.

Polk opened the icon when it popped up on-screen.

"Check it out," Gibbons said.

Keying the number in quickly, Polk verified that the account existed. More work would have to be done to get further information. But the number and the account certainly looked real enough.

"Jesus!" Donnan whispered.

Feeling elated, Gibbons turned to Donnan. "Roger, go see Sam about a ball."

Without a word, Donnan left the command center.

Xander prepared a pot of coffee on the machine that had appeared with one of the Ivans after he'd woken from his nap yesterday afternoon. Jet lag was a bitch, and the coffee had helped. As he waited for the pot to brew, he found his sunglasses and slipped them on, cutting down on the morning glare that stabbed needles into his brain.

Judging from Gibbons's silence at the other end of the video cell phone, Xander knew his success with Anarchy 99 had wowed the agent. But he kept a shit-eating grin from his face with effort. Not that he was humble, because he wasn't. Success spoke volumes for itself, and he knew he had success in spades and by the *cojones*. Bragging about that success would enable Gibbons to deduct style points, and Xander wasn't going to do that.

Opening the avenue for further discussion was feasible.

"Stolen cars, night clubs, prostitution, extortion," Xander said, naming some of the crimes he'd found out about last night. "What's so special about these guys? We got criminals like them in the U.S."

On the small screen, a dark cloud covered Gibbons's scarred features.

Okay, bro, Xander thought, *you're definitely holding out on me*.

"Your job is to gather intel," Gibbons said. "Not ask questions."

The reply stung a little even though Xander had figured it was coming. It wasn't exactly like he was Johnny G-Man. He kept his features blank and his voice flat. "Well, I did my job. So now I'm going home."

Saying that made him feel a little lost. Getting to know Yorgi and Yelena and the others had been exciting and interesting. The buzz he'd gotten off last night's confrontation had been a lot different from anything else he'd ever been involved with.

"Not yet," Gibbons said.

Xander started to rebel.

"You're a victim of your own success, Triple X. I want you to get closer to these guys."

"Wait a minute," Xander protested. "They're cool, but not that cool."

Gibbons ignored him. "Get inside their castle. Go deeper. I'm sending a man over with a care package to help you out."

Still not going to tell me what this is really all

about, are you? Xander paced and shoved his face toward the video cell phone's viewer. "I thought we had a deal."

"Do this for me and you can go home."

Xander laced his response with sarcasm. "So much for your word. Hey, next time you send someone to save the world, make sure they like it the way it is." He punched the End button, cutting off the transmission.

Despite less than an hour of sleep, Xander felt good. From Gibbons's tone, he knew he'd been more successful a lot faster than the agent had expected. *I'm a freakin' natural, bro. Poppin' air and doin' the spy biz, it's all natural talent.* He poured himself a cup of coffee and toasted himself. "Shaken and stirred."

Hanging around ferreting out more secrets from Yorgi and his quirky little bunch—and maybe spending time swapping insults with Yelena—suddenly seemed interesting. Especially when that course of action also meant he might dig out whatever little private agenda Gibbons was working from.

SPY 2.0: MISSION UPGRADE

32

"Are you Triple X?"

Trying to get around the painful headache rocking his brain from not enough sleep, jet lag, and partying all night the night before, Xander turned slowly and gazed at the man who had spoken. The fact that gunfire kept erupting all around him didn't help.

According to the dossier Gibbons had sent through e-mail, the guy asking the question matched his picture. Standing a few inches short of six feet, he had dark hair cut in a corporate style. He was in his early thirties, dressed in a dark suit, but he still carried a nervous, boyish candor.

"Don't call me that," Xander instructed.

The man hesitated for a second, then brightened. "Ooooh, a code name. I get it."

Irritation and fatigue, not to mention a pounding head, made Xander's temper dangerously short. He'd tried going back to bed after Gibbons's call, but Milan Sova, with the Ivans in tow, had come calling. Apparently, Gibbons hadn't screwed around about sending the "care" package he'd promised.

After Xander had showered and gotten dressed, the Czech police guys had driven him downtown to the main Prague police station. They stood in the basement training area now. Several Czech policemen practiced on the shooting range on the other side of the huge room.

"Who are you?" Xander asked, thinking Gibbons couldn't possibly have sent the guy standing before him.

"I'm Agent Shavers." Shavers offered his hand. "Toby Lee Shavers." When Xander didn't move to take the proffered hand, the guy looked at his hand self-consciously, then dropped it back to his side. He carried a large case in his other hand.

"Oh," Xander said. "You're the care package."

Shavers nodded and waved Xander toward a table he'd evidently commandeered. Other unmarked cases sat on the table and on the floor nearby.

"You must rate pretty high for Gibbons to send you all this stuff," Shavers said. He grinned hopefully. "It must be great out in the field, huh? You know, being a secret agent. License to kill, the danger, the women. How long have you been with the Agency?"

Xander held up two fingers. "Two days."

The good-old-boy smile disappeared from Shavers's face almost instantly. "You're shittin' me! No way! No effing way, dude! That sucks!"

Xander shrugged, figuring the guy totally understood about getting his life derailed by Gibbons or someone like him. "Yeah, it sucks, but it beats jail."

"Jail?" Shavers still hadn't regained control of his feelings. "You've been in jail?"

Xander didn't answer.

"I spent six years in a windowless NSA basement as a weapons engineer. I got a degree from MIT, man! Phi Beta Kappa." Shavers paused. "Where'd they find you? Sing Sing?"

Tired of listening to the man's grating voice, Xander said, "Show me your stuff before I hurt you."

Retreating to one of the cases, Shavers knelt and worked the combination locks. When he opened the case, a large revolver resting in a foam cutout gleamed.

"I made my rep with this one a few years back," Shavers said. "My multi-purpose, multi-function field sidearm."

"Oh," Xander said with enthusiasm, "I like this."

Shavers looked surprised and seemed to warm a little. "You do?"

"Yeah."

Shavers unlocked and opened another case. Nasty-looking darts lay lined up in color-coded regimental formation inside the case.

"See," Shavers said, "the pistol has all these different loads. Something for every secret agent situation. The green ones—dutura knock-out darts." He slammed a fist into his palm. "Pow! Guy goes down for twelve hours. Wakes up and doesn't know who he is, where he is, with his head splitting like a cord of firewood." He laughed uproariously, drawing the attention of a few Czech police officers passing by.

Xander glared at the green darts. "I've been shot with those twice. I should punch you in the face."

Shavers stopped laughing and cleared his throat.

Panic welled in his eyes. "I was just following orders."

Shaking his head, Xander shrugged. He couldn't
blame Shavers.

Getting back on task, the agent pointed to other
darts in the case. "These red ones, tranquilizer and
blood splatter darts. All the appearance of a kill shot
with no aftereffects. I call them 'the Lazarus Loads.'"

"Catchy name," Xander said, throwing the guy a
bone. There was no reason to be nice, but there was
something about Shavers that reminded Xander of
other guys he'd known growing up. Guys who
hadn't made it out of the projects because they'd
been too naïve. "Copyright it."

"Nice." Shavers smiled like a little boy who'd just
been rewarded. He waved toward the case. "You've
also got your exploding darts, your radio surveillance darts, and of course your regular .44 caliber
rounds—if you should want the real thing." He
winked and nudged Xander conspiratorially. "Wet
work. You know what I'm talking about."

Xander ignored the comment and took the pistol
out. Holding the weapon out at arm's length, he discovered the weight was considerable. The pistol
wasn't something he'd want to take out and wave
around for a while, and the silver finish was more
eye-catching than he would have liked, but the
weapon felt solid and reliable in his fist. He expertly
released and spun the cylinder.

"Knocked over a few 7-11s, have we?" Shavers
asked.

"Nah," Xander admitted, flipping the weapon's
cylinder back into place. "I had my leg in a cast for
three months. All I did was play first-person-shooter

Vin Diesel stars as Xander "XXX" Cage, the notorious underground thrill-seeker.

NSA Special Agent Augustus Gibbons (Samuel L. Jackson) believes Xander is the right man for his latest mission.

First, Xander must pass Gibbons's tests of his abilities and judgment in a diner "shootout" . . .

. . . then on a cocaine plantation in Colombia.

Xander is sent to Prague to infiltrate "Anarchy 99," a group of criminals led by the dangerous Yorgi (Marton Csokas).

By convincing Yorgi that he's shot a Czech cop, Xander wins his trust.

Xander gets closer to the criminal organization than any American agent has before.

But Yorgi's girlfriend and Anarchy 99 member, Yelena (Asia Argento), is suspicious of their new American associate.

When Xander and Yelena find each other snooping around the castle, it's clear they both have secrets.

Soon Xander's cover is blown, and he and Yelena need to make a quick exit without getting shot.

Despite his orders to return home, Xander sticks around to see what Anarchy 99 has planned.

He gets his GTO equipped with the latest in spy gear.

In the basement of Anarchy 99's castle, Xander can't believe his eyes.

Yorgi's plans for world destruction are near completion.

The only chance for survival is XXX.

video games." Not every stunt came off exactly right. His current situation in Prague was a prime example of that.

Moving on, Shavers opened another case that contained a pair of high-tech binoculars that looked capable of searching for life in other dimensions.

"Here's a good one," Shavers said, taking the binoculars from the case. " 'Eagle Eyes.' Nine different enhanced vision modes." He lowered his voice to a whisper. "Check this out, dude. *Penetrator* mode." Setting the controls on the binoculars, he handed them to Xander and nodded at a group of female Czech police officers gathered at the firing line of the basement's shooting gallery.

Taking the binoculars, Xander gave into his curiosity. He put the binoculars to his eyes and looked at the female police officers. Focusing on a pretty, hardbodied brunette, he pressed the power button.

Despite the way Shavers had been acting, Xander hadn't known what to expect. Every pre-teen male talked about X-ray glasses and what they'd do with a pair of them if given the opportunity, but each guy figured out pretty quick that X-rays meant seeing bones through clothing, not naked and forbidden flesh.

Shavers's gizmo worked differently. Sure, Xander could see bones through clothing and flesh—to a degree, but there was a healthy amplitude of flesh as well. He stood frozen for a moment, studying the luscious curves revealed through the binoculars.

"I think I'll hang on to these," Xander said.

Shavers grinned. "Thought you'd like those." He reached inside a final case and whipped out a small package. "Put the finishing touches on it just last week."

On closer inspection, Xander found that the package contained bandages. "Come in real handy if I skin my knee."

Shavers flashed him a quick, mischievous grin. "Watch, Mister X, and learn." Gripping a bandage's vinyl backing, he stripped the bandage clear. A spiral of primercord lay in serpent's coils under the gauze. "Enough primercord in here to blow a hole in a bank vault, vaporize a person, whatever an undercover agent such as yourself should ever need."

Looking at all the technological weaponry, Xander felt a little awed. Sure, he'd seen movies where sophisticated and urbane guys with British accents toted similar stuff around. He'd never in his life thought he'd actually see stuff like it.

Shavers brought out a small electronic device that almost disappeared in his hand. "This is the detonator. *Star Trek*, dude! Have a sense of humor with your work, that's what I say. It can also suck out a computer hard drive in ten seconds flat . . . and let you store fifty thousand of your favorite songs."

"I don't have fifty thousand favorite songs," Xander said.

Shavers remained positive. "It's just an option. Here we go." He turned and slapped the opened bandage on a big wooden crate that had airline markings. "Smack!" He glanced at Xander. "Stand back."

Xander moved, not willing to stand anywhere near the explosive bandages.

"A little farther," Shavers encouraged, walking back with Xander. "Farther."

Xander kept moving, staying one step ahead of the enthusiastic agent.

Without warning, Shavers pressed a button on the small device he held.

Ka-boom!

The explosion shattered the wooden crate in a heartbeat. Everyone in the basement target range dove for cover, leaving Shavers standing all by himself. Sawdust and splinters swirled around the agent as he turned to face Xander with a proud smile. He spread his arms wide as if expecting applause.

"Cool, huh?" Shavers asked.

Xander stared up at the man in disbelief. He stayed on the floor for the moment, remembering that Shavers still had access to a whole box of explosive bandages. Xander knew the Czech cops weren't going to be happy with the impromptu demolitions demonstration. Between the two of them, Xander figured he and Shavers had a good chance of alienating the whole country.

He wondered what Gibbons would do about that. But that led to wondering why Gibbons would think someone like Shavers—with all the gear he was packing—would be necessary. What the hell was Anarchy 99 interested in that was drawing so much heat?

"What do you think?" Shavers asked.

"This is all great, dude," Xander said, looking at the spy gear, "but all I'm supposed to do is buy ten cars."

33

"So what do you think?" Kolya asked.

Standing in the warehouse where the meet had been scheduled, Xander pulled his fur coat a little tighter against the cold and studied the nine cars he was purchasing with Gibbons's money. He walked along the cars, taking time to survey each one.

"Looking good," Xander stated. The cars were all cherry, all looking slick and glossy.

"Looking *good*?" Kolya acted like he couldn't believe the response. "They're beautiful."

"Okay," Xander replied. "They're beautiful." They hadn't shown him the tenth car yet, the one that he'd chosen for himself. He didn't know what that meant yet. But he was grimly aware that Yorgi had posted guards around the warehouse's inner perimeter.

Yorgi had put in a brief appearance after Kolya and Viktor had brought Xander to the meet, then he'd gone upstairs to the office that overlooked the warehouse proper. Yelena and Kirill were up in the office as well. Xander had seen them through the big plate-glass windows.

Yelena was attempting to verify the money transfer for the cars. And Kirill—

Xander glanced up at the window and saw the cold-blooded killer staring down at him. The coal of Kirill's cigarette glowed orange. Xander felt like he had a target tattooed on his face. He knew what Kirill was doing up there, and he knew that Kirill's jealousy over Yelena would let the assassin bust a cap and never look back.

Except maybe to piss on my grave, Xander thought.

Yorgi stood in the warehouse and looked at Yelena. The soft blue glow of the notebook computer screen reflected in the plate-glass window. Yorgi spoke, then Yelena looked up and shook her head. A moment later, she stared at Xander.

Disappointed, Xander told himself. *That's what she is. But is it because the money hasn't gotten there, or is it because Kirill is gonna cash me out?* He felt his heart beating strongly in his chest. *This is all a stunt, babe. You got the nerve and you got the moves. Ain't nothin' here that you can't do if it comes down to it.* He wore the pistol in his waistband under his coat. If it came down to it, Kirill wasn't going to be the only one busting caps.

In a way, Xander figured, he was right where he'd always promised himself he wouldn't be when he'd been growing up. He was playing with gangsters. There was no percentage in playing with gangsters.

Never had been, and never would be. At least he was free from the deal to a degree. He was playing with someone else's money, and he'd never see the cars again after today. All that mattered to him was getting out alive in the next couple of minutes.

Yorgi came down the rickety wooden stairs leading to the second-story warehouse office. Keeping his hands in his coat, he asked, "You like the cars?"

"Yeah," Xander said, knowing what Yorgi's hands were on inside the coat. "The cars are dope. You like the money?"

Cocking his head, Yorgi said, "I love money. It's just that I don't have it."

Xander didn't know what to say to that. In a way, he'd screwed Gibbons over, and maybe he'd screwed himself over. He'd assumed Gibbons had access to deep pockets, but that might not have been the case. Gibbons hadn't said either way, but the cold-hearted son of a bitch probably wouldn't.

Everybody gets surprised this way, Xander thought. He was deeply aware of how Yorgi stood squared-off with him. The Anarchy 99 leader had a pair of brass balls, there was no doubt of that. *So what's the deal? He gonna try and do me himself, or does he think Kirill is that good?* Of course, there were also Kolya and Viktor standing in the warehouse to deal with.

Xander felt the pressure building. His heart rate increased and he felt fluid and loose. And part of him was so hooked into the rush that he couldn't let go. However things went down, he was going to deal face-front.

Yelena stood in the upstairs office and knocked

on the window. Her knuckles slapping the glass echoed in the warehouse. When Yorgi looked back at her, she nodded. Her eyes drifted to Xander's, then she turned away.

Despite the tension, or maybe because of it, Xander put a smile on his face. "What did you think? That I wasn't good for it?"

Smiling back, Yorgi said, "Not for a moment."

Xander reached into his coat pocket and took out a folded piece of paper. "There's a cargo ship waiting in Rejika. But I only count nine cars here. You're one short."

Accepting the piece of paper, Yorgi said, "Come with me."

Warily, Xander fell into step with the man. Together, they walked to the back of the warehouse and came to a long object covered with parachute silk.

"This one mine?" Xander asked.

Yorgi pulled off the silk cover, revealing a gleaming black GTO muscle car. "Car number ten," the Anarchy 99 leader said.

Grinning out of real pleasure, Xander ran a hand along the GTO's curved flank. "That's what I love about this job. The perks."

Opening the passenger door, Yorgi slid inside. "Come on. Get in."

Eagerly, Xander opened the door on the driver's side and started to crawl in. Feeling eyes on him, he glanced up and spotted Yelena staring at him from the warehouse office.

When she saw that he had noticed her, Yelena turned away.

Kirill lit a new cigarette from the butt of the last, then breathed out against the glass, masking his features in smoke for a moment. He didn't turn away.

Xander slid behind the GTO's steering wheel. The keys hung in the ignition. He started the car, listening to the deep rumble of the powerful engine. He grinned more widely.

Turning to look at his passenger, Xander said, "You're all right, Yorgi."

Yorgi cocked his head as if the car weren't anything so special. "Everything is all right with enough vodka." He reached into the glove compartment and brought out a bottle.

Guy comes prepared, Xander thought. *You got to give him that.* But he knew that Yorgi had been prepared if the deal had gone sour as well. That knowledge took part of the glow off the moment of success.

Detective Milan Sova crept across the sloped warehouse roof where he had trailed the American agent. The slope of the roof and the worn soles of his shoes made footing difficult.

Sova's grudge against the American agent had grown over the last two days. The Czech detective's own efforts against Yorgi and Anarchy 99 had lasted for more than a year, and he had almost nothing to show for that time. His career with the department hung by a thread, and it existed only because no one else had felt that they could make any headway against the organized crime group.

That had changed once the American agent's own success at getting inside the group had become known to the few department heads involved with the joint effort regarding the American CIA. Now, those same department heads were expecting Sova to pull off miracles of his own.

Panting, winded from the exertion of climbing the warehouse, Sova paused and hunkered down beside one of the dirty windows that lined the structure's rooftop. He took a camera with a long zoom lens from the case he carried strapped over one shoulder.

Once he had the camera ready, he leaned forward and used his shirtsleeve to clean a section of the glass pane in front of him. The warehouse below was lighted well enough that he could see the American agent and Yorgi seated in a black car.

Sova set up his camera and started snapping pictures. The Ivans were set up in the construction zone across the street from the warehouse. They were manning a parabolic microphone, hoping to overhear and record some of the conversations taking place inside the structure.

Staying with the viewfinder, Sova focused and snapped shots quickly. He took pictures of the American agent and Yorgi seated in the car.

"Smile, *blbecku*," Sova whispered in English. Using the American agent's mother tongue mixed with his own language somehow seemed more insulting.

Then he took pictures of Viktor and Kolya standing by the transport trucks loaded with Italian cars. Finally, he moved around to get a better angle to photograph Yelena and Kirill in the upstairs office.

As Sova shifted again, reaching for a fresh roll of film to trade out the one in the camera, the long line of glass panes—eighteen of them in a three-by-six stack—dropped from their moorings.

No! Sova thought, trying to freeze the falling glass in midair through a supreme act of willpower.

The panes fell twenty feet to the concrete warehouse floor below. The crash of shattering glass filled the warehouse, echoing back up through the empty space in the roof where the panes had been. By that time, Sova was running for his life.

34

The liquid smash of glass startled Xander. He spat out the drink of vodka he'd chugged from the bottle Yorgi had offered. Swiveling his head around, he spotted the cracked lake of glass shards spread across the warehouse floor. He looked up just in time to see a shadow sprinting in front of the other windows.

"What in the hell?" Yorgi exploded.

Xander's senses were in overdrive. He heard the hiss of metal against leather that warned him Yorgi was going for his gun even as he spotted Kirill and Yelena bolting down the rickety wooden stairs from the upstairs office with pistols drawn.

Having no choice, knowing he had a slim chance at best of surviving the coming encounter, Xander reached under his coat as he stepped out of the GTO. He fisted the shiny pistol and thrust the weapon out before him, reaching over the top of the muscle car as Yorgi did the same.

They stared at each other over the barrels of their pistols. The standoff didn't last long, though. Kolya, Viktor, Yelena, and Kirill arrived and pointed their weapons at Xander as well.

"What's going on, my friend?" Yorgi's pistol remained steady. His voice was quiet and polite.

"You tell me!" Xander commanded. "You got a sniper up there or what?" He kept both eyes open, staring immediate death in the face, and held the pistol in a firm grip. His finger rested easily on the trigger, like he'd been pulling guns on people all his life.

It was the adrenaline, he knew. The drug slapped into his system and his body moved, mirroring strategies he'd used on arcade games and video shooters. Maybe his style lacked a little something, but at the range separating them, he wasn't going to miss.

Yorgi's gaze remained level. "He's not with us, Xander. He must be with you."

"Bullshit!" Xander rolled the pistol's hammer back with his thumb, lessening the amount of pressure needed to snap the firing pin through the chambered bullet. "You get your boy off that roof or I swear to God I'm gonna give you another hole to breathe out of."

Yorgi stared a moment longer. Then he lowered his pistol, waving to the others to do the same. Only Kirill looked disappointed.

"All right," Yorgi said. "If he's not yours, let's go get him together."

For a moment, Xander hesitated. He didn't trust Yorgi much. Maybe the Anarchy 99 leader had secretly signaled Kirill to put a bullet between his eyes when he lowered his weapon.

Hold it together, bro, Xander told himself. *Ain't no getting out of this without somebody getting killed. Sometimes you just gotta trust the rush.* He lowered the hammer on the pistol, then nodded.

Without a word, Xander slid behind the GTO's wheel. Yorgi dropped into the passenger seat, holding his pistol in his lap. Shifting the powerful V-8 into gear, Xander shoved his foot down on the accelerator. The engine responded immediately, roasting the tires on the rough concrete floor as he came around in a tight 180-degree turn. When he straightened the wheel, he blew through the blue-gray smoke left by the tortured rubber.

Kolya hit the powered garage door opener just in time to allow Xander to get under the door without losing paint. The GTO snarled out into the street, sprawling like a charging hound dog for a moment, then grabbing traction and hurtling down the street like a bullet.

Xander scanned the street, spotting the Ivans taking cover behind a bulldozer. Yorgi hadn't seen them because he was peering at the warehouse roof. Xander knew he wouldn't have seen them himself except that he had his eyes on the road.

But with the Ivans in the area, that meant the guy they were chasing was probably Sova. And Xander had no idea what the hell he was going to do about that.

Running flat-out, pushing himself almost past the point he could handle his headlong sprint across the warehouse rooftop, Detective Milan Sova brushed past a brick chimney, aiming himself at the location of the wrought iron ladder he'd spotted earlier. His breath burned the back of his throat. The fear that filled him left a sour metallic taste in his mouth.

If he were caught by Yorgi, he had no doubt that the Anarchy 99 leader would kill him on the spot. Yorgi or his group had killed other Czech policemen as well as the American CIA agents.

He caught the first rung of the ladder and threw himself down, feet moving rapidly. Spotting a rain gutter next to the ladder, he jumped to the pipe and slid toward the ground. The camera fell from his shoulder and shattered on the cobblestones below.

Ignoring the broken camera, knowing the film was ruined, Sova dropped to the alley and ran. If he could reach the Ivans, he felt certain they could help him get out of his present situation.

He didn't hesitate at the end of the alley, bolting straight across for the construction site on the other side. Before he took two steps into the street, the growl of a powerful V-8 engine shredded the silence trapped between the buildings.

Glancing back over his shoulder, Sova saw the black muscle car squeal around the corner. The vehicle fishtailed for just a moment, then came at him like a rabid beast.

Suddenly, there was nowhere to run. The American agent would sacrifice him to keep his own cover. Sova knew that in his heart even as the car gained on him.

"Son of a bitch!" Yorgi exploded. "That's the cop from the club!"

Fifteen seconds of fame, Xander thought sourly, *and look how much they can screw up your life.*

Before Xander could say anything, Yorgi shoved his pistol out the window, following it with his arm, head, and shoulders. He lowered the pistol, drawing a bead on the fleeing Czech detective.

Damn it! Xander thought. His brain worked furiously, giving him only one option. He switched his pistol to his left hand and took the steering wheel in his right. He spun the cylinder till he had one of Shavers's Lazarus Loads under the hammer instead of one of the .44 Magnum rounds. He floored the accelerator and yanked the wheel hard right, sending the GTO into a sideways skid that put Yorgi on the other side of Sova.

Before Yorgi could aim across the top of the GTO, Xander leaned out the window, shoving the big silver pistol in front of him. After hours spent in arcades, aiming and firing on the fly was almost instinct. But the way the pistol bounced in his hand wasn't something that could be programmed into an arcade facsimile.

Less than a heartbeat after the detonation of the bullet, the round caught Sova between the shoulder blades and knocked him facedown on the cobblestone street. Crimson stained the back of the detective's coat.

Sova flailed weakly for just a moment, eyes white with fear and disbelief. Then his head lolled and he went limp.

Knowing Yorgi might be tempted to pump another round into the downed Czech policeman, Xander dropped the pistol into his lap, jammed the gearshift into reverse, and backed into the street away from Sova's body. Throwing the GTO into a skid, Xander cut the wheel sharply, accelerated and changed gears again smoothly, and had the muscle car hurtling through the street away from Sova.

Xander passed the other cars streaming from the warehouse and saw Yelena's face. He was surprised to see revulsion tightening her features. But then again, she didn't know he'd only shot Sova with one of Shavers's Lazarus Loads.

The crimson staining the back of Sova's jacket was just dye. With the narcotics released into his body, the Czech detective had no choice about going down.

Yorgi glanced at him from the passenger seat for a moment, then slid his pistol out of view. "Most people talk a lot," he said. "Few are up for the moment." He paused. "Welcome to Anarchy 99."

Xander concentrated on his driving and didn't say anything. If he had to kill his way into the inner circle of Yorgi's criminal organization, he wondered how many he'd have to kill to get out.

35

Hours later, Xander stood at the railing of a second-story balcony of another club owned by Anarchy 99. Yorgi hadn't told him that the criminal group owned the warehouse-turned-club. That information was immediately apparent from the attention Yorgi and the others received from the staff.

Upon arrival, they had been escorted to the best table in the establishment, then watched as the security staff evicted those unfortunate to have chosen that table. Viktor helped out with the evictions, roaring with pleasure and scaring off all but the tough guy wannabes and those too drunk to know better.

Xander's attention was drawn to the gyrating bodies out on the dance floor. The stage was decked out as a high-voltage electrical testing center. Artificial lightning lit up over the crowd, throwing sparks in all directions. Thunder hammered from the huge speakers.

Glancing at Yelena, Xander found the woman still wasn't looking at him. They hadn't talked since the warehouse, where they'd swapped a quick hello when he'd arrived. None of the others had talked about Sova, or about why they would have been spied on by the Czech police. But Kolya had invited him to their place—at least, the place where the group was currently staying—for the night. Xander thought maybe he would learn more there, but the situation was a hell of a lot more dangerous. Looking at Yelena again, he thought maybe things were a hell of a lot more complicated, too.

At the table, Yorgi waved at Xander to join them. Crossing the distance to the table was simple enough. The *mafiya*—the Russian version of the mafia—that Yorgi controlled cleared the way for Xander.

Xander took a seat at the table and had to wave away a cloud of smoke that Kirill blew in his direction. "Why do you do that to yourself?" Xander asked. "That cigarette is gonna kill you one day."

Kirill smiled thinly and talked around his cigarette without removing it from between his lips. "I like smoke better than air. If I could, I'd smoke in my sleep. I will still do it after it kills me. I am smoke."

Shaking his head, Xander turned to Yorgi. "You were talking about Anarchy 99. What's up with that? Sounds like a motorcycle gang."

Yorgi shook his head. "No. It's what we've been living since 1999, when we left the Army of Mother Russia." His eyes took on a heaviness that Xander had never seen, but his voice remained neutral, as if he were talking about someone else. "So many of our comrades died in combat, and we said the hell with this shit. They die for what? Politics? Whose politics? Not ours. So we decide from then on to do what we want, when we want. In their honor, we call ourselves Anarchy 99."

The story conflicted with the details in the briefing that Xander had gotten from Gibbons. Yorgi's words had a ring of sincerity. But so had Gibbons's, and there was the matter of the dead CIA agents.

Yorgi rolled up his shirtsleeve and revealed a stylized tattoo that read ANARCHY 99. "There's an old punk song. It says, 'America stands for freedom . . . ' "

Grinning, recognizing the song, Xander got into the stanza with Yorgi. " 'But if you think you're free, try walking into a deli and urinating on the cheese.' "

Yorgi stopped in surprise and started laughing.

" 'Anarchy Burger,' " Xander said. "By the Vandals."

"You got it!"

Feeling totally at home, Xander leaned back in his chair. "I'm with you. But what are you gonna do? There's rules and government everywhere. Always has been, always will."

Yorgi's gaze flattened and turned cold. "Maybe not always. You never know." He turned and called over his shoulder. "Yelena!"

Only a few feet away, standing at the railing staring down at the dancers, Yelena turned her attention to Yorgi. Kirill stood next to her, as quiet and close as her own shadow. His cigarette glowed bright orange in the club's darkness.

Yorgi pointed at Xander. "Make sure he doesn't get lonely."

Distaste flickered across Yelena's beautiful face.

Although he didn't show any emotion, Xander knew Kirill wasn't happy about the situation either.

Part of Xander relished the idea that the cold-blooded killer was put off, but he realized that he was toying with sudden death as well. And actually, maybe that realization made everything a little more exciting. Now that Yelena was really keeping her distance from him, he felt even more drawn to her.

Yelena crossed the short distance to the table. She stood with her arms folded, gazing down at Xander with hooded eyes.

Yorgi captured the wrist of a young woman passing by. A smile split the young woman's face and she went with Yorgi willingly onto the dance floor.

Xander stood and held his hand out to Yelena. "You wanna dance?"

Yelena turned and walked away from him.

At first, Xander was just going to let her go, but he knew that he couldn't. He went after her, knowing Kirill was following him with gunsight eyes.

Xander caught up to Yelena within a few steps, managing to make his way through the crowd of gyrating bodies. He felt Kirill's eyes centered between his shoulder blades the whole time, and he couldn't help thinking of the last CIA agent who had encountered the group and what had happened to the man.

"Where we going?" Xander asked as he caught up with Yelena.

She glared at him but said nothing.

"You heard the boss," Xander reminded. "You gotta keep me company." He knew his words were true and that she had been given an order, not a suggestion. Even though Yorgi appeared to be getting along with him, and even trusting him to an extent, Xander knew the Anarchy 99 leader didn't trust him completely. The man would have been a fool to do that.

Yelena stopped at the bar on the other side of the upper floor and ordered a drink.

"Make it two," Xander told the bartender as he pushed in beside Yelena.

When the drinks arrived, they downed the shots together. Yelena slammed her empty glass down and walked away.

Shaking his head, Xander went after her. *Damn, she's stubborn.* He caught up to her in a few short strides. "It's gonna be like that, huh?"

She made a point of ignoring him.

"If you're mad at him," Xander said, thinking maybe she was upset because she used to be Yorgi's girl but had been shown the door, "don't take it out on me. I've been trying to figure out the deal between you two all night. Are you his slut or what?"

Dark fire flashed in Yelena's eyes as she wheeled on him. For a moment he thought she was going to slap the hell out of him.

"Exactly," she said in a bitter voice. "I'm his slut. If you'd pay me as much, I'd be your slut."

Xander wondered if that was the truth. Even though he couldn't put Yorgi and Yelena together romantically in his mind, it didn't mean that hadn't happened. Love and attraction were funny that way. Maybe Yelena had gotten in close to Yorgi, been his lover for a while, but that hadn't lasted. Only when the dust had settled on the relationship, maybe Yelena had proven too valuable to let go because of her computer skills. And maybe she had gotten addicted to the money and lifestyle. She'd chosen to stay for the cash, but her self-esteem had taken direct hits.

For a moment, he felt sorry for her. There was nothing that hurt more than love. And that was the one big stunt Xander had never tried himself. Wipeouts on that one were seriously intense.

Still, he was drawn to the hurt side of her. Just as he knew that if she'd known what he was thinking she would have hated him for it.

As the silence stretched between them, Yelena turned abruptly away again.

Xander followed after her doggedly, trying desperately to figure out how to reach her. Yelena was a puzzle, and he was determined to figure out her secrets.

Huge spools of thick copper wire cordoned off the back section of the warehouse. A couple dozen portable chemical toilets filled the area, and lines of dancers and partyers stood before them.

Not knowing what else to do, but knowing he had to do something, Xander grabbed Yelena's arm and pulled her around. Before she could respond in any way, he caught the back of her head in his free hand, pulled her in close to him, and kissed her full on the lips.

36

Xander didn't know what to expect from the kiss. He thought maybe Yelena would slap him, or maybe attempt to knee him in the groin. But he hadn't expected her to stand there like his kiss was nothing.

The experience was a little humiliating, and it was troubling, too. The cold distance that had erupted from her hadn't been there at any time earlier. Since he'd shot Sova at the warehouse, with her thinking that he'd killed the Czech detective, her attitude toward him had definitely changed.

Xander couldn't get a lock on that. According to Gibbons's information, Yelena had been present the night the CIA agent McGrath got killed in one of Anarchy 99's other clubs. She'd been around when the group members had shot down dozens of other policemen. But nowhere in the reports was there any mention that Yelena had killed anyone.

Suddenly, that discrepancy stood out in Xander's mind. He drew back his head, breaking the kiss.

"Did you enjoy that?" Yelena asked as if they were discussing nothing more important than the weather.

"Yeah," Xander said. And he had. Of course, the whole experience could have been improved if she'd been a little more into the moment. But the kiss had been nice.

"Remember it," Yelena suggested. "Because it'll never happen again." She turned and walked away again.

This time Xander let her go. His mind was racing and he was afraid that if he stayed around the woman she'd be able to see past some of the defenses he had in place. This was different than a stunt. With a stunt, all he had to do was hang it all out there, let everything go. With Yorgi, Kolya, Viktor, and Kirill, he just played a part.

Yelena didn't scan right. She was deeper than the act she put on.

The suspicious part of Xander's mind told him that the woman had her own game running. How deadly that game—and *she* proved to be—remained to be seen.

Yorgi sat at his table and overlooked one of the cornerstones of his empire. Of course, he wasn't building an empire, he corrected himself. Rather, he planned to tear down the existing powers. The time was quickly approaching when he'd be able to do just that. Things at the secret base were progressing quite nicely. Perhaps his team's success was only a matter of a few days away.

The realization made him feel good, but absinthe made him feel better. The combination of drugs and alcohol always did. He always felt so much more alive when he was under their influence.

He heated a spoonful of sugar over a candle flame, watching as the crystals took on heat and started to glow blue. When the sugar was ready, he dropped the spoon into the glass of absinthe, stirred, and set the alcohol on fire.

A moment more, waiting till the mixture reached perfection, and he blew out the flame and drank. The heated liquid rushed down his throat to his stomach, then exploded on contact. The effect was immediate, seeming to kick open doors inside his mind and reconnect him to the environment of the club in whole new ways.

Kolya and Viktor joined him at the table. His brother sat down with a grin on his face, waiting till Yorgi focused on him.

Yorgi nodded.

"So what do you think of Xander?" Kolya asked. "He's insane, but I like him."

"I like him, too," Yorgi said. Images of the way Xander had brought the car around and shot the policeman in the back in the street danced inside his head. The American was utterly ruthless. And that, Yorgi felt, was something to be admired.

"Good," Kolya said, "because I already invited him for the weekend."

Yorgi started to protest. Things were moving very quickly regarding the American. Still, the money had been there for the cars, and Xander was unlike most men Yorgi had ever met. Maybe things would be improved by closer inspection of the young extreme sports athlete.

At that moment, Xander returned to the table.

Yelena was nowhere to be seen. Yorgi had expected the two of them to hit it off, and suggesting Yelena keep him company had been the perfect opportunity for the two of them to talk. If they were so inclined.

From the irritated look on Xander's face, Yorgi gathered that things hadn't gone exactly as he'd planned. Yelena could be that way, though. Yorgi knew that from experience.

Yorgi waved at the club, taking pride in one of the things that he had created. "Check it out! A thousand people in my club all doing what they want when they want. That's anarchy, buddy. No rules."

At that moment, the huge electrical testing devices that were set up as stage dressing came to life with a hum that would have drowned out a jet engine. The noise was absolutely the loudest Yorgi could get. With the absinthe singing through his brain, he thought for a moment his mind was going to shatter from the experience.

Techno dance music boiled from every speaker throughout the warehouse. The dancers whipped themselves into a frenzy, letting go all tomorrows and living only in the moment.

Yorgi glanced at Xander, seeing the man clearly. Xander was so like them, Yorgi knew. The American lived in the moment, and *for* the moment, just as they did. That was what his interest in the extreme sports that Kolya loved so dearly was all about.

Smiling at Xander, Yorgi said, "The revolution begins." There was no way the American could guess what he had become part of.

37

Hours later, thoughts buzzing around inside his head like shooting stars, Xander drove the GTO up the winding mountain road and tried to stay focused on Yorgi's car in front of him. He liked the way the car handled, and would have enjoyed putting the muscle car through its paces, but there hadn't been an opportunity. He listened to the big engine's muted roar, knowing the high-performance system was barely staying above idle. He felt the same way. The need inside him to do something was growing.

On either side of the mountain road, craggy snow-covered terrain stretched out starkly under the sparse moonlight filtering through the patchy clouds that filled the sky. Yelena drove her car behind Xander, capable of boxing him in.

Another curve of the road revealed a castle sitting ahead. The fortification occupied a cliff near the Vltava River that flowed through Prague. The castle

was also ringed by a high wall that held guard tow-
ers. Knowing the way Yorgi worked, Xander expected the castle to be filled with sophisticated
surveillance gear that monitored the road as well as
the airspace.

Even if Gibbons and the Czech police knew about
the castle, Xander was certain nobody was getting
in without an invitation. That knowledge presented
curiosity and wariness on his part. He had to ask
himself why he'd been invited.

As a result, the adrenaline hummed through his
heart and nerve synapses just like the gasoline
threading through the GTO's finely tuned Quadra-
jet carburetor. Both of them were more than ready
to spring into action, but both of them were being
held down.

A few minutes later, at the other end of the long
road, Xander followed Yorgi's vehicle through the
massive stone doors of the castle. Guards covered
the entrance with machine guns and field artillery.
Video security systems backed them up, relaying information footage to the guard posts.

Inside the walls, a heated fountain sat out in front
of the massive castle. Bikini-clad girls sat in the
steaming waters, seemingly out of place with all the
snow on the ground.

Xander parked the GTO beside Yorgi's car.
When he got out, Xander was unprepared for the
cold air that he breathed in. His lungs tightened in
response, and when he exhaled, gray plumes twisted
before him.

Roaring with savage glee, Viktor strode to the
fountain and reached in for one of the nubile young
women. She came willingly, howling with laughter

and speaking loudly in Russian. Laughing and talking loudly, Viktor cradled the woman in his arms and walked toward the castle.

Xander followed Yorgi toward the main house, aware of Yelena's pointed lack of interest in him. Kirill moved at her side, the wind catching the smoke from his cigarette. Even though the man didn't look at him, Xander knew Kirill definitely had him on his radar.

Kolya roared by, not slowing as he sped up the stone steps leading to the main house. He passed through the doors and disappeared inside.

Following Yorgi inside the main building, Xander was astonished to see how many people were there. Men and women worked in offices in front of computer screens. *Mafiya* hardcases worked security in the hallways, their weapons naked in shoulder holsters or in their fists.

One of the women, a redhead with a wireless headset, approached Yorgi and gave him messages.

Wow, Xander thought, impressed. *Yorgi's crime biz works 24/7.* He was suddenly aware of how much Gibbons and the agency the man worked for didn't know about Anarchy 99. And Xander was grimly aware that he knew even less than Gibbons. He still didn't know what the agent's overpowering interest in Yorgi was. Sure, the crime biz was intense, but there were a lot of other organizations that had more fingers in more pies than Anarchy 99 did.

So what was different?

Xander remained quiet, watching Yorgi conduct business, amazed at how the guy could be so intense, party so hard, and yet keep up with everything that was obviously going on.

Yorgi led the way to a massive hall filled with antique architecture and furniture. As a direct counterpoint, a massive home entertainment center featuring a big-screen TV and a PlayStation 2 gaming system occupied the center of the room near a pool table. *Grand Theft Auto 3* played on the gaming system. Xander recognized the game at once because he'd logged in several hours on the game before beating it.

Spray paint graffiti scarred the ornate walls and ruined all the original décor. A pile of antique vases and pots was arranged like tenpins on one side of the room.

Servants entered the room and brought platters of drinks.

Yorgi turned to Xander with a smile. "Not bad, yes?"

Xander toasted the man with his drink. "Hell of a crib you got here, bro."

Yorgi glanced around. "The original owners, they just one day decide to move out." He didn't offer any explanation as to why they'd decided that.

Viktor searched the room briefly, then gave a yelp of success. He reached behind one of the couches and brought out a bowling ball. The *Sports Illustrated*–swimsuit edition contender at his side bounced up and down and cheered him on as he lined up his shot. Viktor grunted as he released the ball.

The bowling ball flew across the floor and spun into the pile of antiquities. Vases and pots shattered. Brightly colored shards flew across the floor.

"Out with the old!" Viktor roared in triumph. "Make room for the new!"

Kolya yelled in appreciation of the strike thrown by his friend. He jumped up and down and pumped his fist in the air.

Across the room, Yelena kicked a soccer ball. It was a good kick, sailing through the air and smashing Kolya in the face, taking him by total surprise.

"*Yeb vas, a'opa!*" Yelena ordered. "Shut up!"

Kolya waved her off as if she were spoiling all the fun, then walked from the room and disappeared into one of the hallways.

Xander stood and watched, uncertain what he was supposed to do or why he was there. Being inside the castle, if he got the chance to look around unsupervised, had the potential of netting a lot of information Gibbons would want. Of course, getting caught poking around unsupervised also carried the potential of him getting dead.

But the challenge was there. Xander felt the familiar thrill of accomplishing the hard-to-do if not flat-out impossible. Despite the fatigue and the partying, he felt himself amping up. He was willing to bet that he could outlast Yorgi, who had hit the absinthe hard at the club. Viktor and Kolya hadn't been lightweights either.

Xander shifted his gaze to Yelena and Kirill. They were the only wild cards. Kirill had smoked more than he had drunk, so maybe there was some serious oxygen deprivation going on there that would take its toll. But Yelena—

Kirill politely offered to take Yelena's coat. She turned and allowed him. After he slipped the garment off, Kirill walked to a closet in one corner of the room. He paused for a moment, holding the coat in both hands and breathing deeply.

The act disgusted Xander. The hitman was one sick freak. Yelena didn't see Kirill now, but Xander figured she probably knew what was going on. She wasn't the kind of woman to miss much.

Kirill's eyes closed in rapt pleasure. They sprang open again as an almost silent *chuff*, like the cough of a silencer, rang out in the room.

38

The projectile hit Kirill squarely between the eyes, snapping his head back slightly. Bright blue paint burst against his forehead and dripped down the bridge of his nose.

"No!" Kirill yelled.

Xander saw Kolya standing in the doorway on the other side of the huge room with a paintball pistol in both hands. Grinning, Kolya opened fire again, squeezing off rounds as quickly as he could pull the trigger.

Bright blue splotches spread over Kirill as he howled and cursed. At the distance, Xander knew from experience, the paintballs hurt like hell and left bruises. Abandoning the room and the coat, Kirill fled into the hallway, pursued by Kolya.

Beside Xander, Viktor roared with laughter. Yelena stood nearby and tried to remain aloof from everything. Yorgi's attention was consumed by the messages he'd been given.

"What's he got?" Xander asked the big man beside him. "A coat fetish?"

Viktor scowled. "He's in love with her, the dirty fool." He nodded at Yelena. "Smells her clothes like a dog."

"Leave him alone," Yelena snapped. A dark flush spread across her cheeks.

Embarrassed? Xander wondered. He lowered his voice and spoke to Yelena while Viktor swooped upon the girl in the bikini again.

"No wonder you shut me down," Xander said. "With action like *that* waiting at home."

She cut her eyes from him, not deigning to acknowledge his words.

Yorgi started singing and held out his arms. Two gorgeous women came to him, both of them dressed in stunning nightclothes. He closed his arms around the women and looked at Xander.

"I'm tired," Yorgi announced. "It is time for bed. It's getting early." He nodded, indicating the large house around them. "I've got fifty-five bedrooms to crash in, but I have a special one for you. Yelena will show you the way."

Yelena's back stiffened in silent protest. But she started to lead the way.

Xander flipped Yorgi a salute and followed Yelena from the room. They walked through a maze of hallways without speaking. Xander had a lot on his mind, questions about Yelena and her involvement with Anarchy 99, but he knew now wasn't the time to bring them up.

The rest of the house was as vandalized as the other rooms he'd seen. Graffiti stained the walls and remnants of antiques littered the floors.

Yelena halted in front of a bedroom door.

Putting his hand on the doorknob, Xander looked at her. "Last chance to tuck me in."

Shooting him a withering look that probably would have incinerated him on the spot if it had been powered by laser beams, Yelena turned and left.

For a moment, Xander watched the woman go, noting the sensual roll of her hips as she walked. He almost wanted to go after her, but he didn't. If he'd been successful in getting her to talk to him at least, his chances of checking out the rest of the castle would have been nil. For the moment, clandestine snooping promised a definite adrenaline charge.

After shooting Sova down in the street by the warehouse, Xander knew he was working on borrowed time. Either the Czech agent would pull enough strings to get him thrown out of the country, or Gibbons would pull him for being off the hook with agency business and interdepartmental relations.

Or Yorgi would find out that Sova wasn't dead and would kill Xander himself.

Turning his attention back to the bedroom, Xander twisted the doorknob and entered. He was totally unprepared for the beautiful young woman dressed only in a flak jacket and hanging upside down from one of the bedposts.

Flipping down, the young woman dropped to the bed and threw a bump-and-grind number as she hummed. When she finished, she stripped the flak jacket off and threw the garment to the floor. Smiling, she crooked her finger at him.

Xander grinned, crossing the room to the bed and

throwing himself aboard. The next minute, she was
in his arms, her body hot against his. Her lips
sought his, pressing hard.

The things I'm gonna do for my country, Xander
thought. And he threw himself into the moment.

Dawn turned the eastern skies a leaden gray when
Xander disentangled himself from the sleeping
woman and slid out of bed. A chill pervaded the castle, and he was surprised he couldn't see his breath
as he found his clothes. He dressed quickly, feeling
his senses amp up at what he was about to do.

He let himself out into the hallway. He carried the
big silver pistol tucked under his coat and the Tech
Deck in a coat pocket. Since he didn't know the lay-
out of the castle, he had to follow his nose. Starting
with the assumption that the nerve center for the
guard tower and surveillance systems overseeing the
grounds would be somewhere where a purely physical observation would also be possible, Xander
found the nearest staircase and went up.

Most of the rooms in the main building were
empty, but Xander heard stereos, televisions, and
gaming systems running in some of the rooms.
However, no one appeared to be up and about. Evidently, the castle household slept in mornings.

Less than ten minutes later, Xander found a
locked door. The lock wasn't anything fancy. He
used a credit card to void the lock and let himself
inside.

Sophisticated computers and surveillance filled
the room nearly wall-to-wall. Little room was left
over for the workstations and few pieces of furniture. Several monitors showed views of the castle

courtyard, the parking area, the gates, and the narrow road winding through the snow-capped mountains. Huge plate-glass windows allowed bright sunlight into the room and also provided views of the castle grounds and the startling landscape beyond. The river reflected the morning light in splashes of silver.

Taking the Tech Deck from his pocket, Xander used the device the way Shavers had instructed. He aimed the infrared port at the nearest computer, hoping that all the systems were ultimately connected. As Shavers had explained the device's usage, Xander only needed one point of entry.

The Tech Deck hummed as the device went to work. Datastreams slipped across the small viewer. *Come on, come on,* he urged. *You can soak up fifty thousand of my favorite songs in no time flat. Let's get up to speed here.*

Evidently the information in the computers was more complicated than an extended hit list, though. The Tech Deck was still whirring in Xander's hand when he heard a furtive footstep out in the hall. He looked at the door, the only way out of the room, and knew he'd never make his escape that way.

He flipped the Tech Deck off, then turned and vaulted the loveseat, racing for the wall beside the entrance. Ducking down, he hid behind a bank of computers.

He breathed shallowly, his mind flying through all the avenues open to him if he was discovered. Chances were slim that he would make his escape down the mountains, but that just amped him up even more. Slim chances were an addiction.

Moving stealthily herself, Yelena entered the room.

She'd obviously been inside the room before because she made her way to the loveseat immediately. After shoving the loveseat aside, she reached down and pulled the carpet up, revealing a huge floor safe hidden below.

Kneeling, she punched a combination into the electronic keypad. The keypad beeped at her impatiently. After only a moment of hesitation, she tried again and again, pushing upwards of a dozen attempts and growing steadily more frustrated.

As he watched the woman, Xander grew more curious about Yelena. Somehow, in ways that he hadn't quite figured out yet, she didn't fit in with the rest of Anarchy 99. He also knew there was no way she was going to tell him. His only choice was to force the issue, and to do that he was going to have to risk everything.

But that was all right because Xander was all about risk. He stepped out of hiding as Yelena punched in another series of numbers. She didn't see or hear him.

"Try 'open sesame,' " Xander suggested.

39

Reacting as swiftly as a sprung trap, Yelena spun and brought up a blue 9mm pistol in one hand. She pointed the weapon like a natural extension of her body.

Xander stood stock-still, knowing if he moved a fraction of an inch she was going to fire. If she didn't kill him outright, she'd probably wound him and definitely wake the rest of the castle. If she did wound him and he had to make an escape, that little venture would be even more difficult.

Standing there, his heart beating and his senses alive with the adrenaline crashing through his nervous system, Xander hoped he was right. Risking his life was one thing, but simply throwing that life away totally sucked.

That moment crystallized for him, making him realize the confrontation with Yelena was just as exciting as any stunt he'd ever put together. He rode the rush and had to fight the smile from his face. *You're poppin' air here, bro. Time to see if you fly, or if you crash and burn.*

Yelena's eyes narrowed. "You shouldn't be in here."

Xander shrugged. "I got lost on my way to the bathroom. What's your excuse?"

"Yorgi sent me to get something from the safe."

Nodding toward the safe, not believing her lame excuse any more than she had reason to believe his, Xander said, "Looks like you forgot the combination. You'd better go back and ask him." He locked eyes with her. "Unless you're lying, that is."

"You've got a lot of attitude for a man who's just been caught sneaking around. Perhaps we should both go talk to him." Yelena gestured toward the door. "After you."

Xander took a step toward the door, then flicked a hand out, catching the pistol she held. He squeezed his hand around the weapon, prevented her from firing it, and tried to pry her hand loose. Before he could do more than get started, Yelena pulled a second pistol from somewhere beneath her clothing and jammed the muzzle against his neck.

Freezing when the cold metal touched his jawline, Xander chuckled. "Oh, you're good." He shifted and rolled, capturing both her hands and turning her weapons back on her, centering them both on her throat. "But not that good."

Yelena struggled but couldn't escape him.

"Let's try the truth this time," Xander suggested.

After a brief hesitation, obviously acting on her own judgment rather than just the threat he posed, Yelena said, "Look, it's none of your concern. Yorgi pissed me off last night. I . . . I came to take some money."

Choosing to release her, Xander let go of her hands and stepped back, hanging everything out there again, knowing it was the only way to make her come completely clean. He shook his head in disappointment.

"The heartbroken gangster girlfriend?" he asked in disbelief. "That's the best you can do? It's a cute story, but I'm not buying it. You played all the right beats: the pouting, the whole bit. But your eyes gave you away."

She stared at him with traces of curiosity, letting him know he had her attention.

"After I shot that cop," Xander continued. "I saw the look on your face. It made you sick. I knew right then, you don't belong with these guys."

Yelena remained quiet.

"Tell me if I'm wrong, Yelena, but my guess is you're looking for a way out. You're snooping around here for an insurance policy, something to hold over Yorgi's head so he won't come after you when you leave."

"You're crazy," she told him, but her response lacked conviction. "I could go tell Yorgi right now—"

"You could," Xander said. "Trouble is, he just might believe me."

Fear showed in her eyes then.

Xander knew he had her, but he didn't feel good about it. Still, she didn't know that he was in a position to help her. After all, he might have only been in the secret agent biz for a few days, but he had contacts.

"Let's make a deal," Xander said. "I won't tell Yorgi what I saw *if* you come to lunch with me."

For a moment, Yelena held her silence. Then she said, "Do you always resort to blackmail to get a date?"

Xander grinned. *No crash and burn, bro. We're flyin'.* He said, "Whatever works, honey."

Despite the feeling of success, though, he knew the risk in the current situation in Anarchy 99 was reaching the max allowable. They both had secrets, and they both knew the other had secrets. Both of them were in situations where they had little real control. If either one of them went down now, they were going to drag the other one down, too.

Truth to tell, Xander felt good about using his unasked-for secret agent powers for good by helping the woman escape from a harsh situation. Of course, he also figured Gibbons was going to have a cow. But it was about time that some of the surprises and some of the enhanced difficulty factors started going back at the scar-faced guy instead of just coming from him.

40

Seated before the computer terminal in his underwear, Yorgi gazed at the three young women asleep in his bed. His mind stayed sharp and focused in the glow of the absinthe. He hadn't needed the extra clarity provided by the drugs or the liquor to figure out what was before him, though. The computer screen revealed everything he needed to know.

A knock sounded on the door.

"Enter," Yorgi said.

Kirill entered the room and looked with disinterest at the three women piled in the middle of the disheveled bed. He stood quietly for a moment, then asked, "What's wrong?"

Yorgi indicated the computer screen. The header clearly stated the website was property of the Czech Police Department, but he had hacked the site months ago.

"Look at this," Yorgi said. "First we see a cop at the bar. Then the very same cop shows up at the warehouse." He scrolled through the information on the page relating to various ongoing investigations. Files remained open on the three American CIA agents that the group had killed. "The cop gets shot. Of course, I assume they are going to blame me. But who do they blame?" He waved at the screen. "No one."

Kirill stood silently, his head wreathed with smoke.

Yorgi knew the man had been concerned with his own affairs all night, primarily his lust for Yelena, which was doomed to failure.

"I'm in the police mainframe," Yorgi went on. "There is not one e-mail about a murdered cop. No news bulletin. No call to arms. Nothing."

"They would not have overlooked such a murder," Kirill stated.

"No." Yorgi blew out his breath. "That leaves us with only one possibility."

"That no such murder occurred."

Yorgi nodded. "Precisely. And I have to ask myself if he is not a murderer, if he is not a black market dealer, then what is our friend Xander Cage?"

Kirill took a hit off his cigarette. "You think, perhaps, he is another American agent?"

"I don't see how he can be anything else." Yorgi shifted in his chair. He hated to be wrong about things, and he knew Kolya would be disappointed in the outcome. Kolya still craved his heroes. Yorgi was past the need for such things. "There is something I need you to take care of for me."

Kirill waited.

"X claimed he was bored this morning, so he went into town. Yelena also left."

The coal on Kirill's cigarette burned brightly. His eyes tightened slightly, and Yorgi knew the man had put together the two events as well.

"I have a man following X. I know where they are. I want you to take care of this for me." Yorgi returned his gaze to the damning computer screen. "Our friend X won't be bored much longer. His life is about to get very exciting."

Kirill lit a fresh cigarette from the butt of the old one, then turned and walked through the door.

I guess we don't fit in with the usual lunch crowd, Xander thought as he gazed around at the other patrons of the posh restaurant Yelena had chosen for their lunch engagement.

The atmosphere was definitely Old World elegance, plants scattered around antique tables and chairs placed so that diners had optimum room. The tiled floors were Italian marble, and immense ceiling fans hummed as they stirred the air. Huge plate-glass windows offered scenic views of the neighborhood, the buildings and streets, and the mountains surrounding the city.

The patrons on the second floor all wore suits and businesswear. Upscale was their middle name, and probably nobody in the restaurant carried anything as dirty or common as cash.

Xander figured Yelena had brought him there to embarrass him and put him off his game. He studied her across the table, between the tapered candles and over the cut flower arrangement designed to elicit romantic feelings.

Yelena's efforts to back him off through restaurant choice weren't going to work. Xander knew that she wasn't aware of that yet.

"Perogies," Yelena told the waiter, "potato pancakes, fried goose livers, the sausage plate, and a pot of Turkish coffee."

"Garden salad," Xander said when the waiter looked at him.

The waiter paused expectantly.

"Oil and vinegar on the side," Xander added.

Nodding, the waiter took off toward the kitchen.

Yelena shook out a cigarette and lit up. She leaned back in her chair and exhaled smoke as she looked at Xander. "That's how you eat?" She frowned in distaste. "It's like a gerbil."

Xander shrugged. She wasn't going to worry him by talking about his choice of foods either. He'd passed up all the junior high school insecurities while learning to dodge bullets and dealers in the projects. Maybe he wasn't a Martha Stewart graduate, but he'd learned how to live his life and accept himself on his own terms. "I'm from L.A."

She gazed at him with open speculation and some doubt. "A wild man from L.A. who recognizes no laws."

"About the only law I obey is gravity," Xander replied. "And I ain't too fond of that one, either."

Yelena smoked and kept her attention completely on him as if he were some curiosity she was trying to figure out.

"You really don't like me, do you?" Xander asked.

"You?" Yelena shook her head. "No. You're a pig."

Xander laughed. "What about your boy Yorgi? Is he a pig, too?"

"You tell me," she challenged. "You should recognize one of your own kind."

"What if I told you I'm not what you think I am? That I could help you get out of here?"

Yelena's eyes flashed. "I'd say you are assuming a lot. What are you? A mind reader?"

"No," Xander said, deciding to amp up the risk and lay it all on the line. "I'm a secret agent."

41

Yelena stared at Xander Cage, not quite understanding what kind of reaction the man was hoping
for. She knew he wasn't expecting what she did, because she didn't even know she was going to respond that way. She laughed, and she was loud
enough to draw the curious and disapproving stares
of the people around them.

A frown creased Xander's face. "Why is that
funny?"

"It just is," Yelena said. Actually, the idea was
more than just funny; the announcement was ludicrous. She'd gotten to know Xander Cage over the
last few days. He was a product of the streets, lifted
up by his nerve, skill, and need to constantly face
death or injury in the extreme sports he pursued.

For a moment, he looked like a small boy who
had been chastened.

Yelena almost felt sorry for him. His disappointment was nearly endearing. "Look at you," she insisted.

"Yeah?" Xander replied. "It happens to be true. That cop I shot?"

All humor in the conversation dropped away. Yelena had slept fitfully during the night, remembering how the police officer had dropped into the street with bright blood spreading across his back. For all his tough guy posing and posturing, she simply hadn't believed Xander capable of such cold-blooded killing. That act was both unforgettable and unforgivable.

"I faked it," Xander insisted. "I did it to get in with you guys."

"Bullshit," Yelena growled.

Leaning back in his chair, Xander took a large cell phone from his coat pocket. Flipping the device over, he jabbed buttons and seemed irritated that nothing happened.

"I'm telling you," Xander said, "I'm an American operative. I've got the gadgets and shit to prove it." He fumbled with the device. "Hold on a second. This thing opens up."

Almost to the point of getting angry, Yelena reached into her purse and took out her cell phone. "Look. I have a cell phone. I must be KGB." She paused, drawing a withering stare. "Sorry, but you'll have to do better than that."

Her cell phone rang unexpectedly.

Giving Xander another smile, Yelena answered the phone in Russian. *"Da."*

"We think X may be an American agent," Kirill said without preamble. "Do you understand what I'm telling you?"

Suddenly, fear blossomed in Yelena's heart and thudded at her temples. All the months of being afraid, of being found out and killed by Yorgi or one of the others out of hand, came roaring down on her. She felt like she'd been dropped into deep water and couldn't breathe. With difficulty, she kept from looking at Xander.

"*Da,*" she said.

"Don't worry. I am here for you."

That announcement was even more fearful. If Kirill was already there, they didn't have any time to escape.

"I am on the building across the street," Kirill continued. "Bring him outside and I will do the rest." Then the phone clicked dead as he broke the connection.

Stunned, Yelena closed her phone. *Kirill was waiting outside to shoot Xander.* The concept was unbelievable. But once she accepted the concept, and she had to because the only other alternative was to believe that she was either dreaming or had suddenly gone insane—neither of which she could entertain for the time needed to think them—she also had to wonder if Kirill waited outside to kill her as well.

"You okay?" Xander asked.

Yelena thought about Kirill. Of all the members of Anarchy 99, Kirill was the one she most feared. The others—Yorgi, Viktor, and Kolya—those she felt certain she would see coming for her if it came to that. But she had worked hard to keep Kirill hovering around her, fueling his hopes that she might become interested in him. She never would, of course, but the ploy was a cheap enough insurance policy.

Could Kirill kill her so dispassionately? Yelena knew the answer to that question was yes. She would have been a fool to think anything else. That left Xander Cage, self-professed American secret agent. Could that be true?

She took a deep breath, knowing her next few words might forever alter her life, then she spoke quietly. "Let's say you are who you say you are. What exactly can you do for me?"

Xander leaned in toward her and lowered his own voice. "I'm reasonably well connected. What do you want?"

"I want immunity from prosecution," Yelena began, "asylum in the U.S., and citizenship."

"How about a condo on South Beach and a rich boyfriend?" Xander asked sarcastically.

Yelena's pride stung a little but she checked her immediate response. "Those I can get for myself. Now that you know my price, what must I do to get your *help*?"

"My people think Yorgi is up to something. I need to find out what."

Shrugging, Yelena said, "There has been a lot of activity lately. People coming in and out. There's some kind of laboratory in the basement of the castle, but I am not allowed down there."

"Maybe you should get yourself invited," Xander suggested.

Yelena couldn't believe he was making that sound so easy. If getting down there could be done so simply, she would have done it weeks ago. "If I'm going to risk my life, I want guarantees up front."

Xander smiled. "That's what I said to my date on prom night. Know what she told me?"

Yelena remained quiet.

"She said, 'You roll out the limo and the restaurant first. We'll see how you stack up.'" Xander spread his hands. "That's it. Take it or leave it."

Yelena hesitated only a moment. "Okay, but there is one problem. That phone call? They know you're an agent. Kirill is waiting out front."

42

Confusion hammered Xander as he sat looking at Yelena in the restaurant. She'd just come off talking deals with him, then stepped right into the whole Kirill's-waiting-outside-to-kill-you thing like they were talking about dessert. What the hell was it with her that she could come off so calm?

A momentary chill ghosted between Xander's shoulder blades.

Xander nodded like he was used to dealing with stuff like this all the time. *Stunts don't always come off like expected either, bro, so you've had experience in dealing with whacked-out shit before this.* "Yeah, that is a problem, isn't it? Where is he?"

"The roof across the street," Yelena answered matter-of-factly. "You have to get out the back way."

Xander shook his head. "If I go out the back, he'll know you've warned me."

"And if you go out the front, he'll put a bullet through your eye."

Xander considered that, gazing around at all the other people talking to each other over lunch. The whole thing seemed surreal. How could everything seem so normal in here, yet be about to go to hell in a handcart out in the street? Still, there was a definite edge to the situation that drew him on. *It's a stunt, bro. Nothin' but the clock to work out.*

"Either way I go," Xander pointed out, "looks like one of us is screwed." He paused, looking out at the street and putting things together in his head. Just like with any stunt, the piece had to look good and come off right. "You packing?"

"Always," Yelena said.

"Cool, cool," Xander said, listening to the music in his head as he got himself stoked to stand and deliver. He glanced at the waiters carrying shiny silver serving trays over two feet long. The curving stairwell railing in front of the building next door leading to the basement floor drew his eye. His car was parked around back at the other end of the alley.

Everything was doable. Didn't mean that the stunt would come off, but he'd never asked for more than a chance.

Quietly, Yelena watched and waited for his decision, like he was figuring up the tip for the lunch they hadn't received yet.

"We'll go out the front," Xander announced. "Just get up slowly like everything's cool."

"He'll kill you," Yelena warned. "He already hates you."

"Why?" Xander asked innocently. "Because of the chemistry you and me got going on?"

She didn't answer him.

Gearing up mentally, breathing nice and relaxed to keep the blood flow going to his body, Xander got up and followed her to the door. Before he reached the entrance, he spotted Kirill's silhouette against the glare of the noonday sun.

Old gunfighter trick, Xander remembered from an arcade game. His heart sped up when he made out a glassy glint and knew the sun had struck Kirill's sniper scope, but the increase was from anticipation rather than fear. Cigarette smoke drifted from the top of the building.

"What is your plan?" Yelena asked quietly.

"To take a nice vacation in Bora Bora," Xander answered. "But in the meantime . . ." He paused, thinking and watching the building and the silhouette across the street. Sunlight gleamed from the sniper scope again. "Kirill's in love with you, right? He's not gonna fire until he's got a clear shot." That was a big part of the plan.

Kirill lay prone behind the silenced sniper rifle. Both eyes open, shifting visual domination willingly from one eye to the other for close-up inspection of his target and the complete field of fire, he took another hit off his cigarette.

The crosshairs drifted over Yelena's figure, lingering for a moment on her breasts, then moving up to her beautiful face. For months, Kirill had fantasized about kissing her, about taking her into his arms and making sweet, passionate love to her. Those precious few times that she said his name were music to his ears.

He lived for those moments.

And now he would kill for one of them. Surely after he killed the American agent, Yelena would be thankful to him. He could imagine her joy at being saved by him, especially if he confided in her that Xander meant to kidnap her. That brief fantasy was distracting, so he made himself refocus.

He shifted slightly, trying to center the crosshairs over Xander Cage's face. Every time he succeeded and started—just barely started—to take up trigger slack, Yelena seemed to drift back into the way.

Frustration chafed at Kirill as he tried to acquire his target. Even though she couldn't hear him, he spoke to Yelena. "Careful, my darling." He waited because he was good at it, and because death rewarded those who were patient.

His quarry still had to step out into the street.

Xander made his move less than ten feet from the restaurant door. He knew Kirill was waiting, and he figured the guy would wait till he reached the street before taking his shot. Xander wanted to jam Kirill, to turn up the pressure on the guy so he had to perform before his chosen time and spot.

Two waiters crossed in front of Yelena. Xander stepped around the woman, knowing the waiters would provide brief cover from Kirill.

Dropping a shoulder, Xander caught one of the waiters in the side and shoved him into the other waiter. Both men went down in a tangle of arms and legs. Food and drinks scattered in all directions from the big silver serving platters. Glassware shattered against the tiled floor.

"Pull the gun!" Xander yelled to Yelena. "Now!"

They were on the clock, up against time and chance, well past the point of no return.

Reacting quickly, Yelena pulled her weapon.

Xander bent down and caught up one of the silver serving trays that had dropped to the ground. Fisting the tray, he whipped the metal rectangle around to knock the pistol from Yelena's grip. He had to work quickly so that she wouldn't seem to hesitate to Kirill. He trusted her not to pull the other weapon he knew she carried.

"Sorry," he apologized in advance as he doubled up a fist. Giving her no warning, he stepped in and punched her, catching her cheek and her nose hard enough to knock her backward into a dessert tray. Even as the woman fell, he turned to flee, knowing Kirill would have the clear shot at the target he'd been waiting on.

Skirting the fallen waiters, Xander ran for the glass doors of the entrance. He scooped up the other rectangular silver serving platter and glanced up at the rooftop across the street.

Kirill hadn't moved, lying on the rooftop as silent and still as death.

You can't outrun a bullet, bro, Xander told himself as he reached the door. *But he can't hit what he can't see*. As he shoved through the door, he lifted the tray, tilting the shiny surface toward the sun and Kirill.

43

I'm going to kill you, you son of a bitch! Kirill
screamed inside his mind. His attention was momentarily divided between Xander Cage racing for
the restaurant door and Yelena struggling to get up.

Blood flowed down Yelena's beautiful face, mar-
ring her complexion. She fumbled for her pistol,
clawing through desserts smeared across the marble
tiles. The restaurant clientele seated next to her retreated hastily. She stood just as Xander Cage
reached the restaurant's double doors.

Kirill tracked the American's movement automatically with his unaided eye. The restaurant doors
opened onto an outside patio also maintained by
the business. Three dozen tables occupied the patio
area, shaded by colorful umbrellas.

Shifting only slightly, barely keeping restraint on
the rage that filled him, Kirill pointed the silenced rifle at Xander, barely taking notice of the silver serving platter in the American's hands. Kirill dropped

the crosshairs over the American's head, debating
briefly whether to shoot him through the head and
kill him instantly, or shoot him in the throat and let
him drown in his own blood. The neck shot was
riskier, because death might not come instantly and
there was a chance of escape.

Even as Kirill's finger took up slack on the trigger,
the American shoved the serving platter forward.

Kirill grinned maliciously. *Fool! That flimsy piece
of metal isn't going to save you.*

Without warning, the serving tray caught the sunlight and reflected the brightness into Kirill's eyes.
His vision was suddenly filled with pain that
blinded him. He squeezed the rifle trigger, holding
the sights on the last place he had seen the American
and hoping for the best. The silenced rifle banged
repeatedly against his shoulder but made hardly any
noise.

His vision cleared almost immediately and he
spotted Xander darting across the patio. He aimed
again, black spots still swimming in his vision.

Adrenaline surged through Xander as he ran in a
zigzag pattern through the clustered restaurant tables. Bullets punched holes through the glass table-
tops and shattered others entirely. Umbrellas jerked
when they were hit, and the bullets left fist-sized
holes in the bright cloth.

Xander ducked behind a table and brought the
serving platter up to catch the sunlight again. The
reflected light tracked up the side of the building
where Kirill lay entrenched. A vase of flowers on the
table nearest Xander shattered and flew in all directions as the bullet cored through the glass tabletop.

The bright band of reflected light struck Kirill in the face.

Knowing he had another precious second or two of free action without having to worry about being gunned down, Xander leaped up and ran for the long, curving staircase next to the restaurant. If he could make his way to the bottom of the stairs, he felt certain he could reach the alley and the GTO before Kirill could pick him off.

Taking the alley even at a dead run was going to prove too slow. Xander knew Kirill would recover enough to shoot him dead if he took time to negotiate the steps. Bullets struck the pavement and tore through the windows of cars parked along the curb as he ran. Although the sounds of the impacts were louder than the shots fired, he still heard the shots, even with the rifle silencer.

He ran for the metal handrail in the center of the stairs. Leaping into the air, he slapped the metal serving tray under his feet and landed balanced on the handrail. Thankfully, the serving tray was rigid enough to support his weight, and the rail was slick enough to provide the kind of surface he needed.

The platter ground against the handrail as Xander rode the piece of metal like a skateboard. The screech of tortured metal echoed within the stairway area, and sparks shot out behind him.

Bullets broke bricks and tore divots from the mortar, creating a rapid line of destruction that followed him down. The stairs had a landing in the center that didn't have a handrail.

Xander kicked his feet up, grabbing the edge of the platter to bring it with him. Crouched, he sailed across the intervening distance between the sections of handrail.

A statue at the side of the landing lost its head as one of Kirill's rounds found it. Stone shards slapped against Xander, and one of them cut his face. Then he was over the next section of handrail, grinding along it as the cut on his face started to sting.

At the bottom of the stairwell, Xander leaped into the air and let go of the serving platter. He dropped to the cobblestones as the platter clattered away, startling a small party of tourists before thudding up against a fountain with a Poseidon figure spitting water into the reservoir.

A rifle round cored through the stone Poseidon's head. Water leaked through the new hole like blood and spilled back into the fountain.

Xander stayed low, pushing off one wall and hurtling through the alley to the parking area behind the building. Now, if Kirill bought Yelena's story and her bloody nose, they were both good. He ran, breathing normally as his heart met the demands of his body almost effortlessly.

Kirill watched the stairs where Xander Cage had vanished but he knew the moment had passed. The rage within him had locked on with talons as unforgiving as a hawk's.

He has escaped.

Impossible as that sounded, Kirill knew he had to accept that. He slammed a fist against the rifle in frustration.

How had he known? Kirill wondered. *Is he really that good?* The trick of using the serving platter as a means of escape had caught Kirill by surprise. Then he remembered Yelena.

The woman ran, all litheness and beauty as Kirill remembered. She reached the stairs and peered down, tracking the people below with the pistol in her hands.

Lethal and lovely, Kirill thought as he watched her.

Then she turned back to his position and looked up at him. Blood trickled down her face from her nose and the corner of her lip.

Kirill stood and waved her off. Pursuing Xander Cage through the alley would prove fruitless if not suicidal. Noticing that his cigarette had died, Kirill dropped the useless butt and shook out a fresh one. He lighted the cigarette between his cupped palms, then took a deep, soul-satisfying drag to fill his lungs with smoke.

Another time, Xander Cage, Kirill promised silently as he moved across the rooftop and sirens filled the air. *Another time, and you won't be so lucky.*

Xander ran through the alley, dodging trashcans and cats dredging through the restaurant's spoils. He didn't think Kirill would pursue him, and he didn't believe Kolya, Viktor, or Yorgi were involved in the assassination attempt. If the other men had been, they'd have staked out the restaurant, maybe sat down with him and Yelena and watched Kirill take his head off. Or they would have herded him out into the street.

He reached the parking area behind the restaurant, drawing curious stares but choosing to ignore them. The GTO sat in one corner of the lot by itself. The walk had been farther, but Xander had figured the car would be in less danger of getting the door bashed in.

His mind whirled, sorting through the possibilities available to him. For all the gizmos and money Gibbons had thrown at him, Xander couldn't believe how little he could do to help Yelena.

The woman definitely wants to be rescued from the castle of the evil lord, bro, Xander told himself as he keyed the GTO's door locks. Rescuing the princess from the tower was the stuff of arcade games, and maybe a little of the innocence Xander had clung to throughout growing up in the projects and living on the harsh streets.

Leaving Yelena there, knowing she was going to accompany Kirill back to Yorgi's castle, had been hard. Xander didn't know what yet, but he knew he was going to do something about getting her out of there.

Movement caught his attention and deflected his thoughts. As he swung the GTO's door open, the door glass reflected the images of black-clad warriors silently scrambling from a van in the row of parked cars behind him. He tried to turn, knowing he didn't have time to slide behind the wheel of the car. He reached under his coat and fisted the big silver revolver.

Before he could clear leather, one of the black-clad warriors rammed into Xander's back and knocked him into the car. Someone grabbed his wrist and kept him from using the pistol while someone else cupped the back of his head. Before Xander could even try to free himself, the guy holding his head slammed his face against the top of the GTO.

Everything went black.

44

"He's awake."

Xander blinked but still couldn't see anything. His head hurt like hell and he wondered how the guy who'd made the announcement could tell that he'd woken. *Must be some kind of mutant ability.* In fact, he was beginning to believe all the hardcore guys working for Gibbons were some kind of super freaks.

He blinked again and tasted stale air that smelled like old laundry. As his senses returned, he realized someone had bagged his head. They'd also tied his hands behind his back.

You gotta love Gibbons's invitations, Xander told himself. *At least you don't gotta worry about an RSVP.*

"Get him up and get him moving," another man said. "We've got a timetable here."

Xander stood willingly. He didn't even know if he was still in Prague. For all he knew, the shock troops that had banged his head against his car might have also shot him in the ass with one of Shavers's knockout darts. Twelve hours or more might have passed. Yelena might have been thousands of miles away and about to get caught in a crossfire. He figured maybe he was her last chance to get out of the situation she was in and still be in one piece.

Someone grabbed him by the bag over his head. He checked the impulse to fight back. From the way the guy was holding him, he figured he could get one good shot in before they took him down.

But that might not have looked good to Gibbons. So Xander played along. *Stay in the game right now, bro. That's the most important thing.*

He followed the tug, moving at an awkward half-run. If he'd been any less of an athlete, with his head covered and his hands tied behind his back, he would have fallen on his face.

Someone opened a door and opera music blared around Xander. Then he followed the tug again, boots stomping across a hardwood floor. The opera music grew steadily louder.

Abruptly, someone shoved Xander from the side, knocking him over, then shoving him back. Xander braced himself for a fall, prepared to tuck and roll, but he landed in a seat. His pistol was shoved into his waistband. Someone ripped the hood from his head while someone else cut his hands free.

Feeling the cold, fresh air swirling around him, Xander breathed deeply to clear his head. Some of the throbbing pain went away with it. He glanced to the seat beside him and saw Gibbons sitting there.

Xander looked around, discovering he was in a dark opera house and sitting in one of the back rows. The fact that the people up on stage were singing in a language that he didn't understand didn't help him know where he was. He was familiar with the music, enough to know what it was, but didn't like any of it.

The opera house was empty except for Gibbons sitting at his side. The black-clad warriors who had delivered him to the government agent seemed to have evaporated. Xander figured the singers up on stage were going through a rehearsal.

"My favorite kidnapper," Xander said. "Next time just send a car."

Watching the performance on the lighted stage, Gibbons waved at Xander to be quiet.

One of the guy singers hit a note so high and so long that Xander cringed, certain that his eardrums were going to rupture or his brain was going to come through his nose. "Come on, Gibbons. You already broke me. You don't have to get cruel and unusual."

Without a word, Gibbons handed over a plane ticket.

Xander took the ticket. "Where am I going now?"

"Home," Gibbons stated.

45

Home?

The word rattled around inside Xander's head. He couldn't believe he'd heard Gibbons right. Slumping back in the seat, he stared at the ticket in his hand. Then he felt a little more hopeful about the situation. If Gibbons said he was going home, that meant he was still in Prague. He was still near enough to do something for Yelena.

"Your cover's been blown," Gibbons continued. "You're no longer useful."

The announcement stung Xander's pride. "That's it? I'm done?" Hell, he'd barely gotten warmed up, and he'd delivered more goods than anyone else from the government agencies had been able to get.

"It's no trick," Gibbons said earnestly. "Your Tech Deck was gathering data during your visit to the castle. We have enough recon to move forward."

"Move forward with what?"

"A sweeper team."

Xander recognized the term from the video games. A sweeper team went in and killed everybody. "That doesn't sound good."

Gibbons shrugged. "They aren't subtle." He paused. "Don't concern yourself with it, X. It'll all be over soon."

Xander could picture Gibbons's black-clad warriors riding roughshod through Yorgi's castle. An operation like that, Xander figured maybe the warriors could take Anarchy 99, but it would be a bloody piece of business. Yorgi and the others wouldn't give up. They'd make Gibbons's hard guys drag them out of the castle by the boot heels.

And somewhere in the middle of all that, Yelena wouldn't stand a chance.

"Gibbons," Xander said in the calmest, most serious voice he'd used in years, "you gotta call it off."

Gibbons stared at him.

"These guys aren't as bad as you think," Xander went on.

"You got in with them by shooting a cop. How good can they be?"

"Okay," Xander said, granting the man that because he didn't want to argue points, "but there's a complication. The girl, Yelena."

Gibbons broke out laughing, only keeping it quiet enough to keep from disturbing the rehearsal.

"What?" Xander demanded, feeling angry.

"I should have seen this one coming," Gibbons said. "There's always a girl."

"Yeah," Xander said defensively, "well, she wants out. I sent her back to get more Intel." *More or less.*

Gibbons shook his head. "It's too late to play favorites, Xander. The cards have been dealt."

"But you don't know her." Anger crept into Xander's tone and he knew that. The problem was, he just couldn't control the anger. "You don't know any of them."

Gibbons studied him for a moment, his face turning hard as shadows swathed his features. His words came out hard and flat and cold. "I've met a lot of bad people in my day. Funny thing about them, for the most part they don't look any different than anybody else. Evil can have a very pleasant face. Sometimes even a beautiful one. But behind that beauty can hide all the ugliness that humanity has to offer. Believe me. I learned the hard way."

"You're so full of shit," Xander exploded. "I've hung out with these guys. You don't know what you're talking about."

Maybe Yorgi, Kolya, Viktor, and Kirill were killers, but given their experiences in the war and being betrayed by their government, maybe they were entitled to a degree of craziness and outlawry. The whole world was crazy. And Gibbons and his pals had started the cowboy crap by sending secret agents snooping around. Having a license to kill also meant having a license to be killed. Nobody playing the game could cry foul.

And Yelena wasn't like them. She was innocent. At least, she was as innocent as Xander had come close to in a long time.

"Maybe so," Gibbons conceded.

From his tone, Xander knew the man was about to stick it to him.

"By the way," Gibbons continued. "That bank

number you got us? Your friends made several cash transfers to a group of Soviet chemists who specialize in biological weapons."

Xander didn't want to believe what Gibbons was saying, but he knew it was true.

Rising and turning from Xander, Gibbons said, "Go home, Triple X. That's an order."

Xander sat and watched the man's back disappear into the shadows that filled the opera house. His head hurt from getting slammed against the car. More than anything else, he felt confused. The feeling was new to him. Since he'd grown up he'd figured he knew the score. He'd learned to trust his instincts and feelings regarding himself and others.

He lay back in the darkness for a time. *You're not a quitter, bro. You never have been, and you never will be. But this thing, maybe it's just more than you know right now. Maybe you should just let this one go by.*

But he kept remembering Yelena's face and knew that she was in a tower somewhere back in Yorgi's castle. Maybe she wasn't hanging around waiting to be rescued, but he didn't think she'd turn down the offer.

46

Xander walked through the Czech Police Department hallways, surprised at how well he knew the way. According to his travel arrangements, Detective Sova and Agent Shavers had to escort him to the airport to get him through Customs.

Shavers and Sova stood beside an unmarked police car. Neither man looked sad to see him go.

In fact, Shavers looked positively cheery. "Looks like this is *adios,* huh, buddy?" the agent said. "Back to the low life for you."

Xander ignored the guy. During the taxi ride back from the opera house, he'd had plenty of time to think about things. He didn't like the way he felt about himself or about the way he was leaving. He was a player, not some grade school kid to be dismissed so casually out of hand as Gibbons had done.

Evidently mistaking Xander's reticence as anger and maybe the willingness to pop him one, Shavers looked a little nervous. "Hey, it's probably for the best. We aren't all cut out to be G-men."

"I cannot say I am sorry to see you go," Sova said.

Big deal, Xander thought. *Guy hasn't gotten over getting his chops busted twice.*

Sova opened the police car door and waited expectantly.

Xander stood his ground. The open car door stood for commitment either way. In or out, a couple of steps would set the die.

"You wanna speed it up, lightning?" Shavers asked. "Plane's leaving. Gibbons told you to get your butt out of town."

And maybe that was what decided Xander. He wanted to think that maybe his decision was based on his need to know for certain what was really going on with Anarchy 99 and Yelena. Thinking of them as two separate issues was getting easier. But when he was given a direct order like Shavers had just done through his borrowed authority, hell, Xander couldn't stand that at all.

"Fuck Gibbons," Xander said. Then he turned and walked away. He was on his own and he knew it. Unsanctioned and uncivilized, just the way he liked it.

"Where do you think you're . . ." Shavers started, then stopped himself. "Oh, I am definitely going to write a report about this! And don't think I'll edit out the explicit content!"

SPY 2.0:
EXTENDED PLAY

47

Xander floated and swam down the Vltava River toward the castle on the cliff. Even dressed in high-performance wet gear specially designed for cold-weather diving, he felt near-frozen. The river held crusts of ice along the banks, and small ice islands floated by on the current.

After leaving the Czech police department and grabbing the GTO, Xander had considered the possible approaches to the castle that he had open. Remembering that the castle walls and security system made the road impossible, and since he couldn't pull a plane out of his ass, he'd been left with the river.

A chunk of Gibbons's operating capital had netted Xander the wetsuit and scuba gear. He'd waited for night to fall before entering the water. Clouds shrouded the moon, taking away most of the light and making the night black.

Drawing close to the bedrock of the cliff under the castle's shadow, Xander kicked off his fins and swam to the abbreviated bank. The river current had swept away everything, leaving no sand or plants, even wearing away at the rock. In time, maybe hundreds of years, he knew the river would take the cliff, too, weakening the rock till gravity pulled the outcropping down.

He didn't plan on being there that long.

Hauling himself out of the water, he stripped out of the scuba gear and the wetsuit. He balanced on the narrow spit of stone above the river and opened the waterproof gym bag he'd brought to carry spare clothing and his equipment. He dressed in warm black clothing, a black watch cap, and good shoes designed for speed climbing, but left his shoes uncovered. A backpack contained the special binoculars Shavers had brought him, as well as the explosives and spare ammo for the big handgun.

Suited up and ready to go, feeling the adrenaline buzzing steadily in him, Xander leaned into the wall and started seeking fingerholds and toeholds. Handholds and footholds were out of the question. Extreme sports speed climbing was all about finding edges the width of a toe or finger joint, and having the strength to heave the body up in pursuit of the next one.

He pushed and crawled and threw himself upward confidently. The cliff side didn't look any more difficult than a lot of other climbs he'd made. He got into the rhythm quickly, tuning up an industrial metal beat inside his head.

His muscles flexed and warmed as he climbed. The cold wind turned his breath gray, then whipped it away. Within a short time, despite the cold wrapping around the mountain and the snow sitting on top of the broken terrain, he was covered with perspiration under the clothing.

Long minutes later, he reached the base of the castle perimeter wall. His breath rasped against the back of his throat and burned his sinuses dry. He swallowed with difficulty. *You've lost a step or two, bro. Gotta head back to the half-pipes and get your game on soon as you get this piece of biz done and get back home.*

Footsteps echoed along the wall above.

Xander pressed in against the castle wall and made himself as small as he could. The footsteps halted overhead. A lighter flicked, then a soft yellow glow dawned above for a moment.

Kirill? Xander wondered. He slipped his hand into the backpack for the pistol. Then the footsteps went on, leaving Xander pressed against the stone wall. *Come on, X. Halo. Quake. Castle Wolfenstein. You've done this a million times before.*

Those were video games, though, and they didn't quite prepare a guy for an actual planned assault on a real castle. Still, somewhere in that mess was a damsel in distress. Plus, he still didn't believe that Yorgi and the others deserved a cold death at the hands of the black-clad commandos Gibbons controlled. If he could get in and find some kind of proof that they weren't as bad as Gibbons thought, maybe he could save their lives, too. He wasn't going to hold Kirill trying to kill him against them. After all, Kirill had been operating under the presumption that he was the enemy—and maybe a little jealousy.

Go now, Xander thought, adjusting his backpack straps again. *Figure out the hard parts along the way. You know what the objective is.*

He stood and leaned into the wall, finding the fingerholds and toeholds that he needed. Unfortunately, the almost invisible line that he followed up the castle wall also took him out over the cliff's edge. Breathing hard, hoping his fingers would go numb so they wouldn't hurt as much, and yet afraid of that very thing because he might not feel an edge the way he needed to and miss a hold he needed, he kept going and didn't look down. The Vltava River had been there for hundreds of years. It wouldn't go anywhere before he finished the climb.

Moonlight slivered through the cloudbank, briefly igniting the hard metal barrel of some kind of heavy machine gun. Real weapons didn't quite look like the software versions or the hardware used in games.

Xander froze and clung to the stone wall, but he knew he was in trouble. The wind whipped across the wall and dried the sweat from his fingertips to provide a more secure hold, but that breeze also increased his drag. His arms, legs, and back ached from the demanding effort required to climb the wall.

Staying where he was couldn't be done, and going back was out of the question. For one, he didn't think his body could make the climb back without some recuperation time that he wasn't going to get clinging to the cliff side. And for another, he'd come there to help Yelena, not to go halfway and turn back around just because the going got rough. Dropping would only put him in the dark river below and probably attract the attention of the guards.

With only one avenue open to him, Xander continued climbing up. Even with the renewed enthusiasm to reach the top, he barely made it. He slid one hand over the squared-off edge of the castle wall, held himself just a moment on the first full grip he'd had in ten minutes, and breathed. He didn't relax—he couldn't; he needed the extra oxygen to recharge his muscles and break down the lactic acid build-up from the continued exertion.

He reached up with his other hand, shifted, then felt the precarious hold he had with his toes slide out from under him. Back, shoulders, and arms burning with the sudden increased strain, he dangled from the castle wall with only the freezing river waiting below. Instinct drove him to kick his feet against the wall in an attempt to find traction before he was able to stop himself.

Movement overhead drew Xander's attention up. One of the castle guards leaned out and peered down. Xander willed himself to become part of the castle wall and hoped that the shadows would protect him from the weak moonlight.

The guard's eyes widened, and Xander knew he'd been seen.

48

The castle guard tried to bring his rifle around, but Xander lunged upward and roped a hand behind the man's head. Using his weight and strength—and his old adversary, gravity—Xander yanked the guard's head down into the stone wall. The impact sounded as flush and full-throated as a blow from a meat cleaver.

For a moment, they stayed like that while Xander hung onto the man so he wouldn't fall and the guard ground his face against the stone.

Don't let go, bro, Xander told himself. *Even if you hit the deep part of the river and don't freeze to death or get shot before you get out, you ain't gonna get this chance again.*

The guard slid his head from under Xander's hand and drew back. Xander hooked his fingers in the guy's coat, using the man's strength to help him up over the lip of the wall. He rolled, feeling the extra adrenaline crashing through his system, and pushed himself to his feet.

Clutching his bloody nose and moaning in pain, the guard went for his rifle. He opened his mouth to shout.

Xander stepped in, curled a hand into a fist, and punched the guard in the throat, pulling the blow enough that he didn't crush the man's larynx. As the guard gagged and stepped back to cover himself, Xander grabbed the guy's arm and flipped him, bringing him down hard onto the stone wall.

The guard went limp.

Shaking from exertion, afraid that he might have killed the man, Xander bent down and searched for a pulse. He breathed a sigh of relief when he found one. *Never killed nobody before, bro. You got lucky here.* But he knew what he was doing was for the right reason. Yelena was somewhere down inside the fortress below. Maybe she wasn't innocent, but she was innocent enough.

He breathed deeply, recovering his strength. The post-stress quakes from the climb faded rapidly. Maybe he wasn't in top form, but he'd never allowed himself to get far from there.

Gazing down at the unconscious guard, Xander knew he had to do something with the man. The guard could wake at any time and sound the alarm.

A quick search of the machine gun nest turned up an empty Thermos. Hoping that the container held enough buoyancy, Xander slipped the Thermos inside the guy's coat, running it from armpit to armpit across his chest. He buttoned the coat tightly over the Thermos, then picked the guard up and heaved him over the side.

Xander peered down into the darkness and watched the unconscious guard splash into the river. The noise didn't carry far. Although the guard disappeared beneath the river's surface, he bobbed up again, his face turned up toward the hidden moon. The makeshift buoy kept him from drowning as the river carried him away.

Regrouping, Xander crouched down and studied the castle's inner courtyard. Guards patrolled the grounds on foot while mounted video cameras swept the area. Xander trotted along the wall, staying low and out of sight, and reached a set of stairs that led to the courtyard.

At the bottom of the stairs, he paused to allow a video camera to sweep by, then broke cover and raced toward the line of vehicles beside the main house. No one was in the heated fountain out front.

As he crept along the line of motorcycles and cars, Xander broke out Shavers's box of explosive bandages and adhered them to the gas tanks. In case he had to beat a hasty retreat from the castle, he wanted to limit pursuit. That was a textbook exercise in every video game he'd played.

He left one of the motorcycles near the front of the mass bandage-free and took time to strip the ignition wires so he could jumpstart the machine easily. If the time came for a hasty retreat, the motorcycle would be ready.

As he got ready to move, a shadow fell across the white carpet of snow in front of him. The crunch of footsteps came closer. Even with the dim light, the snow-covered landscape increased visibility.

Across the open area, Xander watched as a security video camera panned toward him. The footsteps kept coming closer, then stopped. A flashlight beam suddenly flicked on and played over the ground, picking out Xander's boot impressions.

Busted! Xander realized. He drew the silver pistol. The weapon only held dutura knockout loads. Breathing shallowly, Xander waited crouched in the shadows of the motorcycle behind him. He watched the video camera panning toward him again. *All in the timing, bro.*

The guard stepped closer, moving cautiously. The shadow of his rifle cast a hard line across the crystalline surface of the snow.

Xander saw the toe of the guard's boot pass the edge of the motorcycle as the video camera started sweeping away from the area. He launched himself into motion, grabbing for the rifle barrel as he stood.

The guard tried to squeeze the trigger, but Xander shoved the rifle butt back into the guy's face and rocked his head backward. Before the guard could recover, Xander had the pistol up and firing. The knockout dart pierced the man's chest and put him down immediately.

Xander slipped the big pistol back into his waistband, then picked up the guard's rifle and hooked his fingers into the guard's coat as the video camera came back toward him. He dragged the man's unconscious body behind a truck and left it there.

After waiting on the camera to veer away again, Xander ran for the main house. Before he took more than a few steps inside, he heard voices coming toward him. Hurriedly, he stepped into one of the dark and empty rooms off the main hallway and flattened against a wall.

Yorgi and Yelena passed by the room, flanked by Kirill, Kolya, and Viktor. They walked with purpose, with the same intensity of a group of stunters approaching the starting line of a motocross track, a snow-covered hill, or a twisting street set up as a luge run.

Xander understood that kind of intensity, but he knew Yorgi was motivated by something other than amping up the adrenal flow. Remaining quiet, Xander watched them pass through the front entrance. Moving silently, he followed.

He paused at the front entrance and stepped into the shadows framing the doorway. Yorgi remained in the lead with Yelena at his side. Xander listened, but they were speaking Russian and he didn't understand. He didn't hesitate about following.

49

Yelena kept pace with Yorgi as they crossed the inner courtyard of the castle grounds. Her nose still hurt from where Xander Cage had hit her, and she thought she might not forgive him that, but she also realized that his blow might have saved her life. Although Kirill had vouched for her, she felt certain that the bruises that showed on her face were more convincing.

When Yorgi had asked her why she had gone with Xander, she'd replied that she was only doing what he asked her to do. After all, her watching the American had been Yorgi's idea, not hers. She thought that Yorgi believed that she had been attracted to him on a physical level.

She walked beside Yorgi, conscious of the others around her. She didn't know whether they were there because they had nothing else to do, or because they were going to be her executioners. The heaviness of their presence weighed on her.

Pausing at the bottom of the staircase leading to the main house, Yorgi stepped into the shadows and turned back toward the building. The heavy wooden door to the basement level stood barely revealed in the darkness.

A primitive wariness coiled in Yelena's brain as she watched Yorgi take the heavy padlock in hand and insert a key. She jerked her head up, looking at the main entrance above, only then realizing that she thought she'd seen movement.

But there was nothing. Only the shadows occupied the main entrance.

Aware that Yorgi was looking at her, Yelena turned her attention back to him.

"Once you go through this door, Yelena," Yorgi said, "there is no going back. You're with us to the end. Are you sure that's what you want?"

Yelena tried not to hesitate, but she knew the kind of men with whom she had surrounded herself. She'd taken care to know them well. Only Xander Cage had been a surprise to her.

"I'm sure," she replied. The grim finality of her words filled her with an apprehensive chill colder than the blowing snow in the courtyard.

Yorgi studied her a moment more, then shoved the door open and waved her inside.

Yelena entered the basement, surprised to find that the way was actually a passage hewn through solid rock.

"The original builders of the castle," Yorgi said, flipping a switch on the wall, "built their home to withstand enemies as well as diverse elements." He raised the lantern.

The darkness retreated down the throat of the

passageway. The light revealed steps cut into the solid stone. Depressions in the stone testified to the long years of use.

"The passage goes down a long way," Yorgi said, taking the lead. "By the time we reach the bottom, we'll actually be below the level of the river. You'll notice that the cold grows with every step you take."

Yelena silently agreed as she followed him down. She felt the arctic chill bite into her bones and hollow out feeling. That worked in her favor somewhat, though, because the fear thrumming inside her felt isolated. As they passed, warm yellow light brushing up against the tool-scarred gray slate rock, she noticed that some areas were shored up by brick masonry. Her mind raced, trying desperately to guess what Yorgi might have hidden in the basement. After months of observation, she still had no clue.

The sound of their shoes and boots striking the stone echoed and rolled in the subterranean passage. Near the bottom, the dim light brought out runs and coils of new pipe mounted in brackets on the wall. The pipes passed into and out of the stone, precisely fitted into the holes that had been drilled.

That, Yelena thought, *is not original handiwork.*

Yorgi halted in front of a solid steel door that would have looked at home on a nuclear submarine or a starship. The entrance definitely didn't belong in the basement of a medieval castle. He punched a complicated sequence of numbers into a digital touchpad.

The door hissed open, moving on a well-lubricated track. The rectangle of light fell into the darkened passageway, bright enough to hurt Yelena's eyes. She noticed another door to the left of the main entrance and guessed that a supply or storage room lay in that direction.

Yorgi entered.

Trepidation whirled inside Yelena with sick intensity as she followed.

Cautiously, Xander followed the weak light to the bottom of the stairs in the tunnel through which he'd followed Yorgi, Yelena and the others. He pressed his ear against the stainless steel door. Machine sounds—clanking, whirring, and thuds—echoed on the other side of the door.

Even if Shavers's electronic lockpick could get him through the digital touchpad, Xander figured getting into the next room without knowing what was there first was risky. *And stupid, bro. You got to know.*

Looking around, he spotted the room next to the hermetically sealed door. Crossing the distance, he put a hand against the steel surface and felt heat from inside.

Boiler room. Gotta be. Can't expect whoever's working down here to do without hot water for showers and stuff. Xander took out the electronic lockpick and put the device to work on the lock. Less than a slow three-count later, the lock *snikked* open and he let himself inside.

Pipes and tanks crowded the boiler room. Whatever the need actually was, a large amount of hot water got used. The heat trapped inside the room was sweltering.

Two steps into the darkened room, Xander tripped

over a half-empty vodka bottle and sent a stack of European pornography magazines tumbling to the floor. Cigarette butts lay scattered around the floor as well.

While the boss isn't looking, Xander thought. *Impromptu break room.*

Glancing around the room in the dim light coming from the hallway, he found a folding metal chair against one wall. He set the chair up in the middle of the floor, giving himself a clear view of the cinderblock wall that had been built between the boiler room and the hidden room next door. Shrugging out of the backpack, he placed the bag on the floor between his feet and took out the sophisticated binoculars.

He raised the binoculars to his eyes. When he activated the lenses, the first images he saw were skeletons of people and the interiors of huge machines in the next room. Dialing the power down a bit, he put flesh back on the bones of the people.

Focusing on Yelena, seeing at the surprised look on her face, Xander couldn't help but be entranced by her naked body. *Great piece of hardware.* Getting back on task to find out what Yorgi was up to took an effort of will. Before he did, though, he used the binoculars' camera function to get a few digital photographs. *Ain't nothing wrong with appreciating beautiful graphics.*

Then he dialed the binoculars down so that he could just peer through the wall. The room on the other side was a huge laboratory that had been sectioned off.

A sinking feeling filled Xander's stomach. Whatever scheme Yorgi was into was huge. *The guy's bad news, dude. You don't find somebody spending this kind of money to help out the rest of the world.*

He remembered Gibbons's last conversation with him. *Your friends made several cash transfers to a group of Soviet chemists who specialize in biological weapons.* Xander was betting that those biological weapons would look a lot like the teched-out laboratory he was looking at.

The only good thing Xander saw was that Yelena looked surprised.

50

Astonished, Yelena gazed around at the underground lab. Judging from the fresh score marks on the ceiling and walls, the original cavern had been vastly enlarged. Not all of the area could be beneath the river level. Catwalks crisscrossed the open area above, burdened with lights and equipment.

Clear plastic water filtration tubes covered all available wall space. Ten-foot-tall impeller fans were built into either end of the room, and there was still a lot of wall space left.

Smaller labs occupied space on the left and right of the room. Both of those labs looked airtight. Thick glass filled the observation windows. Looking through the windows, Yelena saw white-coated lab personnel working with canisters containing chemicals. Both labs resembled mini-refineries due to the metal pipes running everywhere within them.

The unmistakable centerpiece of the room was the twenty-five-foot submarine-looking vehicle that hung from chains and hoists above a railroad track. The vehicle was finished in white. A pair of huge electric fans stuck out on either side of the machine. A diesel engine showed at the aft end. Two hydrofoil keels, folded up tight against the vehicle's hull at the moment, looked like skis. Solar cells, barely seen from Yelena's position, glinted along the top of the vehicle.

Staring at the railroad tracks beneath the hanging vehicle, Yelena assumed that the device could be taken in and out of the room by flatbed railcar. The other end of the track led under a door. Yelena assumed that the track eventually led to the river.

A casual observer, Yelena thought, might make the mistake of assuming that Yorgi had financed a private sport submersible. But she knew that it had to be much more than that.

As she watched, a lab team rolled up to the vehicle on a wheeled gantry and began attaching a rocket launcher carousel. The carousel mounted on top of the vehicle but clearly had the ability to be retracted and safeguarded within.

Suddenly, Yelena forgot about being cold. Fear filled her, not just because of where she was and the risks she was taking, but because of what the device would probably be used for as well.

"This is *Ahab*," Yorgi announced. He smiled as he gazed at the vehicle. "Think of it as a solar powered torpedo. It can circumnavigate the globe to reach its target through an onboard computer system operating by a global positioning satellite link. It only comes up to gather sunlight or to do its business."

"And what is its business?" Yelena asked, because she knew Yorgi would expect her to.

"Dropping off presents to all the good little boys and girls," Yorgi answered.

A thousand questions slashed through Yelena's brain, but she knew she could never ask most of them. Before she could say anything, a chemist came out of each of the individual labs.

One of the chemists carried a glass canister with blue liquid in his arms and the other carried a glass canister with yellow liquid. Both men crossed to a small cart that supported a rocket that looked the right size for the launcher being fitted into *Ahab*.

When the rocket was properly fitted back together, one of the chemists rolled the cart over to Viktor. Pulling the cart, Viktor went to *Ahab*, hoisted the rocket over his shoulder, then used the hydraulic gantry to raise up to the hanging submersible. Almost tenderly, Viktor placed the rocket within the carousel. He shoved the carousel into line with the launcher. The clicks echoed ominously over the electric hum that filled the cavernous lab.

Kolya entered the main chamber carrying a large box marked CHAMPAGNE. He placed the box on the nearest lab table and began fisting bottles from within.

Viktor roared gleefully as he lowered himself on the gantry. "Everyone! Time to toast your excellent work!"

Yelena felt hypnotized and powerless as she watched the workers leave the two labs. The workers even pushed a man forward from their ranks. Evidently the man had been their supervisor and now found himself embarrassed to be drawing so much attention.

"Drink up!" Kolya said, passing bottles out. "You're all getting a surprise!"

Yorgi tapped Yelena on her shoulder. "This way," he said.

Thinking that Yorgi wanted to talk to her somewhere away from the noise of the lab workers who were now in full celebration mode, Yelena followed him into one of the small labs.

Once inside the lab, Yorgi studied her intently. "You are truly with us, Yelena?"

"I've always been with you." Yelena was still surprised at how easily the words came to her lips. They had taken her in when so much confusion had gone on in her life and she hadn't known where to go. Now, they were the source of so much confusion, and still the words came to her.

Smiling, Yorgi shut the door and used the touchpad to seal the room off.

Paralyzed, not certain what was coming, Yelena looked out at the lab crew. Several of the members were shaking up the champagne bottles and hosing each other with white foam. None of them had noticed that Yorgi and Yelena were gone, or that Viktor, Kolya, and Kirill had locked themselves in the lab on the other side of the main room.

Striding to a control panel, Yorgi pressed a button. Out in the main room, the rocket that Viktor had loaded onto the submersible suddenly raised into firing position. Some of the lab workers noticed the launcher's operation and began telling others. When the rocket's thruster system ignited and spewed three cones of blue flame, they all turned.

Slowly, as if realizing what was coming, the lab workers stared at Yorgi and the others sealed in the smaller labs. Yelena felt their stares as well, and the guilt twisted through her because she was glad she wasn't where those people were.

Kolya's cold voice dripped with maniacal humor over the public address system. "Surprise!"

Stunned, Yelena watched as the rocket launched from *Ahab* and sped straight to the stone ceiling, narrowly missing two catwalks on the way. A virulent gas cloud formed and drifted back down over the room as klaxons shrilled and warning lights flashed.

The people inside the main chamber ran to the exits but couldn't open them. Then they ran to the lab doors and beat on them, crying out for assistance.

In the safety of the other lab room, Kolya pantomimed that he was choking himself. He stuck his tongue out and grabbed his throat, pawing at Viktor, who only laughed at him. Then Kolya couldn't hold back any longer and started laughing as well.

Helpless and horrified, Yelena tried to distance herself from the emotions swirling within her. She couldn't help those people; she had to help herself. Outside the thick glass of the observation windows, the lab workers grabbed their throats and worked their mouths, gasping for breath and dying by inches. She watched them as they twitched and convulsed, then died and fell. Even with everything she had seen in Russia during the worst of the social upheaval, this was far beyond the worst thing she could ever imagine.

She wanted to live, and she didn't think she was going to be given the chance to do so. She stood, frozen and silent, afraid of what Yorgi was going to do next.

When the last lab worker had dropped and now lay still, Yorgi approached the control panel again. He pressed buttons and the big impeller fans at either end of the room started working.

"They did their jobs," Yorgi said, staring out at the corpses. "Now they were a liability. We don't need anyone talking about our business." He turned and looked at her. "Right, Yelena?"

Mechanically, she nodded, knowing she couldn't say what was truly on her mind. He might suspect, but he would also believe that he had branded her with the deaths of those people. She had no options remaining.

Grinning mirthlessly, Yorgi approached the PA system and keyed the transmit function. "Is it just me?" he asked with feigned innocence. "Or did they not seem to enjoy their surprise? Water filtration in progress."

Outside the lab, the huge impeller fans dragged the gas cloud from the room.

"The fans will pull the gas from the room," Yorgi said, "then filter it through the water tubes. Once pushed into the water, the nerve agent becomes dissipated and harmless. You have nothing to fear as long as you stay in here for a few minutes." He glanced back out into the main chamber where all the corpses lay scattered like broken dolls. "To accomplish what I mean to do, Yelena—what *we* mean to do—sacrifices have to be made. Those people are the beginning of the necessary sacrifices."

And how many more are you going to choose to sacrifice? Yelena thought, though she didn't dare voice the question.

Looking out over the corpses on the floor of Yorgi's secret lab, Xander thought for a moment that he was going to be sick. Dozens of people had died; and he had *watched* them. Only the sheer disbelief of what he had just seen kept him from flipping over the edge and losing it completely.

Through it all, Yelena had stood there frozen. She didn't even try to stop Yorgi from setting off the rocket. *Maybe she didn't know.* He tried to believe that, but growing up in the hard underbelly of the city as he had, he knew that kind of thinking was just a pipe dream that could get him killed. He had to think she was part of it now. She'd gone down into that basement with Yorgi. She'd known something bad was there.

And she'd wanted to be part of it. He had to remember that. But his thoughts swirled up inside his head, making him feel almost powerless. Choosing a course of action had always been easy for him. All he did was just move on to the next and bigger stunt.

Gotta get outta here, bro, he told himself. *Gotta get moving so you can let Gibbons know about this.* Even if the black-clad warriors the government agent had access to stormed the castle without being seen, Xander was certain they weren't prepared for something like Yorgi's killer gas. Those men would come, and they would die.

Xander scanned the submarine-type vessel and considered what the vehicle meant. Judging from the sub's size, the vessel wasn't intended to carry a crew, and if there wasn't a crew on board, the thing had to be remote controlled. But controlled to do what? He looked at the launcher, realizing the carousel could hold a lot of rockets. In a moment of crystal clarity, he realized that Yorgi could rendezvous with and re-arm the craft.

So what are the targets?

Even as the question entered Xander's mind, shoe leather scraped out in the tunnel passageway on the other side of the boiler room door. He shoved the binoculars into the backpack, scooped a strap up over one arm, and ran deeper into the room. Avoiding the hottest pipes as best he could, he scrambled to the top of one of the tanks, then up into the rafters supporting the pipes and connections.

A guard entered the boiler room and said, "Gregor." He spoke in Russian, calling out to Gregor again.

Missed one of his buddies, Xander thought. He hung balanced in the rafters, body aching all over from the harsh climb up the cliff only a short while ago.

The man reached to the wall and flipped on a light switch. Dim yellow light flooded the room. Unfortunately, one of the lights was positioned behind Xander. His shadow fell over the guard, drawing the man's attention immediately.

52

The guard looked up at Xander and started to pull his rifle to his shoulder.

Reacting instantly, Xander swung down from the rafters and drove his feet into the guard. The rifle clattered away before the guard fired. Xander got his feet under him as the first guard called for help.

A second guard entered the room and pulled a pistol from his hip. Spinning to meet the new threat, Xander swept the second guard's hands aside with an arm and headbutted the man in the face. Still moving, Xander ripped the pistol from the man's hands and tossed the weapon away, then swept the man's legs from under him with a foot.

Turning his attention back to the first guard, Xander leaped on the man just as he closed his hands over his rifle. Xander shot a leg out, performing splits, and caught the rifle with his left foot, sending the weapon sliding under a boiler unit. Grabbing the man's shirtfront with one hand, Xander doubled his other hand into a fist and punched the guard three times in quick succession. When the guard went limp, Xander released him.

Breathing hard, knowing that getting out alive depended a lot on getting out quietly, Xander looked for the second guard. The man had gotten to his feet and retreated rather than sticking around to help his friend. Xander hurled himself in pursuit, hearing the guard's ragged breath whistle through his broken nose. The man gagged and coughed as he tried to cry out.

The man reached a red switch on the wall. Knowing the button couldn't possibly mean any good, Xander threw himself at the man, hitting him with a full bodyblock and driving him from the wall. They both fell, arms and legs flailing, as klaxons screamed to life behind them.

The guard's head slammed into the wall and knocked him unconscious. Listening to the klaxons keening around him, Xander knew it was already too late. There was no finesse left. He had to escape or die. He pushed himself to his feet.

Yelena heard the warning klaxons shrilling inside the sealed lab. The noise was muted somewhat, but still very discernible. She looked at Yorgi.

Yorgi looked calm and collected. He made no move for the sealed door.

"Someone has breached the security systems!" Kolya yelled over the PA system.

Glancing over at the other lab, Yelena saw Kolya step forward as if to open the door.

"Wait!" Yorgi commanded, locking eyes with his younger brother.

Kolya halted, but clearly didn't like the order.

"Fifteen more seconds!" Yorgi said. "If you go out now, there is still enough gas to kill you!"

Disgustedly, Kolya hammered the thick, protective glass with his pistol butt. He paced impatiently and screamed as if he'd gone insane.

"Get ready," Yorgi said.

Yelena pulled her pistols, wondering who had dared attack the castle. Her first thought was of Xander Cage, but she figured if he had any sense he was long gone from Prague and was on his way back to Los Angeles.

In the hallway, standing above the unconscious body of the second guard, Xander opened the big pistol and shook out the knockout loads. He quickly replaced them with explosive rounds from his backpack.

Just like in the games, bro, he told himself calmly. *Security klaxons are nothin' but bad news. They alert every wandering monster in the area to come and try to climb up your ass.* He snapped the cylinder shut and even managed a grin. *Just means one thing: Time to break out the KFA. Killer fuckin' ammo.*

He spun like an Old West gunfighter and fired a round into the powerbox he spotted on the wall beside the boiler room door. The box went up in an explosion of electrical sparks that looked like a Fourth of July fountain.

The tunnel went dark.

Cool-cool, Xander thought, turning at once and streaking up the passageway. *Cover of darkness works for me.*

Before he'd gone two steps, the backup emergency lighting flared to life with harsher illumination than had been there before. No shadows remained.

"Three more seconds," Yorgi said, standing by the door. "Two . . ."

Yelena stood behind him, ready to cover him as a panel of lights turned green.

"Go!" Yorgi yelled. "Go go go!" He pushed against the door and ran out into the main chamber, stepping on bodies without a second thought.

Yelena followed him, but she avoided all the bodies. Her nostrils flared as she tested the air. One side was still packed with coagulated blood from Xander's fist earlier, but she couldn't smell anything in the chamber. Whatever the rocket had contained had been odorless or the fans and filtration system had worked extremely well.

Viktor and Kolya led the way through the main door into the tunnel leading to the castle courtyard. Yorgi was at their heels, with Yelena behind him. Kirill brought up the rear, hovering over her protectively, silently letting her know he was there.

But is he there because of his feelings for me? Yelena wondered. *Or because even after this Yorgi doesn't trust me?* She had no way of knowing.

Viktor and Kolya opened fire at once. Empty shell casings spun and glittered in the bright emergency lights.

Looking up the winding stone steps cut through the mountain, Yelena spotted a lone figure sprinting up the steps. She recognized Xander Cage at once.

Lines of bullets chopped into the sides of the tunnel and closed in on the fleet-footed American. Then he spun, dropped to one knee, and raised a big silver pistol in both hands. He fired three times.

Viktor and Kolya didn't even bother to step back, obviously thinking at the distance that marksmanship with a handgun was out of the question. Instead, at least one of the rounds hit the pipes mounted on the walls. Small explosions ripped through the pipes and clouds of steam boiled out into the hallway.

Caught in the heated spray, Viktor and Kolya screamed in pain and dodged back into the lab, driving Yorgi, Yelena, and Kirill back inside ahead of them. Luckily, Yelena only felt the heat of the spray and didn't get burned as Kolya and Viktor had.

While the steam emptied, they reloaded their weapons. Then, when the way was clear, they took off howling in pursuit.

Yelena trailed them, running hard across the drenched stone steps. Xander Cage wasn't going to get off the castle grounds alive. There was no way. She knew the American was by himself. Secret agent or not, he didn't have much experience. He was too naïve, too green, and to a degree he wore his heart on his sleeve. A man like that wouldn't live long in a trade such as the one in which he found himself.

She would hate to see him die when Yorgi and the others caught up with him. But she knew that was what would happen in only minutes.

53

Xander ran and the adrenaline rush pounded in him like a live thing. Pain didn't exist in his world anymore. Neither did fear or uncertainty. He rode the high, pulling the feeling along now instead of being pulled.

Movement ahead of him gave him a split-second of warning. He lifted the big pistol and cracked off his last two shots. The explosions ripped through the tunnel. He'd missed the man he'd been aiming at, but the explosive rounds had detonated against the wall behind the guard.

Instead of one guard, the smoking bodies of two guards spilled down the stone steps.

Xander didn't know if the men were alive or dead, and didn't care. After seeing the people executed in the labs, there was precious little mercy left in him. He'd never killed before in his life, but he was ready to start tonight.

He bent down and grabbed one of the submachine guns the guards had been carrying. A quick glance assured him that the magazine was almost full and that the weapon was ready.

At the top of the steps, bullets still gouging the walls and stone steps behind him as he ran, Xander burst through the door. Guards raced through the courtyard while others manned searchlights mounted on the outer wall.

Xander pounded through the snow and soft ground, aiming for the motor pool of motorcycles and cars. He slung the machine pistol over his shoulder. Reaching the motorcycle he'd left without a booby trap, he threw a leg over the seat, toed the gearshift into neutral, then bent down to touch the bare wires together. The wires sparked just for an instant before the powerful engine roared to life.

Slamming the gearshift down into low and taking in the clutch, Xander dropped his left foot and let out the clutch again. The big knobby back tire chewed through the snow and into the earth below, grabbing traction immediately.

He roared through the courtyard, spotting Kolya and Viktor running from the basement tunnel entrance. Tracer fire suddenly lanced the night ahead of Xander, drawing his attention to the guard in the tower over the main entrance.

Xander veered away from the line of bullets ripping craters in the earth. Another guard on a catwalk ahead fired at him. Shaking the machine pistol loose into his left hand, Xander kept his right hand on the throttle and steered. He fired the machine pistol on the fly, trusting his instincts, amazed at how he almost hit the guard and sent the man scrambling for cover.

Mind working furiously, knowing none of the gates would ever open for him, Xander spotted a line of stairs on the same wall as the main gates. Like the stairs he'd followed down after his climb from the cliff side, these stairs were narrow and short, and they ran almost to the top of the wall.

Xander only considered the path for an instant, then he twisted the throttle viciously and sped toward the stone steps. He glanced over his shoulder as he started his final approach, not wanting to get blindsided by something he didn't see coming.

Kolya ran to one of the motorcycles and took off in immediate pursuit.

Remembering how the man had mimed choking while people died outside the lab in which he'd been hiding, Xander popped a wheelie, knowing Kolya would take the move as a dare. Then he leaned forward and stood up on the pegs as the motorcycle shot up the makeshift ramp.

The ride jarred Xander to the core, but he hung on grimly because the stairs were the only way out. In the next second, he was airborne, streaking for the wall, knowing he had the clearance to get over.

A shadow flitted along the top of the wall beyond the stairs, materializing into a guard that raised a machine pistol. Muzzle flashes lit up the man's arms as he cradled his weapon and fired.

Reacting automatically, Xander pushed back from the motorcycle, kicking the pegs forward so the bike would leave him as he released the handlebars. Flying through the air, closing on the guard still firing away with the machine pistol, Xander reached for the seat with his right hand, hooked it with his fingers, and straightened out in a Superman seat grab. His body was horizontal, straight-out behind the motorcycle.

A handful of bullets struck the motorcycle and tore through the air where he would have been seated if he'd remained on the bike.

A one-handed Superman seat grab on a motorcycle! Xander exulted. He was wired inside, ready to howl at the moon. *You are one gnarly, crafty dude!* And it didn't even matter that there wasn't an audience for the stunt. He stunted for himself, and once he had a move, that move was his to keep forever.

Even as that realization hit him, Xander saw the guard coming into view as the motorcycle flew over the wall. He pointed the machine pistol in his left hand by instinct and fired on the fly. The pistol jerked in his fist and the bullets hammered the guard over the side of the wall.

Xander was conscious of Kolya roaring toward the steps after him and of the guard falling down the wall. Throwing the empty machine pistol away from him, Xander hauled himself back toward the motorcycle as he headed toward the earth. If he didn't recover the bike he knew he'd be in no shape to try to get away. His best hope would be that the impact would kill him because after what he'd seen in the castle's basement he knew there'd be no mercy at Yorgi's hands.

Pulling himself forward, Xander grabbed the handlebars and released the seat. He slid back into position on the motorcycle just in time to keep the bike straight when it hit the ground. He hit and the motorcycle went wonky for a moment, but he kept the ride together, managing to bring the motorcycle around in a skidding turn that brought him back facing the castle.

C'mon, Kolya, you sadistic son of a bitch! Don't tell me you didn't have the cojones *to drag your weaselly ass to the line and do the stunt.* Xander dug in the backpack and brought out the Tech Deck. He keyed up the arming sequence for the explosive bandages just as Kolya roared over the top of the castle wall.

54

Kolya had the balls to make the jump, but he hadn't tried to stunt with it. He peered down as the bike descended. When his head stopped swiveling, Xander knew Kolya had spotted him.

Xander held up the Tech Deck as Kolya dropped from the apex of the jump. *Just letting you know it's coming, asshole.* Then Xander pressed the button.

The motorcycle's gas tank exploded, turning Kolya into a flaming comet blazing across the night sky. Off-balance and already blown to hell, the motorcycle and the corpse came down all wrong.

Maybe killing Kolya didn't make up for all the people who'd gotten killed in the lab only minutes ago, and maybe most of those people weren't exactly working on the side of good, but Xander felt a little better all the same. The world was a screwed-up place to live in for the most part, but it damn sure didn't need cold bastards like Kolya living in it.

The motorcycle's flaming front tire rolled by Xander.

"Choke on that," Xander told Kolya's corpse. Knowing that Yorgi and the others would be along to pick up his trail at any moment, he turned and roared toward the long, winding highway that would take him back to Prague.

"Kolya!" Yorgi cried out, pulling the wheel of his vehicle over immediately toward the burning motorcycle only a few feet beyond the castle's wall.

Seated in the passenger seat of Yorgi's car, Yelena felt a momentary chill ghost through her. The body might well have belonged to Xander Cage. She didn't know how the American could have expected to survive such a feat, even with all the training he had in extreme sports.

The rapidly disappearing ruby taillight in the distance told her that one rider had gotten away, though. And in the next instant Yorgi's headlight played over the smoking ruin of Kolya's biker leathers.

Yorgi stopped the car at the side of the road and walked slowly down to his brother's corpse. Unmindful of the flames, he ripped the motorcycle from Kolya, then knelt and gently picked his brother up.

If she had not just seen Yorgi kill so many people and seen Kolya dancing around laughing at those dying people, Yelena might have felt sorry for the brothers. But she didn't. They were madmen.

Yorgi stood holding his brother. Moonlight turned his tears silver.

Viktor raced over to them, putting his hand on Kolya in disbelief. "Yorgi," the big man bellowed, pain sounding in his voice, "we must go after him." He glanced at the lone taillight. "He's getting away."

Yorgi made no response.

"Yorgi?" Viktor tried again.

"No!" Yorgi said. "He was in the outer room. He saw nothing inside the lab. We stay and carry out the plan."

"Forget the plan!" Viktor yelled. "I want to get my hands on him!"

"I said no!" Yorgi exploded. "He is dead already. It is just a matter of time." He glanced up, locking eyes with Yelena.

He is going to test me, she knew. She could see it in his eyes.

"Yelena," Yorgi said. "You go. Take care of the details. Kirill, help me take my brother inside."

Kirill moved forward silently, a wraith shifting across the snowy landscape.

Without a word, not knowing what she was going to do, Yelena slid behind the wheel of Yorgi's car. She closed the door and put the transmission in gear. Gazing in the mirror as she took off in pursuit, she watched Yorgi carrying his brother's body back into the castle.

Then she glanced back at the road. The motorcycle's taillight had vanished up ahead. As she put her foot on the accelerator, she wondered who would be more surprised at the turn of events: her or Xander Cage.

She also wondered what she was going to do about the American. Since he'd had no backup at the castle, she knew his foray there hadn't been sanctioned. Perhaps he could do nothing for her. And if that was the case, she had to seriously consider killing him to keep her own lies intact.

It was an interesting position in which to be.

Xander drove back to the apartment he'd been assigned a few days ago when he'd first arrived in Prague. He couldn't believe the time had been so short. At the moment, it felt like he'd been in the city forever.

His only other option had been to return to the Czech police department. That hadn't seemed a good idea. He figured Sova and Shavers would have bundled him up with a knockout dart and put him on the next plane out. And there was no telling what Yorgi would do with an extra twelve hours of operations time. If he woke up then. He felt like he was cratering now, worn completely to the bone.

He left the motorcycle in the alley by the building, figuring that it would be long gone by morning. Down the street, two winos standing by a trashcan fire were blowing kisses at an old woman. Although he couldn't understand her angry words because they were in another language, Xander got the gist of them. The winos ignored her and kept blowing kisses.

Somehow, seeing the old woman verbally abuse the winos reminded Xander of Yelena. Had she known what she was getting into tonight? Had she known about the basement lab before she'd gone down there? Had she been a willing party to the slaughter?

Not knowing the answers to the questions bothered Xander a lot. He entered the building and went up.

As he neared the top of the stairs inside the building, Xander saw a soft light glowing under his door. Knowing he hadn't left the lights on, he reached to his waistband and took out the big pistol. When he pushed the door open while taking cover behind the doorframe, he found Detective Milan Sova seated in the overstuffed armchair.

The detective had his feet up on one of Xander's luggage cases. He sat patiently, glaring at the door, but Xander knew the man had a serious mad on.

"Sova?" Xander said, tucking his pistol back in his waistband and stepping into the room. "What the hell are you doing here?"

Sova appeared to consider the question for a moment. "First, you set me up in the bar. Then you shoot me in the back."

Xander nodded in total sympathetic understanding. "My boss does it to me, I do it to you. It's a vicious circle." He couldn't help smiling.

"You think it's funny?" Sova demanded.

"I actually do think it's funny," Xander admitted. "Nothing personal. I did what I had to do to get inside. You're a cop. You understand. We're all on the same side here."

A slow, nasty grin spread across Sova's face. "I'm sorry. I switched sides." He lifted a machine pistol he'd had hidden beside the chair.

Xander started to move, but Sova waggled the weapon and motioned for Xander to put his hands up. Tired and washed out, knowing he'd never be able to free the silver pistol in time, Xander put his hands up.

"You pushed me too far, Triple X," Sova went on. "I had a very interesting offer from Yorgi today. And my government doesn't pay quite as well as Yorgi."

Okay, bro, it's all about money here. I can get with that. "Well, I can make a call," Xander said. "My government pays a whole lot better than—"

Anger darkened Sova's face as he cut Xander off in midpitch. "Did you think you could just stroll into this business one day and have all the angles figured out? You're a dreamer."

Xander thought about the dynamic of the situation. "So you're gonna shoot me?"

Sova shrugged, enjoying being in control. "Where do you want it? The head to be quick? Or the chest for an open casket?"

Considering the options, Xander asked, "Can I think about it?"

Gunfire ripped into the room so suddenly Xander thought Sova had fired without warning. Then he saw that a line of bullets blasting through the closed door chewed into a lamp, a picture, and finally smashed Sova back into the overstuffed chair. Tufts of material floated from the chair's back as bullets ripped through.

Sova fell forward in a lifeless heap as the door opened and Yelena stepped through, still holding her smoking pistols.

55

"What the hell are you doing?" Xander exploded. "You could've killed me!"

A calm look filled Yelena's face as she shrugged and coolly reloaded her pistols. "I heard you talking. I could tell where you were in the room."

Then Xander realized that actually Yelena probably should be killing him. Totally lost, he ignored the pistol in his waistband and sat on the bed. "I don't know what's going on anymore. Everybody's changing sides."

The Ivans stepped into the room, flanking Yelena. And things were so weird to Xander that he didn't even blink twice at that.

"What are you doing with the Ivans?" Xander asked. "How do you even know these guys?"

Yelena knelt beside Sova and felt for a pulse.

Xander could have told her she was wasting her time.

"There's something I didn't have time to tell you before," Yelena said. "I'm an agent as well."

"You're what?" Xander couldn't believe it. That was about the last thing he'd seen coming.

"I'm an agent for FSB—Russian Intelligence. Same as your CIA. I've been undercover for two years."

"Two years? What was the plan? To wait until Yorgi and his homicidal friends die of old age?"

"There was no plan," Yelena said. "A year and a half ago, the intelligence section gets reorganized and I stopped getting orders. They forget about me. I stay and I wait like I was told, but I hear nothing. I do what I must to survive."

Xander shook his head, thinking about all the dead people in Yorgi's castle basement. "I've been an agent for a week, and my boss hasn't changed. He needs to know what we know right now."

". . . and they named the thing *Ahab*," Xander reported over the Tech Deck linkup. "You got the pictures. That's all I know. Your turn: what's going on here?"

Augustus Gibbons was a happy man. He scanned the workstations that had been turned over to his control in the Blue Ridge Mountains command center. Shutting down Yorgi and his doomsday weapon was becoming one of the biggest operations he'd ever handled. And the operation looked to be one of the most successful.

Greg Donnan was nowhere around to see the event happening.

Gibbons grinned anyway. Even if he stayed away,

Donnan would still hear about the op through the agency grapevine. All the really good ops got talked about that way.

The monitors showed the pictures of the submersible vehicle Xander had shot while inside the castle, and the intelligence teams had already located similar vehicle schematics for study. The tech-geeks were already buzzing about the vehicle's specs, such as the diesel engine, the fact that speed had been sacrificed for stealth, the solar power, and the probable capacity of the launch rack.

"This submarine's function," Gibbons said, feeling that Xander had earned his right to the Intel, "is to deploy a binary nerve agent called *Silent Night*. The gas was being developed by the Soviets. The formula was thought lost."

"Well," Xander said, "it's not lost anymore. I knew you had something you weren't telling me."

"And it can kill millions," Gibbons went on, pacing the floor as his mind worked at a furious speed. A lot still remained to be done to get troops deployed over in Prague to handle something like this. "Some of those Soviet scientists apparently felt the need to manufacture the stuff and sold it to the highest bidder."

"Anarchy 99," Xander said.

"Exactly. We knew they were up to something. You found out what it was. That was excellent work, X."

Xander was quiet for a moment, and Gibbons knew the guy was putting the rest of it together. "There never was a sweeper team, was there? You *wanted* me to go back."

Gibbons smiled. That part had been risky, and at

the time he'd hated playing that card. But Xander had come through like Gibbons had hoped he would. The agent had just never figured Xander would have done it so quickly or he would never have come back to the States. Now one of the people he had to get back to Prague was himself.

"Hey, if I told you *not* to jump off the Empire State Building . . ." Gibbons said.

"Yeah," Xander replied, nodding. "I'd definitely do it."

"I inspired you," Gibbons said. I'm an authority figure. That's what I'm supposed to do."

"You're a sneaky bastard, is what you are."

Gibbons grinned again. "That's what people tell me." He paused, trying to keep up with the influx of information the techs were turning up on the submersible design. "Look, my team is on it now. It's time for you to come home, Triple X."

Xander moved the Tech Deck back, widening the video pickup to include the woman sitting beside him. "What about Yelena?" he asked.

Gibbons sobered. "I don't have the authority to give her asylum . . ." He saw the woman tense. ". . . but I promise you it'll be done by the time you get here. Come home, Triple X. That's a real order." And he meant it. Without another word, Gibbons broke the connection and the video screen turned gray.

He just hoped Xander took the order. Now was not the time for him to be a rebel.

56

"Does that mean I'm going to America?"

Xander studied the Tech Deck's blank screen as he held the device. Despite the excitement he heard in Yelena's voice, he didn't feel right. Gazing at the blood spot left by Sova's body after the Ivans had carted the corpse off didn't help.

He especially hated what he knew he was going to have to tell Yelena. Looking up at her, he saw the smile on her face start to dim. He felt really bad about that. After two years of palling around with Yorgi and his funboys, she needed some major R&R.

"Let's get some air," he suggested, then stood and guided her out of the room through the window.

They went up the fire escape to the rooftop just as the Ivans were loading Sova's blanket-wrapped body in the back of the little beat-up car they drove.

On top of the roof, Xander couldn't help gazing around at all the steeply angled terra cotta roofs.

"Look at this," he said. "This would make a helluva skateboard park." He pointed. "Could pull some stunts . . . over there . . . to there."

Quietly, Yelena sat on the rooftop only a few feet away. "Talk to me, Xander."

Xander didn't look at her. He couldn't yet. First, he had to string what he was thinking out to her, let him know how he saw things. "How soon can Yorgi launch that thing? *Ahab*?"

"Soon."

Xander nodded.

"You were told to go home," Yelena pointed out. "They're handling it. It's not our problem anymore."

"If Yorgi gets ahead of schedule, it's everybody's problem." Xander couldn't believe he was saying that. He was one of the charter members of the Mind-Your-Own-Freakin'-Business fan clubs. That had been one of the reasons for taking the senator's car, which had gotten him in this whole mess. Now he couldn't even remember the man's name. How whacked-out was that?

Yelena didn't say anything.

Xander turned to her then, deciding to put it to her. Either she was in or out. There was no maybe. It was just like stunting: fly, or crash and burn.

"We gotta delay Yorgi," Xander said.

Yelena shook her head, and he knew she didn't want what he said to be true. "They gave us a way out," she said. Tears sparkled in her eyes as she gazed up at him. "Please, let's take it now while we have the chance."

Xander felt the icy wind whipping over him. He drew some of the cold into himself and tried to freeze it into place around his heart. "I've risked my life for a lot of bad reasons," he said. "This'll be the first time it counts."

Anger colored Yelena's face. "This isn't some stunt. You'll die!"

Xander knew she was seeing her own chances of getting out go down with him. He didn't think the situation would go down that way, but he needed her. "My chances'll be a lot better if we work together."

"You can't ask me to go back there. You can't!" She stood and walked away from him.

Watching her back as she stood there in the moonlight, Xander suddenly felt like the few feet separating them were more like a million miles. But he couldn't let up.

"You know," Yelena said in a harsh voice, "I volunteered for this assignment in the beginning. I fought for it."

"Then finish it," Xander said. *You can't just walk away from this, Yelena. Maybe you don't know that yet, but I do. Yorgi and those guys took too much from you. The only way you're going to go on from here is to get some of that back.* But he couldn't tell her that. She wasn't ready to know that yet.

After a long silence broken only by the gale winds, Yelena turned back to him. Slowly, she nodded. Then she took away the space she'd put between them.

"You know what I told you after you kissed me?" she asked as she slid her arms around his neck.

"Yeah," Xander replied, putting his hands on her waist and pulling her to him. " 'Never again.' "

"I lied," Yelena told him just before she covered his mouth with hers.

For a time, Xander held her in the moonlight of a foreign country. Having her there felt good and right. But maybe that feeling was only so strong because he knew the next day was a coin toss whether he'd ever stand in moonlight again.

SPY 2.0:
OFF THE HOOK

Tired and edgy, wanting to get on with the mission rather than spending time preparing for what he was going to do, Xander went searching for Toby Lee Shavers. As yet, the young agent hadn't been called home to the United States because he was going to be working Gibbons on. When asked, the Ivans had known exactly where to find Shavers.

Shavers sat on the corner of a desk talking to three female Czech police officers who were obviously trying to complete paperwork so they could go home. It was after midnight, but not much after. The Ivans had told Xander that Shavers regularly hung around till shift change at four and at twelve, hoping to get lucky with one of the women.

So far, Shavers wasn't having any luck, even posing as a battle-hardened CIA agent and packing an expense account.

"It's not fun killing a man with your bare hands,"

Shavers was saying to the women. "It's just something you have to—"

Xander grabbed Shavers by the shirt and hustled him off the desk. He kept the smaller man moving, not giving him a chance to balk.

"Hey, hey," Shavers protested, trying to recapture his aplomb.

"I got new orders from Gibbons," Xander said, herding the man toward the stairwell in the basement.

"Looks like someone just hit the jackpot on a black-market munitions dump," Shavers stated sourly as he surveyed the gear lying on the floor in front of the GTO down in the Czech police department.

A small army of mechanics stood behind Shavers.

"Me," Xander said. All the gear came by way of the Ivans. The men had amazing contacts.

The weapons list included .50-caliber machine guns, rockets, ammo belts, a harpoon gun, flamethrowers, mines, and various other items concerning sudden and violent carnage and mayhem. The Ivans had been diligent and they'd been resourceful. They'd even added items to Xander's list.

Xander sat behind the wheel of the GTO. He gestured toward the gear on the floor. "I want all of that"—he patted the muscle car— "in here."

Shavers's mouth fell open at first, then a smile crinkled the corners of his mouth and spread to his eyes. "*Cool!*"

Xander got out of the car and left Shavers with his assignment. His initial plan for getting into Yorgi's castle didn't figure the GTO into it, but he wanted the vehicle ready for when and if it was needed. And if the car were needed, they'd need serious firepower.

The Ivans had gathered at Detective Milan Sova's workstation because everyone there knew Sova wouldn't be coming in to protest. News of Sova's betrayal had spread quickly. The Ivans had also appropriated Sova's computer and his coffee pot. They stared down at the topographical map of Yorgi's castle and the surrounding grounds on the desktop.

"This is a very hard place to get to," the first Ivan said.

"I know," Xander said. "Bet the real estate agent that sold Yorgi the place pointed that out. 'If you're a world villain type, boy do we have a really hard-to-get-to place for you.'"

Neither one of the Ivans appreciated his humor.

"The road is obviously out of the question," the second Ivan said. "Perhaps the river." He traced the river's course with a blunt forefinger.

Xander shook his head. "I used the river last night. And by the time we get this show on the road, we're gonna be looking at daylight. His shock troops won't even need the fancy electronic surveillance gear to see us coming by river."

"Perhaps we could use the road, then," the first Ivan said. "If we had enough vehicles and we moved quickly enough."

"The castle is surrounded with surveillance cameras," Xander said. "If Yorgi sees us coming, he'll launch *Ahab*."

"I know," the first Ivan said. "That's why we cannot get close enough."

Xander tapped the map. "*That's* why I need to

knock out the communications tower at the base of the mountain . . . here." He pointed at the identified tower sandwiched between another peak of the mountainous area and the cliff Yorgi's castle occupied over the Vltava River.

"How will you get there?" the second Ivan asked.

Xander looked at them and grinned. "Anybody here fly a plane?"

Only hours later, Xander arrived with the dawn. He sat strapped into the passenger seat in the cockpit of a small prop plane. A female police officer acted as pilot.

They flew out of the east, with the sun to their backs so they'd be less noticeable. Even if Yorgi's guards spotted them, they weren't a military troop transport, so they wouldn't get much notice. At least, that was the plan.

They got closer to the big mountain reaching up into the sky above the cliff that held Yorgi's castle. A moment later, Xander could see the communications tower that was his target with his naked eye. A guard post occupied the area at the base of the satellite dish. Farther up the steep mountain leading down to the communications tower and the castle beyond, a small warming hut for the guards patrolling the area sat half buried in the deep snow.

The plane took a harsh bounce in a sudden gust of turbulence. The craft slid across the sky out of control for a moment, and lost about four hundred feet of altitude.

Another drop like that, Xander thought grimly, *and we're gonna rack this baby up.*

The woman cop looked at Xander and shook her

head. "This is as close as we can get," she said. "Too much turbulence around the mountaintop."

"That's cool," Xander replied. "I'll get there." He unbuckled from the seat and stood. After checking the parachute harness he wore, he made his way to the back of the plane. He threw the cargo door open.

Howling winds whipped into the cargo area and sucked at Xander. He felt adrenaline hammering through him, amping him up.

Gotta go, bro. Yelena's down there somewhere waiting on you. She trusted you enough to go back. Xander reached back and took a fat snowboard from the equipment racks in the plane's cargo area. He pulled his goggles into place, snugged his woolen cap on, and dove through the cargo door.

58

The bone-chilling winds clutched greedily at Xander has he tumbled through the sky. He angled his body, moving by instinct, and got the snowboard under him. He spread his arms out, catching the wind as he fell toward the snow-covered mountain.

He altered his course, leaning on the board and using his body. Skyboarding wasn't just about the board; the sport was about learning to use the body as well. Skydivers turned their bodies into sprawling masses to slow their descent, or they folded their arms in to become projectiles knifing through the air and gain speed. A diver resisted the air or avoided it. But a skyboarder tamed the air, finding the strengths and the weaknesses of the atmospheric ocean that surrounded the earth, and—for a time— became a master of the winds.

Xander tucked on the board, going low and gliding across the sky. If he'd been on snow, he knew he'd have been cutting powder, spraying a crystalline mist away from the board due to the friction he was pulling. The board left no marks in the air, though, and he had to rely on instinct and experience to guide him.

The ride down from the plane was filled with twists and turns and spins as he found the path he needed. The sound of his passage *whooshed* by his ears. An abrupt patch of turbulence dumped him and sent him sprawling through the sky. Struggling, he used his arms and the board to right himself, regaining control of his plummet again.

He'd kicked loose from the plane thousands of feet up, and that distance dissolved in seconds. The distance separating him from the mountain also lessened. Trying to approach by parachute, even the sport parasail he wore, wouldn't have put him within striking distance of the mountain. The uncertain winds would have blown a parachute far off course. Descending by parachute alone during the long drop would also have given Yorgi's guards more time to see him and react.

The cold burned Xander's face and crusted over his goggles as he whipped through the treacherous winds. He watched the communications outpost and guardhouse. Small figures moved around both structures. Snowmobiles sat anchored out front, and out in front of the warming hut along the outer perimeters of the defenses as well.

Judging himself close enough, the altimeter on his wrist putting him in the danger zone for the drop, Xander yanked the ripcord. Immediately, the brightly colored parachute unfurled from his back and made a canopy. He grabbed the steering cords and juked toward the mountain. Even with the proximity to the ground, the winds still nearly swept him from the sky.

Ten feet up from the snow-covered mountainside, Xander cut the harness loose and dropped. Caught in the wind, the parachute roiled through the sky like a neon-colored jellyfish.

Xander dropped on the snowboard and slid across the snow crust. A steep drop-off that he hadn't seen on the way down suddenly leaped out of the stark whiteness at him, backed by the blue sky beyond and the tree line below. He twisted his body, cutting the board into the crust and sending a rainbow-hued spray out over the drop-off. If he didn't find the traction he needed, he knew he'd be over the drop-off and racing down the steep mountainside before he was ready. At that point, he would have been a sitting duck for the guards waiting below.

He came to a stop at the edge of the drop-off overlooking the communications tower, guard post, and warming hut. Yorgi's castle sat on the broader cliff overhanging the dark blue Vltava River farther below.

The drop-off Xander faced was steeper than he'd been led to believe by the topographical maps the Ivans had turned up. A man couldn't have walked upright without falling at least three hundred yards. Only a brief respite was offered there, because the harsh, broken land fell away again.

When he'd presented them with his plan, the Ivans had told him he was crazy. Xander had responded that crazy was the least of what would be needed to pull off the stunt. He also needed a hell of a lot of luck, and every bit of talent and skill he had.

He took his binoculars from his pack and scanned the guard outpost. Men scattered and ran for the snowmobiles. Along the top of the guard post, video cameras swiveled in his direction.

Aware of the new wave of adrenaline screaming through his system, Xander grinned and put the binoculars away. "Knock, knock."

59

"I'm telling you, I saw something up on that cliff."

Viktor walked to the guardhouse observation window and peered up at the craggy mountainscape that towered over the area. He squinted his eyes and shaded them with a hand, trying to block out the harsh rays of the dawning sun coming up behind the peaked mountain.

"What do you think you saw?" Viktor asked.

"A parachute," the monitor guard replied.

Turning his gaze to the bank of video camera display monitors, Viktor walked over to the man. The guardhouse had been there for years. Yorgi had paid for a major tech overhaul when the communications tower had been built, but he had maintained the hardwood floors and stone walls.

The tech tapped computer keys. "Here."

Leaning over the man, Viktor watched as the video footage rolled back. Then he saw the bright splash of color against the pink and blue dawn.

"Can you magnify the image?" Viktor asked.

"No. I tried. The program fuzzes out the picture when I try to increase the pixelation."

A motion detector suddenly blared out a warning.

Viktor stared at the nearby monitor. "Where is that coming from?"

"The mountain peak," the tech replied, checking the monitors before him.

"You can increase power to one of the cameras, yes?"

"Yes."

"Get it done." Cold fury roiled inside Viktor. Kolya's death was already hours old and hadn't been avenged the way it should have been. Yelena had returned from the city with news that she had tracked Xander Cage to his apartment. During the gunplay, the American had killed Detective Sova before Yelena had in turn killed him. Xander Cage had died much too quickly at Yelena's hands. That fact rankled Viktor. Yorgi should have cut him loose and let him avenge Kolya.

On another monitor, telescopic crosshairs suddenly appeared. Swiftly, the video camera's point of view locked on the mountain peak and zoomed in.

A lone figure stood there in a snowsuit.

Viktor recognized the cocky posture of the insufferable son of a bitch even before the camera revealed Xander Cage's features.

"Sound the alarm," Viktor ordered.

The monitor tech hit another key and klaxons blared to life around the outpost. Men galvanized into action, springing up from other rooms in the building with weapons in hand as they raced to the snowmobiles outside.

Viktor grabbed his own AK-47 and joined his men. Yelena had lied about the American, the big man realized. He had to wonder what else she had lied about. But Xander had landed alone, perhaps on some foolhardy American Old West daydream.

Straddling his snowmobile, Viktor yelled over the crash and thunder of the high-performance engines. "Take him alive!" He smiled as the men nodded. "I'm going to kill him for a very long time." When he twisted the throttle, the snowmobile shot forward and raced toward the steep incline where Xander Cage stood.

Xander stood at the edge of the drop-off and surveyed the phalanx of snowmobiles barreling in his direction. Snow clouds followed behind the men and machines as they sped up the steep incline. Viktor's bulk and mass were too unique to miss.

Even though he wasn't moving and the only wind in his face came from the howling gales surrounding the mountains, he knew he was in mid-stunt. He had been into the stunt since he'd leapt out of the cargo plane.

In truth, he didn't know if the snowmobiles could climb the steep grade, but he was certain the tracked vehicles would bring the riders within shooting distance. Forcing himself to do deep exhalations, clearing his lungs of all residual carbon dioxide build-up so he could take fresh oxygen in and get pumped, he grinned at the adrenaline surge that ripped through him.

Time to get down to it, bro. Xander reached into his coat pocket and pulled out the HE grenade he'd packed. The high-explosive grenade was the only true weapon he'd brought for his assault on the communications tower. If the HE grenade wasn't enough, he was a dead man. *Could be you'll be a dead man before this is all over anyway.*

But he didn't let himself dwell on that possibility. That was in the future. He was all about living in the *NOW.*

Keeping his front foot locked on the snowboard, he pushed off with the other foot. At the same time, he pulled the pin on the HE grenade and tossed the explosive onto the cliff. Instead of staying in the snow as he'd thought it would, the grenade slid over the snow crust and came toward him. He bent his knees and leaned back with the fall as he went over the incline's edge.

At first, Xander dropped like a rock. The snowboard barely skimmed the frozen crust. The snowboard's edge carved divots from the surface, then the grade eased, allowing him contact with the snow. Behind him, the tumbling HE grenade gained ground, hopping and skipping across the snow.

Xander forcibly looked away from the bouncing explosive. When the grenade exploded, and he was sure that the device would, he didn't want to lose his sight to flash-blinding. He stared at the snowmobiles, watching as men lifted sidearms and started shooting.

A deafening roar rolled over the mountainside.

Xander whipped his head around, falling off-balance just for a moment and having to dig his fingers into the snow to retain his footing on the board. Looking up, he watched as the face of the snow sheet draped over the mountain spiderwebbed with cracks that were still moving.

Without warning, the entire face of the crust tore away from the mountain. The huge mass shattered and broke as it hammered against the side of the mountain. Skidding and skipping, the falling snow knocked still more snow loose, adding to the mix that roiled down the mountainside. The wave of destruction gathered mass, then speed.

Xander felt the earth shake under the snowboard. Glancing forward, he saw that the snowmobiles had slowed to stops. The guards stared up at the avalanche with open-mouthed astonishment. Their study of the unnatural phenomenon didn't last long; they heeled their vehicles around and headed back to the outpost.

Hunkered low over the snowboard, his knees bent and his upper body centered over his spraddle-legged stance with his arms out at his sides, Xander leaned into the run, willing himself to gain momentum. The dulled, growing roar behind him was a constant reminder that death dogged his heels. He'd started the avalanche that he hoped would wipe out the communications tower, but he had no control over the lethal wave of snow and rock.

60

The avalanche grew larger than Xander had counted on. He'd known from snowboarding and being around ski resorts that snow could often be dangerous as the weather started to warm or snow accumulation had grown too great. The information the Ivans had gotten on the weather conditions around the mountain had suggested that both were true.

He'd planned on the HE grenade starting an avalanche, but he hadn't counted on the avalanche ripping trees from the ground or pulling massive boulders free. Yet that was exactly what the avalanche did.

The monstrous carnage fell behind Xander, then rose again from its own body, rising and falling like a live thing, as forceful and regular as a heartbeat. The mountain fell like cooked meat from a T-bone. The trees and boulders, shorn of their moorings, knocked and tore others loose as well.

Xander knew he had problems that he hadn't counted on. As fast as he was on the board, as skilled as he was on the snow, he couldn't go any faster—and the avalanche gained on him, pounding the earth like a ravenous beast in pursuit of prey.

Tracking movement in his peripheral vision, Xander caught sight of an uprooted tree tumbling and skidding at him from the left. Shattered and broken limbs, stark white at the breaks where the bark had torn away, chopped through the snow like spears.

Xander leaned on the board, stabbed a hand into the snow for a moment to create additional drag, and veered away from the twisting, stabbing tree. The sharp spikes missed him by less than three feet, but the move had cost him more of his lead in front of the main body of the avalanche. Spitting snow crawled down the neck of his ski suit.

Leaning again, Xander avoided a boulder that bounced down the mountain. The boulder caught up with one of the snowmobiles, smashing man and machine before careening on. Xander avoided the crimson stain spreading across the snow, wanting to avoid the possibility that a piece of the crushed snowmobile might trip him up.

He glanced over his shoulder and snow mist pressed into his face. The avalanche towered thirty feet high easily. The thing was so huge and roiled so much in the center that distance perception was out of the question.

Damned freakin' close, bro, Xander decided. *And it's getting closer. You can bet on that.* He turned his attention back to the downhill run. Another uprooted tree slid toward him on an interception course. Spotting a rise ahead of him, Xander steered

for it. The wider he veered, the more ground he lost
to the avalanche, and he knew he was almost all out
of lead.

He hit the ledge expertly, going for a full 360-de-
gree diving flip over the tree because he didn't think
he could ramp over it. On the other side of the tree,
he landed off-balance. Reacting quickly, going for
time on the run now rather than style points, he
threw himself over onto his side, bent his knees
slightly, and heaved himself onto his feet again.

He regained the board almost effortlessly, but
he'd lost more of his lead. The avalanche breathed
around him now, covering him in spitting mist and
stinging ice crystals.

To his right, he passed one of the guards' snowmobiles. A heartbeat later, the avalanche of crushing snow overtook the snowmobile. If the driver
screamed, Xander never heard the noise.

He was almost on top of the warming hut before
he recognized the small mass jutting up from the
field of cascading snow staring to race by him. He
knelt and popped up, catching the top of the warming hut in a rail slide that put him airborne.

The speed and angle at which he hit the warming
hut shoved him high into the air. Helpless, he
watched as the avalanche gained more ground he
knew he'd never make back. The cascading snow
caught another snowmobile, picked the craft up,
and slammed it into another snowmobile. Both men
and their machines disappeared at once.

Xander hit the ground hard, and tried desperately
to keep control of the snowboard, but he couldn't
hold it together. He pushed himself up and tried to
get going as the avalanche overtook him.

For a moment, he was buried in whiteness, and maybe even part of him figured it was all over. But only for a moment. He wouldn't quit, *couldn't* quit. Ever since he'd been born, he'd been made for the struggle to live outside the rules, to break convention. Accepting life as it was handed to him would have kept him inside the projects, would have turned him into somebody he didn't want to be.

And above all other things, Xander Cage was a fighter.

He kept the board under him out of sheer willpower and an amazing display of skill. Briefly, as he stood in the whirling tube of shifting snow that kept falling forward like an ocean curler, he thought about Rashonn. *You're missing one gnarly stunt, babe.*

He never saw the next jump, only felt it as the snowboard crunched up under his feet and propelled him skyward. He didn't even know what he hit. But in the next instant he was through the snow and on top of the avalanche. The snowboard bucked and tossed underfoot, but it held the shifting surface of the avalanche's leading edge.

From his new vantage point, feeling the adrenaline high buzzing in him, Xander watched as the back row of fleeing snowmobiles was overtaken. The avalanche was merciless, pounding down on the men and machines, tearing them from sight between heartbeats.

The snow rushed on into the small copse of trees before the communications tower and guard post. The trees went down like toothpicks, torn from the ground with ease, their clusters of roots jutting and gnarled up like the deformed hands of old arthritics.

Spotting the communications tower ahead, not so tall now that he was riding the crest of the avalanche, a desperate plan entered Xander's mind. Even with his skill, he knew he couldn't hope to ride the avalanche down. The mass of snow was tearing through trees at the moment, but the avalanche would peter out, leaving the tonnage of snow and rock still plenty of impetus to bury him.

He reached down and unlocked his boots from the snowboard. Then, as he came within reach of the satellite dish at the top of the communications tower, he leaped. He caught the dish with both hands and pulled himself aboard, feeling the shudders running through the structure.

Holding steady, hoping the communications tower could weather the blunt, unyielding force of the avalanche, Xander stared out at the wave of destruction that overtook the snowmobilers.

Viktor was blazing through the line of guards, unaware of the guard desperately holding onto the back of his snowmobile. One particularly bad bounce made both men and the machine airborne. The snowmobile wobbled on the way down.

Viktor's head turned around to look behind him, evidently feeling the drag. When he saw the man desperately clinging to the snowmobile, he pulled his pistol and shot the guard through the head.

Xander inhaled and exhaled heavily as he tried to recover his breath. He held onto the satellite dish because the communications tower kept quivering from the continuing impacts.

Obviously hoping the guard post would prove substantial enough to handle the avalanche, Viktor drove his snowmobile through the huge plate-glass window. The snowmobile overturned inside the building.

Maintaining his precarious hold on the satellite dish, Xander watched as Viktor scrambled to his feet and turned to watch the oncoming snow wave. The avalanche smashed into the building, filling the structure with snow.

Before he could see what happened next, the avalanche slammed into the communications tower as well. For a moment, Xander thought the structure might actually withstand the assault. Then the anchors gave way, and the tower fell over.

Xander had nowhere to go and could only watch helplessly as the blinding whiteness overtook him and pushed him under.

61

Grimly, despite the all-consuming cold and unflinching whiteness around him, Xander fought to breathe. The crushing weight of the snow held him down, filling his nose and mouth. He tried to move and couldn't.

C'mon, bro. You got more to give than this. He twisted his body again, heaving himself in the snow. Satisfied that he could move, keeping a tight rein on the panic that filled him, he concentrated. *Gotta pay attention, X. Gotta know which way is up.*

He paid attention to gravity, the one law that he'd never been able to break, the one true constant in his life that he'd tested time and time again. Deep in the water and during free fall on a skydive, gravity didn't exert such a strong pull on him, but any time he'd stunted on the ground, he'd been aware of the force pulling him back earthward.

He felt it now, and he fought against it as he clawed his way up through the snow. His lungs burned from lack of oxygen and spots spun in his vision. Getting through the snow was challenging; steps had to be made—packed down and shaped—to support his weight. At least he wasn't trapped inside the moving avalanche.

Before he expected the crust to be there, his hand plunged through. Galvanized by the nearness of the surface, Xander clawed his way up, breathing in the fresh, cold air that followed along the opening his arm had made.

Long seconds later, he pushed through to the surface. Gazing around, he was amazed at the damage the avalanche had done. The communications tower was definitely down, completely buried except for a small portion of the top.

Sitting on his haunches, taking deep breaths and knowing any movement required on his part at all was going to be too much, he stared at the guard post. Snow had filled the building, but Viktor's tattooed arms stuck out from inside. The other window Viktor had been trapped against was covered with bars. He hadn't escaped and had drowned in the snow.

After a moment, Xander became aware of the Tech Deck beeping in his coat pocket. In disbelief, he took the device out and answered it.

"Gibbons," Xander said, "long time no talk. You wouldn't believe my day."

Jet noises sounded over the communications line, but they were receding. Xander figured Gibbons was at an airport, already on his way. Still, getting a team into the area would take time. And Xander didn't know if the avalanche was going to buy enough.

"And you wouldn't believe mine," Gibbons assured him. "I've flown to Prague twice in one week keeping tabs on you, Triple X. I've been calling for an hour. You mind telling me what's going on?"

Looking farther down the mountain, Xander saw guards filling the castle grounds. The main doors opened to allow four-wheel-drive Jeeps, motorcycles, and snowmobiles to speed out toward the avalanche-stricken outpost and communications tower.

Xander shrugged, knowing he didn't have time or energy to get away from the advancing troops. "Snow-covered fortress. Army of bad guys. The usual."

"Your orders were to go home," Gibbons insisted. Was I unclear at all?"

"I guess I got confused. Sometimes go means stay. Sometimes stay means go. You really should work on your communication skills."

Gibbons paused. "Satellite puts you near their mountain compound. Don't make things worse by doing something stupid. You can observe, but do not get involved."

Xander looked back at all the destruction he had caused. The first wave of Yorgi's guards on snowmobiles had almost reached him. "It's a little late for that now."

"Listen to me very carefully, X. I admire what you're trying to do." The sincerity in Gibbons's voice was real. "You've come a long way since we met. But my team will handle it from here. That is a direct order."

The three guards on snowmobiles pulled up short of Xander and pointed their assault rifles at him. They gestured for him to stand.

Xander had to speak over the popping, deep-throated roars of the snowmobile engines. "We don't have that kinda time, boss. Yorgi know we're on to him. I've gotta go now. There's three guys with AK-47s staring at me."

He closed the Tech Deck and dropped the device back in his pocket, then he raised his hands and waited to be taken prisoner. It was the most restful thing he'd done in what seemed like forever, but he knew it wasn't going to remain that way.

Yorgi was going to be pissed.

62

Xander entered the castle anteroom at the head of a squad of guards. They hadn't tied him up, but he knew he wasn't going anywhere without getting his brains blown out. He stood in the anteroom and gazed out through the window. As luck would have it, the view he had was of the avalanche-covered outpost and the downed communications tower.

The sight wasn't exactly the last thing he wanted to see on earth, but it was okay.

Thudding footsteps announced Yorgi's arrival.

Xander turned to face the man. Frustration ached deep within Xander that he couldn't meet the man on more equal terms, but he wasn't afraid. Even if he died in the next few minutes, that was a few more minutes the Ivans had to put the second wave together now that Yorgi's security system was down.

Knowing that felt pretty good.

Yorgi crossed the room with Kirill at his heels.

Without a word, Yorgi doubled his fist and hit Xander in the face.

Staggered by the blow and feeling his cheek split, Xander took a step back, then straightened again. He glared into Yorgi's eyes, barely able to restrain from launching himself at the man. *Don't be so quick to die, bro. String this out. Make it work for you. This asshole's gonna get his ticket punched.*

"That was for Kolya," Yorgi snarled.

Kirill lit up a fresh cigarette and dropped the butt of his old one to the floor. He seemed a little jovial.

Xander spat blood at Yorgi's feet and squared himself. "You forgot Viktor. I greased him up on the diamond run."

"I don't forget anything," Yorgi said. "And neither will you when I'm finished with you." He drew back his fist and smashed Xander in the face again.

The powerful impact left Xander dazed. *Okay, man's got a pretty good punch. I'll give him that. But if I wasn't already beat up from the mountain and his goons weren't all over the place, I'd be throwin' him a beatin' about now.*

"Bring him," Yorgi commanded.

Two guards flanked Xander and dragged him after Yorgi. Kirill remained only a few feet away, smoking and watching Xander with bright interest.

Putting it together, aren't you? Xander thought, looking at the man. *If I'm alive, then Yelena was lying. And Yorgi ain't gonna be none to fond of her either.*

Yorgi led the way into a large library. The windows were huge, requiring the use of the fireplace in the center of the back wall. Shelves almost twelve feet high held thousands of books. Small built-in ladders gave access to the stacks. Rugs covered the polished hardwood floor.

Yelena sat behind a hug desk, her notebook computer open before her. She looked up at their approach. Her shock to see Xander was apparent to everyone in the room.

"Yelena, my sweet dove," Yorgi said with false sincerity. "Do you notice anything strange about X?" He gestured to Xander. "He looks slightly less than dead."

Without a word, Kirill took out his pistol and pointed the weapon at Yelena.

"Yorgi," Yelena protested, getting to her feet, "I thought he was—"

Yorgi slapped her, driving her to her knees. He stared down at her as she rubbed her jaw.

Xander held himself in check. Yelena was no wallflower. And she was armed. If Yorgi continued to get physical, she'd know when she'd had enough.

"You disappoint me, Yelena," Yorgi roared. "After last night, I thought you'd finally come over. But you're still a slave to your police masters."

Yelena looked at Yorgi with genuine surprise.

"Do you think I didn't know about you all along?" Yorgi asked. "My contacts back home told me you were coming. You show up undercover and, I must admit, you play your part to the hilt."

Color stained Yelena's cheeks, not all of it from the slap.

"When it's time to be cruel," Yorgi went on, "you are cruel. When it's time to be passionate, you are very, very passionate indeed. I could have killed you, but I thought this would be so much more fun. To twist you and use you how I see fit. And to be honest, you went much farther than I ever expected you would for your country." He ran his hand through her hair.

Xander watched Kirill beside him, knowing the man was watching his dream fall apart. The killer's face was devoid of emotion.

Yorgi turned his attention to Xander. "And you. Why do you have such a problem staying away, my friend? Did you miss us that much?"

Buy time, Xander thought. *Get him talking. Yorgi is an egotistical son of a bitch. You've met guys like him all around the sports scene. Use his own ego against him. Buy more time for the Ivans.*

"What's the gimmick, Yorgi?" Xander demanded. He coated his words with sarcasm. "That's the part I don't get. You gonna hold the world hostage? I didn't think you were dumb enough to go with that hack cliché."

A shocked look filled Yorgi's face. "You think I'm after money?"

Xander shrugged.

"I'm trying to give a gift to the world," Yorgi said. "Anarchy. True freedom. I'm going to eliminate all the rules."

"So all by yourself," Xander challenged, "you're going to destroy every government in the world." He shook his head, showing Yorgi he didn't believe a word of it.

"Easier than that," Yorgi said. "I'll get them to destroy each other. The first attack takes out Prague." He raised his shoulders and feigned a puzzled look. "Nobody knows who did it or why. Then our friend *Ahab* continues unseen down the Vltava

River, finds his way to the North Sea and begins his world tour. London, Jerusalem, Beijing . . ."

Xander exchanged a quick glance with Yelena. When they'd been talking, they'd never thought about that. The whole campaign they'd put together with the Ivans had been to keep Yorgi from foraging into international blackmail. No one thought he'd use the Silent Night biological like this.

"We end with a trip up the Potomac River," Yorgi said. "To your Washington, D.C. Ten cities, ten countries, and still no one knows who to blame. So they make up their own answers. These guys attack those guys, those guys invade these guys. Soon the whole world is like your wild West cowboy days. No rules, no law, everybody free to do whatever they want."

Listening to Yorgi's plan, Xander knew it was possible. With the current world political climate, even Gibbons walking into the United Nations with documentation regarding who was responsible for all the mass killings wouldn't keep international paranoia from unleashing violence. Old enemies would be at each other's throats and people would die. Maybe the world Yorgi was describing would come about.

Xander pushed the horror out of his mind. That wasn't going to happen. He wouldn't let it. All he had to do was hang on for a few more minutes till the Ivans arrived.

"Wow," Xander said. "And here I though *anarchy* was just something cool to put on a T-shirt."

Anger and a lack of understanding filled Yorgi's face. "What's with you, man? You used to be one of us. You broke all the rules. You didn't sell out to anything or anyone. That's what Kolya said about you. Of all people, I thought you'd understand what I'm trying to accomplish."

"Oh, I get it all right," Xander retorted derisively. "For the betterment of humanity, you're gonna start World War Three. You're a regular humanitarian."

"You know," Yorgi grated, "for someone who thinks himself so clever, I'm shocked at your stupidity. I've got a regiment of heavily armed men and you come snowboarding down here in broad daylight like some kind of—"

When Yorgi stopped speaking and swiveled his head to the bank of gray-fuzzed security monitors on the library desk, Xander knew the game was up.

Yorgi stared out the windows and up the mountain to where the communications tower had stood. "—like some kind of diversion," he whispered. Then he spun, drawing his pistol and aiming at Yelena.

Yorgi's move caught the attention of everyone in the room. Taking advantage of the distraction, Xander threw himself forward, knowing he'd never beat a speeding bullet.

Then an explosion slammed into the castle, seeming to rock the huge building. Glass blew out of the windows, ripping drapes down and becoming a cloud of deadly shrapnel that ripped into the guards. The ones that survived dove to the floor for cover.

63

Startled by the explosion, Yorgi fired anyway, but his shot went wild, missing Yelena by several feet.

Xander grabbed the woman, throwing them both to the ground behind the huge library desk. Yelena recovered quickly, pulling her pistols from hiding and blasting away immediately.

Under fire himself, Yorgi had no choice but to retreat.

Xander threw a shoulder under the heavy desk and managed to flip the furniture over as a temporary shield. Bullets thudded into the wood with hollow booms and peeled away long splinters. He took one of Yelena's pistols when she handed the weapon to him, wishing he had the silver revolver he'd been given. The exploding loads would have come in handy for clearing out the opposition.

"Sounds like the Ivans got here," Xander said, leaning out long enough to shoot one of the guards.

"They're dependable," Yelena said, shoving a

fresh magazine into her weapon. "They always have been."

Yorgi yelled in anger and hammered the desk with a line of fire.

Grabbing Yelena by the shoulder, Xander took advantage of a lull in gunfire and retreated back into the book stacks. The thick books and the shelves themselves provided adequate defense. Yorgi yelled to his men, urging them on.

Last stand, bro, Xander thought, looking around the library. *Didn't exactly have this one figured.*

Then men in Czech secret police vests stood outside the library windows and hosed Yorgi and his men with assault rifles. The castle guards went down in droves, hammered by the flying bullets. More Czech police cars roared through the snow covering the castle grounds on that side of the main house.

Yorgi's line broke and ran. Kirill stepped around the corner with a 40mm grenade launcher over one shoulder and fired through a window. The warhead leaped from the launcher and streaked toward one of the police cars as the men inside got out. The orange and black fireball rocked and overturned the police car, covering the vehicle in flames. The gas tank exploded a moment later.

Glancing around a corner of the stacks, Xander watched Yorgi grab Kirill by the shoulder and pull him from the room.

Yelena leaned around the corner and fired her weapon as fast as she could pull the trigger. The pistol cycled dry as two guards collapsed but Yorgi and Kirill escaped.

Xander let out a sigh of relief. All they had to do

was wait till the Ivans mopped up the place. Gibbons could have whatever was left over.

"Come on," Yelena said, snapping the slide into place.

"Come on where?" Xander asked. "They're beaten. They're giving up."

Yelena shook her head. "It's not over."

"What do you mean?" But Xander was already starting to put it together. Yorgi wasn't the type who'd walk away from a fight.

"They've gone to make the launch," Yelena declared tersely. "The Ivans don't know how to find the basement."

Xander looked at the pistol in his hand. "We need more firepower."

Nodding, Yelena ran down the aisle then along the wall. She pressed a security touchpad on a wall covered with exotic woodwork and a section swiveled around to reveal racks of weapons and explosives.

Xander handed the pistol back to Yelena, then armed himself with pistols and a sub machine gun. He hefted a small satchel of C-4 over one shoulder. *Is that it, bro? You gonna play the hero? You ain't never looked after nobody's skin but your own. That's what you learned to do. Ain't been nobody out looking after you.*

But when Yelena turned and ran across the library, he was on her heels.

64

Yorgi stooped and picked up a submachine gun from one of the dead guards blown out into the hallway by the hail of fire from the arriving Czech police. Yelena had betrayed him in a bigger way than he ever could have imagined. But he'd thought she'd come around to him, to his way of looking at things. He knew she'd been abandoned by her spymasters, and hadn't had any contact with them for the last year and a half.

How could she find it in herself to believe that he should be stopped? The world was filled with madness. People were no longer free. She of all people should have realized that. She'd been a slave to Russia, and she'd been a slave to him.

Xander Cage had changed that in her, though. Somehow the American had given her some kind of false hope. That had to have been the case. Nothing else made sense.

Yorgi prepared the submachine gun, then picked

up a bandolier of extra magazines. He concentrated on *Ahab*. Once the submersible launched, there would be nothing they could do to stop it. Silent Night would kill thousands of people in minutes and the death cruise would continue.

He smiled in spite of the bullets hammering into the castle's stone walls. Some of the intruders had breached other rooms in the building. Yorgi heard the sound of gunfire cascading down the hallways. He looked at Kirill, who was stripping weapons from a dead man.

"There will be many of them outside in the courtyard," Yorgi said.

"Then we will kill many of them," Kirill said. His voice was colder than normal. His eyes held no emotion.

Yorgi knew the man had lost a lot when he realized Yelena would never be his. But that was good. A sense of loss made a man even more willing to die for something he believed in. Kolya's death filled Yorgi with the same resolution.

Leading the way through the main hallway, Yorgi killed two Czech policemen who didn't see him coming. He ran across their falling bodies, listening to the muted cough of Kirill's pistol as another policeman stepped around the corner and Kirill's bullet took him full in the face.

Reaching the stairs outside, Yorgi's gaze swept the staggered line of police cars and the pockets of battle, individual sites of death and dying. The sight pleased him. Soon, the whole world would be locked in such battles. He and Kolya would have their revenge against the world.

He paused at the entrance. Going down the steps

without getting seen was out of the question.

"Let me," Kirill said.

Yorgi stepped aside as Kirill hauled up a 40mm grenade launcher from another dead guard. He extended the weapon into firing position, then shouldered the tube. He aimed in a heartbeat, and squeezed the trigger.

The rocket leaped from the launcher and exploded against one of the police cars. Debris from the vehicle and the ground sent guards and policemen ducking for cover.

Yorgi threw himself around the corner, then vaulted the side of the stairs. He crashed to the ground beside the basement door but managed to keep on his feet. Kirill landed behind him a moment later.

Before the Czech troops could recover, Yorgi had the basement door open and was running down the tunnel. The damage Xander Cage had done the night before hadn't been completely fixed, but the lights came on when he flipped the switch.

At the bottom of the tunnel, he keyed the touchpad to enter the bypass code. The hermetically sealed door hissed open and he charged through before the section had totally recessed.

Gazing up into the catwalks above, knowing the police would follow through the lab door, Yorgi turned to Kirill. He locked eyes with the man, both of them knowing what he was about to ask.

Kirill took out his cigarette pack and shook one out. He examined the pack, as if surprised to find that he'd taken the last one. With no emotion, he crumpled the pack and threw it away, then lit the fresh cigarette from the butt of the old one.

"Hold them off as long as you can," Yorgi said.

Kirill nodded and shouldered the sniper rifle he carried. Without a word, he started up the nearest catwalk to take up a position.

Yorgi turned and ran toward the big metal hatch that closed the docking area off from the lab. A smaller door, inset in the center of the hatch, held another security touchpad. *Ahab* was inside, already in the water and waiting to be sent on its way.

He keyed the touchpad, only then realizing that he had left the door to the main lab open to the tunnel. But that was no matter. The first few policemen through the door were going to die under Kirill's rifle.

As the small door centered in the big hatch opened, Yorgi flipped switches off on the nearby control panel. Most of the lights inside the lab went out. Kirill was lost in the darkness on the catwalk. No one would see him, and the rifle's silencer also held a flash-hider.

Yorgi went through the door and sealed it from the other side.

Xander peered around the corner of the main entrance. A three-round burst of gunfire knocked chips from the stone only inches away. He ducked back, watching Yelena pull back on the other side of the entrance.

Raising his voice, Xander yelled, "Yo, Ivans! I come in peace, bro!"

A quick shout in Russian quieted all the guns.

Xander peered around the corner again, halfway thinking he was going to get his head taken off. Instead, he saw both Ivans standing at the forefront of the action.

Xander and Yelena went through the doorway, hurrying now, taking the stone steps two and three at a time. He scanned the dead men lying at the foot of the stairs, hoping to find Yorgi and Kirill there.

"You guys were right on time," Xander said.

"We are always on time," one of the Ivans said.

"What about Yorgi?"

"He escaped," the other Ivan said.

"Where?" Yelena asked.

Both Ivans pointed to the basement tunnel.

"That's where the lab is," Yelena said.

One of the Ivans waved, and a small group of policemen vanished into the tunnel. Xander fell in behind them, matched by Yelena and followed by the Ivans.

The tunnel was eerily abandoned. For a moment Xander thought Yorgi and Kirill had managed to get away. Then gunfire opened up in the lab ahead.

Staring through the open doorway, Xander watched as a half-dozen policemen went down in less than that many seconds. All of them had been shot in the head and most of them were dead before they hit the floor.

One of the policemen remained alive, jerking and crying out for help. A young policeman tore from the ranks in the tunnel outside the lab. One of the Ivans reached for the man but couldn't grab him in time.

The young policeman ran inside the lab and reached the wounded man. He let his weapon hang by the sling as he hooked his hands under the wounded man's arm.

Then the unmistakable coughing whisper of a silenced round echoed inside the cavernous lab. The young policeman dropped as crimson emptied out the hole in the back of his skull. As his body dropped, another round killed the wounded man.

"Kirill," Yelena said.

Xander glanced inside the lab but saw no sign of the man in the darkness. He also didn't see Yorgi. With Kirill in position somewhere in there, Xander knew there was no way they could continue the pursuit.

"I'm sick of that guy," Xander said.

Yelena sniffed. "He's smoking," she said.

Xander detected the acrid stench of Kirill's cheap cigarettes as well.

Turning to one of the policemen near her, Yelena pointed at the rocket launcher the man carried. She asked something in Czech that Xander didn't understand.

The man nodded and Yelena took the launcher from him. "Heat-seeking," Yelena told Xander as she fitted the tube over her shoulder with obvious skill. She waved the tube around, not exposing herself to Kirill's field of fire.

A red light showed on the rocket launcher, then a *peep* rang out.

"The weapon has target lock," Yelena said, and she fired.

The rocket *whooshed!* from the tube.

65

Senses amped to the max, living on adrenaline at the moment, Xander saw the rocket close in on Kirill's position. Xander couldn't actually see the man, but he spotted the cigarette coal an instant before detonation. Kirill must have figured out what was drawing the warhead too because he tried to throw the cigarette away.

The rocket impacted against the catwalk and blew out an entire section. The plastic pipes ruptured, sending out steam and scalding water. Other sections of computers and machinery erupted into sparking flames.

Kirill's smoking and broken corpse hit the lab floor a heartbeat later.

"I told him that cigarette was gonna kill him one day," Xander said into the silence that followed the deafening explosion. His ears still rang with the sound.

Yelena tossed the rocket launcher and led the way

into the room. She stopped at the huge metal hatch over the railroad section on the other side of the lab. Spotting the security touchpad, she pressed buttons in rapid sequence. The red FAILURE light kept coming on and the system beeped at her.

"He's locked us out," Yelena said in frustration. "This keypad doesn't work anymore."

Xander stared at the big metal hatch as the Ivans and several Czech policemen began pounding on it with their weapons.

When he heard the pounding against the big metal hatch covering the entrance to the lab, Yorgi only smiled and continued his work. Getting through that door wasn't going to be easy.

He walked *Ahab's* length, carrying the internal hard drive that had already been loaded with all of the submersible weapon's programming. He knelt, opened the access hatch, and seated the hard drive. For the moment, *Ahab* sat at the end of the railroad tracks on a conveyor system that could lower the vessel into the water.

The docking area was half-submerged with water that held *Ahab* and the cigarette boat in which Yorgi intended to make his escape. The cigarette boat was a high-performance smuggler's craft of a design that had been built since the 1950s. They were constructed only for two things: racing and smuggling. Or perhaps only one, if a person looked at the situations properly.

Track lighting hung from the ceiling of the cave. Only the lighting and some of the docking equipment were new. The previous owners of the castle had kept the dock hidden behind a cleverly constructed gate that fed directly out into the Vltava River. Yorgi had found it necessary to invest in reworking the doors as well, but the secret had remained his after he'd killed the construction crew that had done all the work.

The door pounding stopped.

Thinking the Czech police had given up, Yorgi dropped from *Ahab* and crossed the wooden dock to the waiting cigarette boat. He cast the mooring lines off, then moved to the control panel for the conveyor system that held *Ahab*. Escape was only minutes away.

Yelena slapped C-4 blocks against the metal hatch. If there was a rhyme or reason to her method, Xander couldn't see it. Of course, he'd never worked with plastic explosives before.

"Be careful what you shoot at," Yelena advised as she strung wire between the charges. "If you hit *Ahab* you could release the nerve agent."

"Normally," Xander said, trying to emulate her coolness, "I hate people telling me what to do, but you're generally informative."

Yelena ignored him, taking care with her project. When she finished, she said, "Okay. Take cover."

At the controls of the conveyor system and the dock, Yorgi pulled a lever. The system operated smoothly.

At the opposite end of the dock, the huge doors that allowed access to the river slid apart. Sunlight glimmered out on the river. Prague lay only a short distance away.

He pushed another lever on a remote control

panel, then turned and watched as the conveyor system holding *Ahab* tilted forward and dropped the submersible into the water. Using a pocket remote control, he turned *Ahab* around and pointed the submersible in the direction of the gates.

And in the next moment, a series of explosions rocked the cavern, bringing stalactites down from the ceiling. Deafened and totally surprised, Yorgi turned and watched as the big hatch blew loose from the cavern wall and toppled into the dock area in a cloud of choking dust.

Wired to the max, Xander exploded from cover and raced across the empty space in the wall where the metal hatch had been. He carried the sub machine gun in his arms.

On the other side of the doorway, he peered through the choking dust and spotted *Ahab* in the middle of the water. Yorgi threw himself into a waiting cigarette boat and threw the craft into overdrive, easily outpacing the sluggish *Ahab*.

At Xander's side, Yelena raised her weapon, then hesitated and turned to Xander. "He's out of my range—but not yours!"

"Here's where a thousand hours of Virtua Cop are gonna pay off." Xander raised his weapon and unleashed the magazine on full-auto. Bullets hammered the cigarette boat, chewing through Plexiglas, windows, and coaming.

Some of the rounds also caught Yorgi at the controls, knocking him down. The boat raced out onto the river, then out of control. Yorgi stood and took a remote control from his pocket.

In the next instant, *Ahab's* engines kicked to life.

Slowly at first, then with increasing speed, the submersible rose up out of the water on the hydrofoils. Not cutting back on power at all, *Ahab* veered out of the cavern and onto the river as though possessed.

Not possessed, Xander realized. *Preprogrammed.*

Out on the river, the submersible kicked in with everything it had, picking up speed and skimming across the top of the river.

"Aw, shit," Xander said. He stared out at the cigarette boat as it headed for the riverbank.

Yorgi was coughing blood now, and crimson stained his face. Still, somehow he managed to sing. "I am an antichrist. I am an anarchist . . . I wanna be anarchy!"

The cigarette boat rammed the bank and exploded, becoming a rolling fireball that spread over the snow-covered landscape. The dock gates closed automatically, plunging the dock back into low lighting and cutting off sight of the submersible speeding away.

"This day keeps getting better and better," Xander said.

"We've got to stop that thing," Yelena said.

"I know," Xander said. He turned and ran for the lab. "There are cars out in the courtyard. And the road follows the river back into the city. It ain't much, but that's all the chance we have."

66

As Xander reached the courtyard, breathing hard but steadily, he watched Toby Lee Shavers get out of the GTO in the middle of the battlefield. The young agent peered around in surprise. He'd been assigned with the Ivans and given instructions to bring the car in. When Xander had left Prague, Shavers didn't know if the work would be finished.

Shavers looked incredibly worn and tired. He also looked like he was in shock. His eyes got big when he spotted Xander, and he threw out an accusatory finger.

"X! Jeez, there you are!" Shavers said.

Xander's heart pounded with exhilaration. The car was faster than anything the Czech police had. And if the vehicle had been amped up with all the stuff Xander had asked for, maybe it would give them the chance.

He stopped at the car and peered in at the dashboard. With all the additions Shavers and his team had made, the car looked like the cockpit of a fighter jet.

"You really screwed me this time!" Shavers yelled. "Gibbons didn't authorize this! He's gonna hang us both out to dry!"

Xander turned to the man and kept his voice level. "Agent Shavers, I'm giving you a field promotion." He passed the young agent the empty sub machine gun. "Take over here. Finish the mop-up. You're in charge."

Shavers accepted the weapon and his face lit up. "Yes, *sir!*"

Xander slid behind the GTO's wheel as Shavers began yelling orders. Yelena slid into the passenger seat. Xander put his foot on the accelerator, bringing the car around in a tight U-turn and speeding back through the open main gate. He rocketed onto the road leading back to Prague.

Ahead, he could see the city in the distance. To the side, in the middle of the river, was *Ahab* perched on the hydrofoils.

"There it is." Xander pointed. "You got the guided tour of that damn thing. How do I shut *Ahab* down?"

"I don't know," Yelena yelled back over the roar of the wind and the engine. "The controls are in a panel on top. But how would you even get to them?"

Xander shook his head as he pressed the accelerator down further. "One crisis at a time. Put a CD in, will you? I need to relax."

Operating on automatic pilot, her attention riveted on the speeding submersible, Yelena slid a CD into the player. High-speed punk metal filled the GTO's interior.

"Much better," Xander said. His senses sang to him, riding the adrenaline rush that filled him. He was in mid-stunt, with the hardest part of the course to go, and he didn't see himself failing. "All right, how about the car? Looks like we could take out the Death Star with this thing. Anything here we can use?"

Yelena searched the car and turned up a book on the floorboard. "Shavers left instructions. Flame thrower, mini-bombs, exploding hubcaps . . ."

Xander nodded, feeling a little proud. "Those are some dope options."

"Mini-machine guns, rocket launchers." Yelena shook her head. "You can't use any of those. The only way to safely dispose of the nerve agent is in deep water. The chemicals will break down and dissipate."

Xander reached into his pocket and pulled out his Tech Deck. Gibbons answered almost immediately. "Silent Night is on its way to Prague," Xander announced. "Where are you?"

"I'm heading downtown right now," Gibbons answered. "This is hero time now, Xander. Can you get to the submersible?"

"I'm gonna try," Xander said. "If I can't you'll be the first to know."

Gibbons stared at the Tech Deck in his hand. He sat in a Jeep with a Czech general beside him. Agent Polk rode in the rear deck. The general drove, whipping through the traffic with his sirens blaring.

"Should we evacuate, sir?" Polk asked over the siren's scream.

"Twenty minutes to evacuate one point five million people to a distance of five miles," Gibbons mused. He looked at the general. "General, better scramble some air support. We may have to blow this thing out of the water." Maybe they'd lose Prague, but there were other cities on the weapons hit list as well that could be saved if the air strike was successful in destroying *Ahab*.

"But, sir," Polk said, leaning forward, "if the pilots hit the target—"

"I'm well aware of the ramification, Mr. Polk," Gibbons said. "And if they don't destroy *Ahab* now, it'll surface again in nine other cities. We're all dead anyway unless our friend pulls off a miracle."

And Gibbons was reminded of Sam Tannick's question about whether a wild dog could be taught to be a guard dog. Xander Cage had risen to meet the demands till now. But had the bar been raised too high?

"Keep checking the book," Xander said as he drove. The city was only a short distance ahead, growing closer by the second. "There's gotta be something we can use."

Yelena flipped the page. "It's all useless! Smoke bombs, a harpoon gun, parachutes built into the seats in case you drive off a cliff."

Xander spotted a jack-knifed eighteen-wheeler lying on its side in the middle of the intersection ahead. Several pipe metal carts filled with potatoes were scattered around. No one was in the vehicles.

They were all standing on the street corners talking to each other, waving their arms in accusation.

"We've gotta get through this," Xander said. "You said rockets. Hit those now."

Yelena consulted the book. "Rockets. Number 22." She reached forward and hit a switch on the dash.

Flamethrowers belched fire from the GTO's front grill. The slipstream caught the twisting flames and splashed them back across the windshield. The heat baked through and bathed Xander. He reached over and flicked off the switch.

"Sorry!" Yelena yelled. "Not 22. 32." She leaned forward and hit another switch.

67

Xander felt the GTO quiver as the rocket launchers loaded up. The headlights plopped out, the left one shattering on the street beside the muscle car. In the next instant, twin contrails jetted from the front of the GTO.

Both rockets streaked toward the overturned eighteen-wheeler, screaming defiantly till they ended in a double explosion. The destructive force lifted the truck and trailer into the air and broke them apart.

Xander steered for the gap, shooting through as flaming potatoes rained from the sky. He glanced to the side, spotting the submersible standing on top of the river, leaving foaming wakes behind it.

With the straightaway, they'd gained on *Ahab*, but as they closed on downtown Prague, the streets became twisting meandering routes. Prague was an old city, and had grown in layers as more and more people had come to live there. City planning hadn't

accounted for all the growth, or the need for trans-
portation ease.

Xander drove with his foot on the floor, knowing
he couldn't ease off because they were racing the
clock and the clock never stopped. Time was the
hardest opponent of all to beat, and he knew they
were running out of it. But time was when a true extreme sports guy threw what was left of the rule-
book out the window.

"Careful!" Yelena said, drawing into a ball
against the passenger door as Xander swept out into
the oncoming lane and passed the car in front of
them. "Watch the traffic!"

Xander stared coolly at the truck racing toward
them. The driver was laying on his horn.

"You call this traffic?" Xander cracked. "This is
nothing." He juked back in ahead of the car and let
the truck go by with inches to spare. Adrenaline
filled him, making him tingle with energy. The
closer to death he got, the more alive he felt. And he
never felt more alive than at this moment. "I know
traffic. I'm from—"

"You're from L.A.," Yelena said. "I know."

Xander took another corner, heading away from
the river for a moment. He scouted the streets open
to him, roared past an open-air market, and pulled
back onto an access street that put them next to the
river again.

"Take the wheel," Xander said.

Yelena looked at him. "What?"

"Take the wheel. C'mon, move it." Xander
locked the cruise control, one of Shavers's additions,
and stood up in the seat. As Yelena slid over, he slid
under her. He plucked the car manual from her

hand as she settled in. A quick flip through the book gave him the information he needed.

"What are you doing?" Yelena asked.

"I got a plan."

"What kind of plan?"

Turning to the rear seat, Xander pulled the seat-back down. Weapons covered the back of the seat in neat order. *Bro, if you live through this, you gotta tell Shavers he does dope work.*

"Get as close to the river as you can," Xander said. Ignoring the pistols, assault rifles, and shot-guns tucked behind the seat, he took out the harpoon gun. "I'm going over."

"You're what?" Yelena stared at him in the rearview mirror.

Xander checked the harpoon gun. A full spool of metal cable hung from the front of the weapon. The harpoon had wicked hooks designed to penetrate and catch hold of whatever it hit.

Knowing there was no time to explain, Xander hit the canopy release. The GTO's hardtop blew off like a fighter jet's canopy right before ejection. Only Shavers hadn't put ejection seats in the car.

Xander shoved his arms through the straps of the parachute seat. He clipped the harpoon gun to the chute harness, then swiveled in his seat and took aim at *Ahab*. He rested his finger on the trigger and squeezed.

The harpoon leaped from the gun with a pop, then the cable paid out behind the shaft with a whirring buzz. A heartbeat later, the curved head penetrated *Ahab's* side.

Xander watched as the cable exhausted the spool.

"Turn around, Yelena," he said. "Get as far away as you can!"

She didn't look at him, having to concentrate entirely on her driving. "I'm staying with you!"

"That's gonna be kinda hard," Xander said as he stood and stepped back onto the trunk. He pulled the parachute's ripcord. "I'm outta here."

The wind caught the parachute, stopping his forward motion and yanking him from the speeding GTO. For a moment he thought he'd judged the harpoon gun's reservoir wrong, that he was going to end up hitting the street and get dragged to his death by the submersible racing across the river.

Then the cable slack drew tight, pulling on the parachute harness with a jerk, yanking him like a kite high up into the air. *Ahab* wasn't slowed at all.

For the first time, Xander noticed the military jets in the sky overhead. *Gibbons's back up team,* he thought grimly. *Has to be. And here I've gone and tied myself to the target. It's all or nothing, bro. Fly or crash and burn.*

Then he noticed the stone bridge less than a hundred yards in front of the submersible. *Ahab* was going to make the bridge, but Xander knew he was going to be scraped off at best, or smashed and broken against it. Either way, a few minutes after that and Silent Night would descend over the city and he'd be dead along with most of the downtown area's populace.

68

Thinking quickly, Xander took the shoulder sling from the harpoon gun and looped the leather over the straining cable attached to the shaft buried in *Ahab's* side. He pulled the parachute release and kicked out of the harness.

Swinging out while holding onto the leather sling with only one hand, Xander kicked his legs and tried not to lose control of the downward slide to the doomsday weapon. He smacked into *Ahab* an instant before the parachute hit the stone bridge.

The impact against the bridge destroyed the parachute but didn't break the cable. Instead, the parachute tangled and fell into the river. Once the folds filled with water, the parachute created a major drag on *Ahab*. The submersible shuddered with the effort of remaining up to speed.

Then the cable sheared with a loud *ZING!* In that moment, *Ahab* was loose and running free again, closing in on downtown Prague.

With grim determination, Xander climbed to the top of the submersible. Yelena had told him that the control panel was on top of the craft during their flight from the castle. Staying low on the submersible, clinging tightly because the craft was being battered by the rough surface of the river, Xander crawled to the access panel.

Not finding any purchase on the access panel, Xander drove his fist into it, hoping to warp the cover in its setting so he could create something to grab onto. Nothing budged.

Thunder crackled in the sky. When he looked up, he spotted the military jet contingent streaking through the wild blue. At the moment, they reminded Xander of vultures, there to deal with whatever was left of what he couldn't handle.

Ahab juked really hard to the left unexpectedly. Caught by surprise, Xander nearly rolled off but managed to catch the row of solar panels and keep himself aboard.

When the hatch slid open, he thought maybe he'd managed to disrupt the locking mechanism somehow and trigger the release. But as the rocket carousel revolved and three rockets poked their snouts up in preparation to launch, he knew the ignition sequence had started.

Augustus Gibbons abandoned the Jeep at the edge of the park that he'd selected as his point of no return. Once *Ahab* made that distance, he was going to order the jet strike.

The park was old, but drew the neighbors out into the sun and to the river. Most days, the park was probably a peaceful place, a place for dreams and relaxation. Today, though, Gibbons knew, the park was most likely ground zero for one of the deadliest attacks ever against civilization.

He ran, passing old men playing chess in front of a café across the street and bundled up against the slight chill in the air. On the other corner, children chased each other through a crowded piazza near an open-air farmer's market filled with vendors and prospective buyers haggling over the price of fruits and vegetables and poultry.

"Agent Gibbons," the general's voice came over the Tech Deck.

"Sir," Gibbons responded. He gazed at the teenaged couples walking hand in hand along the riverbank. God, had he ever been that young?

"I've got word from the pilots," the general said. "Your man has made it onto the device."

Gibbons couldn't believe it. How the hell had X managed that?

"They also tell me their weapons are locked onto the target," the general continued.

"Wait," Gibbons said. "Just a little longer." Either way it went, the people in the park were dead. *He* was dead. Gibbons wasn't afraid of dying. Maybe he didn't take the risks that Xander Cage did with his sports interests, but Gibbons had known he'd agreed to give his country at least one death when he signed on. But he didn't want to take all these people with him.

"You're almost out of time," the general argued.

"And I've got a man in position to shut that damn thing down. I'll make the call. That's what I was put here for."

As he watched, *Ahab* sped closer, and he could see

Xander struggling on top of the device now. Then the sound of the approaching submersible rolled over the park, drawing the attention of everyone there and startling a group of pigeons into flight.

No one in the park knew they could be dead in the next few seconds. And he'd be the one that called it.

C'mon, X.

Xander stared down into *Ahab's* weapons bay. He saw the control panel and leaned in to get a closer look.

"They're all in Russian!" Xander glanced around wildly. *Give me icons. I'm a freakin' genius with icons.* But there weren't any icons either. "Down! Which one is down?"

Suddenly, the three rockets that had risen in the bay started mixing blue and yellow chemicals that turned into bubbling black.

"Aw, shit," Xander mumbled, knowing that couldn't be good at all. "No, you don't." He reached down and yanked the first rocket from the launching tube. As he did, the three igniter flames at the rear fired off.

Still holding the rocket, Xander looked up, wishing he knew what the hell he was supposed to do. *This is the part where the spy guy has the ultrasecret superweapon that puts the bad guy's stuff in the toilet.* But he didn't have anything. The only thing he had working for him was the rage against the system, against all the rules that kept him from doing what he wanted to do, being who he wanted to be.

This was Yorgi's sick game, and Yorgi had created all the rules. That wasn't anarchy. That was just changing the game. Just somebody else's rules. And now he was playing along with them, trying to find a way to save everybody and be the good guy. It didn't make sense. He wasn't the good guy; he was just a guy who fought the system, who pushed the limits.

Then, across the park *Ahab* was approaching, Xander saw Gibbons standing straight and tall at the riverbank. The agent was laying his life on the line, too.

I ain't a secret agent, pal, Xander thought. *I'm just a guy who's had enough. I've always gotta go harder, farther, and faster. You picked the wrong poor son of a bitch to play this game.*

He heard his own heartbeat throbbing inside his head, echoing with speed metal music, and he felt the rage in him grow white-hot. He wasn't afraid, and he wasn't going to be afraid.

And he wasn't going to go down without a fight either.

"You want anarchy?" Xander raged. He turned the rocket upside down and shoved it back into the submersible's launcher. "Here's anarchy, asshole!"

With his adrenaline firing, shoving the rocket down into the launcher, Xander stood, holding onto the edges of the hatch. He let his rage go, let himself fight against what was supposed to be, and he stomped the hell out of the control panel.

The computer seized up and started smoking. In the next second, the hydrofoils retracted and *Ahab* slammed into the river.

The sudden change caught Xander off-guard, toppling him into the river.

On the riverbank, Gibbons watched incredulously as the submersible turned turtle and dove into the river. It hadn't fired. He kept that in mind. The damn thing hadn't fired. X had come through with something.

He lifted the Tech Deck and spoke. "Call off those warbirds, dammit! Everybody stand down!"

Tires screeched out on the street. Glancing over his shoulder, Gibbons saw the Russian agent, Yelena, bolt out of the black GTO convertible. Gibbons knew about the car from Shavers's report.

Yelena rushed to the riverbank, searching the water frantically.

Before she could ask, before he could say, a massive explosion filled the center of the river. Geysers of water streamed into the air, then came splashing back down over the river and the park.

As big as the detonation was, Gibbons knew _Ahab_'s deadly payload had to have been completely destroyed. The water had rendered the nerve gas inert and unrecoverable.

But where the hell was Xander Cage?

Xander rode the blast through the freezing cold water of the river. He fought against the impulse to take a breath. The experience was actually a stone-solid rush. Being blown up in the water was a lot different than he'd thought it would be. Earplugs, though . . . if he ever had to do it again, man, he wasn't going to do it without earplugs.

He stared through the river bottom, barely able to make out _Ahab_'s gutted remains. But they were there. The submersible had been spread over the river bottom.

Taking a moment to get his bearings, letting natural buoyancy show him the way, he swam up. He emerged under the bridge near where he'd seen Gibbons standing. Wooden icebreakers built around the bridge supports provided him a resting place. He hauled himself out of the water, too beat to move again for the moment. When he looked up, Yelena was looking back at him.

"He's alive!" Yelena yelled, rushing over to him. Joy filled her face. "He's alive! Over here!"

Then Gibbons was there, rushing right after the woman. The agent looked surprised and relieved, and maybe, Xander thought, a little hopeful.

"X!" Gibbons shouted. Polk was at Gibbons's side. "Polk, get a boat. Get him off of there. He's got hypothermia. Double time."

"Yes, sir!" Polk turned and ran the other way, talking hurriedly into a Tech Deck.

Xander was glad that Gibbons and Yelena reached him. With the cold numbing his body and the aftershock of the submersible exploding still quaking through him and causing some inner ear disorientation, he didn't think he could have held on much longer by himself.

Xander tried to speak, but his words were unintelligible even to him.

"We're gonna get you help," Gibbons said. "Just hang on."

Xander tried to speak again.

"I can't hear you," Gibbons said.

Looking up at the agent, Xander tried to quiet the shaking and muscle contractions that ripped through him.

"I want to go to Bora Bora," he said.

Epilogue

When Xander woke, he was alone. He rolled over in the strange bed and wondered where he was. Seeing the grass hut ceiling above him, feeling the warmth of the French Polynesian climate soaking into him even through the walls of the hut, he had to grin.

One thing he'd learned about Gibbons: The agent was a man of his word. Lying there, nearly freezing to death in the Vltava River, he'd asked to go to Bora Bora. Gibbons had made it happen as soon as Xander had gotten treated for hypothermia, various cuts and bruises, and exhaustion.

And Xander hadn't come alone.

Rolling out of bed, feeling twinges from half-healed bruises, cuts, and scrapes—but those were old friends anyway—he padded across the sand floor to the doorway. He paused and stared out at the blue-green sea and the woman sitting on a towel on the beach.

Gibbons had also come through with Yelena's papers, and he'd reserved the trip to Bora Bora for two.

Yelena sat under the bright sunlight, arms folded around her knees. Her skin held a coppery redness from the sun and the wind gently pulled at her hair. The thong showed off her dynamite curves and the angel tattoo spreading its wings across her lower back. *Surprising where you find angels,* Xander couldn't help thinking.

He crossed the hot sand and joined her on the beach.

She looked up at him, a smile automatically framing her face.

Xander sat beside her and brushed the hair back from her face, feeling the smooth skin against the back of his callused fingers.

"You're awake," she said.

He nodded. "Funny how exhausting relaxing can be."

"Depends on what you find relaxing."

Xander thought about that for a moment, then nodded. "Let's go for a swim."

"Sounds good."

Xander stood and helped her to her feet. "I have a great trick in mind," he said.

Yelena arched an eyebrow warily. "What's the trick?"

"How long can you hold your breath underwater?"

Yelena smiled. "In spy school, they trained us. Two minutes."

Shrugging, barely able to keep from smiling wolfishly, Xander said, "Two minutes. A lot can happen in two minutes." He took her hand in his, then led her to the private dock near the hut.

An electronic chirp drew Xander's attention for just a moment. He looked back at the Tech Deck sitting beside the scuba gear they'd used earlier. Gibbons had insisted that the Tech Deck be brought along.

The screen suddenly flickered to life, revealing Gibbons's scarred face. "Triple X?" Gibbons said, acting like he was trying to peer through the screen. "You there?"

Xander shook his head. Maybe Gibbons was a man of his word, but he was lousy with timing.

"I know you're there," Gibbons continued. "We got you right here on satellite magnification."

Yeah, well, until I hit the transmit button, you don't have me, Xander thought. Maybe he was going to continue the relationship with the NSA for awhile longer, especially for all the adrenaline pump he got out of the assignments, but that didn't mean he was going to play by the rules. Hell, he lived to break those rules.

Another agent—Xander remembered the man's name was Roger Donnan—stepped into the vidlink view. Donnan handed Gibbons a cup of coffee.

Looking up at Donnan, Gibbons said, "Two sugars, right, Roger?"

The agent nodded and didn't look happy.

"Good work." Gibbons turned back to the camera. "Call me, Triple X. We got a whole new thing to talk about." He sipped his coffee. "Oh, yeah, you passed the test. The Gibbons Test. Over."

Xander gazed into Yelena's eyes. She smiled, knowing he wasn't going to make an immediate reply. Whatever Gibbons had on tap could wait awhile. Xander felt the desire to hear what the mission was, knowing that whatever Gibbons had in mind would test him to the limit, but he had other limitations he wanted to test for the moment.

Without a word, Xander pulled her into motion with him. They leaped from the dock and hit the warm water together like they'd been doing it for years. Turning to face each other, with hands and lips exploring and teasing, they held each other in the shimmering blue-green sea.

Secret Agent Guy, Xander mused as he lost himself in the woman. Maybe the job wasn't one he'd have ever figured he'd have, but the adrenaline charges were the bomb. And the perks? He pulled Yelena to him, tasting her, feeling her thrumming excitement matching his. Man, the perks were freaking awesome.